The Happiest Days

Having spent many years abroad teaching English as a foreign language, Iain Manson now lives in west London. His work has appeared in newspapers and magazines on both sides of the Atlantic, and he is the author of three novels, one novella, and one nonfiction book.

The Happiest Days

Iain Manson

Black
Fountain

Published in 2011 by Black Fountain

ISBN-13: 978-0954790912

We receive three educations: one from our parents, one from our schoolmasters, and one from the world. The third contradicts all that the first two teach us.

Montesquieu

Contents

	Prologue	1
1	Crime	2
2	Sex	16
3	Violence	23
4	Religion	36
5	Alcohol	51
6	Travel	70
7	Sex and Violence	88
8	International Relations	98
9	Scandal	115
10	Art	126
11	Sport	138
12	Exploration	153
13	More Sex	163
14	The Supernatural	179
15	Transport	194
16	Politics	216
	Epilogue	235

Prologue: 1950

'So this is him, is it?'

'Yes, this is Thomas.' The tiny creature in her arms began to howl, and she put its mouth to her breast.

'What's he doing with all that hair? Shouldn't he be bald like Linda was?'

'Some babies have lots of hair.'

Walter Cardwell prodded his son doubtfully with an index finger. 'This one's a boy, is it?'

'That's right. So now we have one of each' She brushed a lock of hair from her face and moved the baby to the other breast. 'Well, aren't you pleased?'

'Hmm? Oh... yes, yes, of course.' Mr Cardwell leaned over and planted an awkward kiss on her forehead. He was a powerfully built man of thirty, three years older than his wife. 'Yes, I suppose all babies are a bit ugly, aren't they?'

'Oh Walter! What a thing to say!'

Thomas pulled his head away from the breast, looked at his father for the first time, and began to yell.

'Don't worry,' said his wife. 'He'll get used to you.'

'He's going to have to.'

1 Crime

In fact, I'm not sure that I ever did get used to him. Or he to me. From the start we treated each other as natural adversaries, and I cannot remember a time when I did not believe that the principal reason for his existence was the frustration of my wishes. And he could always count on my mother's support. Together they would make me go to bed when I was wide awake and get up when I desperately wanted to sleep. They would starve me when I was hungry and make me eat when I wasn't. And they would tell me that any food I enjoyed was bad for me, and any food I hated was good for me. Cabbage good, chocolate bad. Liver good, jelly bad. And so on. It was perverse, and the only explanation that fitted the facts was that they were out to get me.

To make things worse, they had the unspeakable Linda on their side. Linda was my sister, two years older than me, and infuriatingly 'clever', always top of the class, and expected to do great things in later life. This famous intelligence of hers irked me from an early age, but it was deep in her attitude to me that the roots of my chronic childhood desire actually to murder her lay buried. Lofty condescension was her style, and 'silly little boy' was her favourite expression when talking to or of me.

She was also alarmingly 'good', in the sense intended by adults when they use the word of children. I, by contrast, was usually 'naughty' and occasionally 'wicked', and the result was that her behaviour was constantly being pointed out to me as a peak I should strive to attain: 'Why can't you be like your sister, Thomas?' 'Oh really, Thomas! You never see Linda doing anything like that.' And so on.

This would have been irritating enough even if her reputation for saintliness had been well earned, but it wasn't. It was just an act that she managed to carry off astonishingly well. She did it by the simple expedient of being bad only when our parents' backs were turned, at which times it was her habit to goad me, quietly and patiently, until my temper snapped, as it always did sooner or later. I would then fill my lungs, screw my eyes tight shut, and express my feelings in a long and tremendous scream. And if this left me unsatisfied, I would launch a physical assault. This she could always resist because of her greater size and coolness, until one parent or the other appeared and saw to it that I was made to suffer for this unprovoked and 'wicked' attack. My sister was a creep.

And so, between them, the other three members of my family constituted a formidable force dedicated to rendering ineffective my pursuit of happiness. It seems unlikely that I articulated it to myself in this way at the time, but I do recall a powerful conviction of being in the right when, at the age of seven, I struck my first real blow of self-assertion. After all, I did like gingerbread.

'Walter, surely you haven't finished that gingerbread already?' My father and I were in the sitting-room, and she was calling through from the kitchen where Linda was, as usual, 'helping' her get tea ready.

'Eh?' My father lowered his paper and contorted his face in a pained effort to make out what she was saying.

'There was big piece of gingerbread in the top cupboard!' she shouted.

'Well, I haven't seen it.' He raised his paper again.

3

I was beginning to get worried. Confident as I was that I had had a moral right to the gingerbread, I knew my parents well enough to be certain that they would not see it that way. And they were bigger than me.

My mother's footsteps approached from the kitchen. She came in, stood in front of me, and fixed me with a steady gaze which I did my best to return. That part of the gingerbread which I had not yet eaten was under my bed, but I was admitting nothing.

'Now Thomas,' she began quietly, 'did you take a piece of gingerbread from the kitchen today? Tell the truth.'

That was all I could take, but before I could say yes, and burst into tears, my father looked up at her with his for-God's-sake-don't-be-so-stupid-woman expression. 'Good God, Doris, how could he have got it from the top cupboard?'

His intervention strengthened my resolve. If he was coming in on my side, I felt able to brazen it out. I widened my eyes. 'No,' I said, my voice suffused with innocence.

As it happened, I had had no end of trouble getting hold of the stuff, even with the aid of a chair, but it had not struck me that they might consider me physically incapable of the theft.

'Well, somebody took it,' said my mother.

I had an idea. 'Maybe it was Linda,' I said. This struck me as brilliant. Simultaneously getting myself out of trouble and Linda into it would be my greatest coup yet.

The plan backfired though. Unable to believe ill of his daughter, my father smelt a rat. In fact, his nose practically twitched as he lowered his newspaper and looked hard at me. 'I suppose he could have stood on a chair,' he said. 'Thomas, you didn't take the gingerbread, did you?'

I was horrified that his support should be so abruptly withdrawn, but I felt committed to my denial of the crime.

'No,' I repeated, shaking my head, 'I didn't take anything.'

There were a few seconds of excruciating silence as they both looked at me suspiciously, and I fought to hold back the tears which threatened to burst forth and betray me.

'Oh well,' said my mother just in time, 'I suppose we can have chocolate cake instead. I'll just be a moment.' She went back to the kitchen. My father looked at me for another couple of seconds, then turned back to his newspaper.

I could have crowed with triumph. Not only had I got away with the theft of the gingerbread, part of which remained to be eaten later, but I had also caused chocolate cake, which I liked even more, to be served instead. It was odd that I had missed it when raiding the cupboards, and my exultant mind now turned to the possibility of stealing later what remained of it, as well. The important thing was to choose a moment when I would not be interrupted, and it struck me that an exciting possibility was to get up after everyone had gone to bed. Why not? I began planning the raid in detail.

A knock on the door brought me back to reality.

'Thomas, open the door for your mother, will you?' said my father, and got up to poke the fire.

Chocolate cake was a speciality of my mother's. This one looked a gem, and I was delighted to note, as we took our places at the table, that the gingerbread I had eaten just an hour previously had done nothing to blunt my appetite. (This proved, incidentally, that I had been genuinely hungry at the time, and had therefore done nothing of which I need feel ashamed.)

'Where on earth has Linda got to?' said my mother as she poured the tea. My father went to the door and shouted for her.

'Thomas!' snapped my mother as I raised my piece of

5

cake to my mouth. 'What have I told you about starting before everyone else?'

'Sorry.' I put it back on my plate.

'At it again, is he?' said my father as he resumed his place at the table. 'Greedy little tyke.'

'And Thomas,' my mother went on, 'when we do start, what are you going to do with your piece of cake before you eat it?'

'Don't know,' I said, unable to think which of her many obsessions was now bothering her.

'Well, you don't put a great big piece of cake like that into your mouth all at once. You cut it up first.'

'But it's not a great big piece of cake. *He*'s got a great big piece, not me.' I pointed to my father's plate with a familiar sense of injustice.

He hit me over the head. 'You just do as your mother says, and don't be so damn cheeky!'

'Language, Walter, please.' My mother had a thing about swearing, however mild.

'Well, he's turning into a right little Teddy boy if you ask me. It's enough to make anybody curse.'

The door opened, and Linda appeared. 'Mummy, look what I found under Thomas's bed.' She held the gingerbread out like an angler showing off his catch.

'She's not allowed into my room!' I cried. 'She's a lout!' I was hazy as to the precise meaning of this word, but it was a favourite of my father's, and it felt as if it expressed what I wanted to say. I was dangerously close to tears.

Turning to me with the expression of extreme piety which she reserved for those occasions on which my behaviour had crossed the frontier between naughtiness and wickedness, my mother addressed me in her quietest voice: 'You know what happens to little boys who steal, don't you?'

In fact I didn't, and didn't want to, but I took the

question to be rhetorical, and stared silently at the table. My sister sat down at her place opposite me. In the midst of my confusion, I could feel her gloating.

'And to little boys who tell lies,' my mother went on.

'I don't care!' I said, knowing I was in the right, and determined not to cry.

My father now weighed in, face and voice saturated in outraged incredulity. 'What did you say?' He leaned back from the table and placed his hands on his hips. 'What did you say? We catch you stealing and lying, and you say you don't care?'

'I was hungry!' I said, and burst into determined tears. I now recalled that I had been famished when I took the gingerbread, that I might have died without it. How could I be blamed for eating to keep myself alive? The injustice of it surpassed belief! And they weren't finished with me yet.

'In future, Thomas,' said my mother, indifferent to my squawks, 'when you want something to eat, you tell me. Do you understand?'

'WAAH! WAAAH!'

'Answer me, Thomas.'

Stemming with a prodigious effort the flow of tears, I resorted to an expression I had picked up in the playground a few days before. 'You piss off!' I cried, and fled.

But my father was after me, and he grabbed me before I was even out of the room. I was hauled back by the collar, and suspended in front of my mother. 'You tell Mummy you're sorry.'

'I'M NOT SORRY I'M NOT SORRY I'M NOT SORRY!!'

So he sat down, and bent me over his knee. Then I was sorry. It was a nasty experience, and I gave up larceny for nearly three years as a result.

~

In that little incident can be seen all the principal ingredients of my early home life: my own attempt to satisfy my legitimate desires, the determined resistance of my parents, and the stab in the back from my sister. It is to this upbringing that I attribute a lifelong sense of grievance.

At the time however, there was no wider context into which I could put my frustration, and when, shortly after the gingerbread debacle, I was told that we were moving from Winterby to a place called Ashminster, I was not unhappy. The move itself promised to be interesting, and I felt I might get on better in a new home.

Best of all, though, was that Linda was dead against it. She burst into tears when informed of it, and subsequently treated us to ostentatious displays of moping whenever the subject was mentioned. And so, even when I too began to have misgivings, I could always cheer myself with the reflection that there had to be a lot of good in anything that could make my sister so miserable. I took care to remind her of it at frequent intervals, and felt that this constituted some measure of revenge for years of suffering at her hands.

When the day arrived however, I was distressed to find that Linda was better prepared for the upheaval than me, for it was now apparent to me that I didn't want to move at all. I was no longer convinced that I hated my teacher, and the thought of going to a new school was beginning to make me nervous. I started to feel sorry for myself, and was glum and uncooperative as the move progressed.

'Thomas, is everything out of your room now?' My mother's voice betrayed her growing irritation with me.

'Don't know.'

'Oh, you're an impossible child at times! I wish I had time to give you a good beating!' She turned away from me in disgust, and went to look at my room for herself. I

8

remained in the kitchen, and watched sulkily as the removal men went about their work.

It seemed to take forever, and yet the house was emptying fast, each piece of furniture leaving a great echoing space as it went outside and into the pantechnicon. I thought of my classmates now in school, and found to my astonishment that I actually wanted to be with them.

'Really, Thomas, can't you do anything to help?' Linda walked past, carrying a pot plant. She was now enjoying herself, and was 'helping' even more ostentatiously than usual.

I felt an access of rage. 'You're a silly cow. Silly cow, silly cow, silly cow!'

'Mummy Mummy, he called me a cow!' She put her burden on the floor, and ran off in search of reinforcements. 'Mummy, Thomas is being rude! He called me a silly cow!'

'Thomas,' called my mother from upstairs, 'don't you dare say things like that to your sister! Now Linda, when Thomas is behaving like this, just ignore him. He's only being silly and trying to annoy you.'

Linda came back into the kitchen to retrieve the plant. 'I'm ignoring you,' she said, nose so far in the air that she was almost looking at the ceiling. 'Silly little boy.'

It was eleven o'clock when the pantechnicon moved off. I was now feeling a little better, largely because Linda's reputation had been tarnished by the breaking of a teapot. Our parents were silent and preoccupied, and I began to feel contemptuous of their sentimental attachment to the house we were now leaving for the last time. And then I made the mistake of going for a final look at my bedroom. In a matter of seconds, I was blubbing like a baby.

'Thomas, are you there? We're ready to go now...

Thomas?' My mother's voice, echoing through the empty spaces, made it all the worse.

'Coming!' I managed to say, with only a slight catch in my voice, but I had no intention of joining the rest of the family until I could be sure they would be unable to tell I had been crying. Deciding I would feel better if I wasn't in my own room, I went out into the passage and closed the door. I stood there for some time, trying to cheer myself with happy thoughts, and finally managed to bring my tears under control.

'Thomas, what on earth are you doing? Are you in the toilet?'

'You shut up!' I cried in rage. It was typical of that woman to suggest something humiliating as the reason for my delay. I decided to kill her, and set off after her. By the time I had reached the kitchen, my temper had cooled sufficiently for me to be prepared to let her live, but she was going to have to watch her step. The great thing was, though, that I no longer felt like crying.

She was waiting for me by the kitchen door. 'Thomas,' she said quietly, 'you do not tell me to shut up. Do you understand?'

With my temper rising again, I tried to push past her in silence, my gaze on the floor, but she grabbed me by the collar and held on. 'I said do you understand?'

'Understand what?'

Now she became really angry, and shook me. 'Understand that you do *not* tell me to shut up, my boy! Well?' She shook me again.

'Yes,' I said sulkily, and she let me go.

My father, with Linda close behind, now appeared from outside to find out what was going on. 'What the hell are you two up to?' he demanded with understandable impatience.

She turned on him. 'You watch your language, Walter!

I've just been giving Thomas a row for the same thing. It must be you he gets it from.'

'Hmh! What's he been saying?'

'He called me a cow!' said Linda enthusiastically, but I ignored her and set off towards the car. All I wanted now was to leave Winterby as quickly as possible.

I heard the house door close and lock for the last time as I tried without success to get into the car. It was, I thought, typical of my father's selfishness that he should never willingly unlock anyone's door except his own.

'Thomas, what's happened to your face?' my mother asked, as she too failed to gain access. I had no idea what she meant. 'Have you been crying? You've been crying, haven't you? I can see what's wrong with Thomas now. He's been crying.'

A terrible and violent fury welled up in me. How could this old bag *possibly* think such a thing? How could she? I filled my lungs till I feared they might burst, and released the most tremendous piercing yell. And as I did so, I drew back my right foot and aimed two violent kicks at the locked door.

My father, who had just taken his place at the wheel, reacted instantaneously. He leapt out, grabbed me before I knew what was happening, bent me over the wing and, under the approving gaze of the other two members of the family, thrashed me till his hand hurt. By the time he had finished, I was howling with pain, humiliation and rage, and this time I didn't care what my mother thought about it.

'WAAAH!!' I yelled, as my father inspected the damage I had done. 'WAAAH!!'

'Look at that! Look what he's done! Isn't that awful?'

'WAAH!' I squawked, beginning to fear he might beat me again.

'Oh that really is dreadful!'

11

'Look, Daddy, he's wearing his heavy shoes too!'

My father was down on his hands and knees, inspecting the damage in detail. He resembled a dog sniffing out a suitable place to cock his leg. 'Scuffed and dented,' he said at length.

'Scuffed *and* dented!' echoed my mother, as if neither type of injury on its own would have surprised her, but the two together constituted evidence of wickedness beyond belief. My sister stood beside her grave-faced, shaking her head slowly as she had seen her father do so often, when evil perpetrated by me had saddened him beyond anger.

But he was not beyond anger now. With a growling noise indicative of intense disgust, he looked round at me and climbed to his feet. 'He should've been knocked on the head at birth,' he said, clenching both fists. 'In fact, I wouldn't mind finishing him off now. What's to stop me?'

I turned and fled. Whether he meant it or not I had no immediate way of telling, but I was taking no chances.

'Come back here!'

'Thomas, come back!'

With another growl, my father set off in pursuit. Now this was the worst move he could have made, because it served only to convince me that my fears for my safety were justified, and I ran all the faster to escape. Off I went round the back of the house.

'Catch him, Daddy!'

'Run, Walter, run! Don't let him get away! Chase him right round! I'll get him as he comes back!'

She did too As I emerged from the narrow path between garage and hedge, with my pursuer far behind, she grabbed me. I screamed and lashed out at her in an effort to regain my freedom, but she held on till my father appeared, and together they succeeded in bundling me into the car. That he did not carry out his threat to do me in was my only consolation.

~

Our new house, which stood half a mile outside Ashminster, was much bigger, and I found it intimidating at first. By contrast, Ashminster itself was just a village, and it took me some time to get used to living in a place so small. My main reason for hating it though, was the school, which had just two teachers, and which took pupils through to the eleven-plus. The contrast with my school in Winterby could not have been greater, and the differences were all in favour of the latter.

The real problem was the headmaster, Mr Blackett, who took the three senior classes, and was the most frightening human being I had ever known. His mood oscillated between anger and rage, and he made frequent use of the cane. When his temper really went, which was often, his face would turn red as a tomato and his roar could shake the windows. Everybody was scared of him, even Gordon Stacker, the class bully, and for me he was a bogeyman, a figure of fear who haunted me in spirit even when absent in body.

My response to his frequent verbal and physical assaults on me was to become timid and withdrawn, at least in comparison with what I had been in Winterby. I began to do as I was told more often and to lose my temper less often, and my schoolwork improved to the point at which I was regularly top of the class – for what that was worth in a class of nine. My parents noted the change in my character with satisfaction, my father once observing in my presence that 'John Blackett's fairly licked him into shape, you know. They were too soft on him in Winterby, that was the trouble. He was getting to be a right little Teddy boy.'

Television was a consolation. We got one as soon as we

arrived in Ashminster, and it was the most wonderful thing to have happened in my life. At first, I would sit in front of it at a distance of two feet, with the volume turned to maximum, but my parents soon put a stop to that, exhorting me to be like Linda, whose self-conscious imitation of an adult viewer would have been perfect but for a slightly overdone look of serious interest in whatever she was watching.

She showed a preference to be seen watching adult programmes, whereas I would take anything just for the pictures and the sound, but only really concentrated on children's programmes, especially *Billy Bunter*. Quelch, Bunter's headmaster, was my favourite character, and it did not bother me that Linda stigmatised all the programmes I most enjoyed as 'kids' stuff', an expression she picked up in Ashminster, and used at every opportunity.

And then our parents got hold of the idea that TV was bad for the eyesight, or at least for the eyesight of children, and our viewing came under rationing. Linda, who could never accept that she and I should be treated equally, reacted even more strongly that I did – '*I* watch serious programmes. All *he* watches is kids' stuff. He should be rationed, not me.' – but they were adamant. Our mother said we should be grateful, this being her usual way of justifying acts of cruelty.

It was fortunate for me that the Bromheads, who lived in the only house anywhere near ours, had a television, and were not afflicted with the belief that watching it might affect my eyesight. They spoke with funny accents, and never took things as seriously as my parents did. I liked them, and got to know them as Keith and Jill.

The best thing about Keith was his sports car. He drove twice as fast as my father, and always gave me a lift back from school if he was passing. As for Jill, she could bake almost as well as my mother, and did not subscribe to the latter's view that cakes, gingerbread and so on should be withheld from me until the 'proper times', when I should receive just enough to make me want a great deal more. Keith and Jill had a baby called Kevin, whom I envied, and a vast tabby cat, who derived her name, Sputnik, from her habit of leaping onto people's shoulders and circling their heads.

Why my parents didn't like them, I had no idea – they never admitted their disapproval openly, obvious though it was – but I was in no way surprised, and put it down to natural perversity. Linda, as was to be expected, took her cue from them.

2 Sex

I was exactly nine years old when I played doctors and nurses for the first and last time.

The only thing that interested me about birthdays was presents – I never forgave my uncle Don for marking the occasions only with cards – and I wouldn't have had a party at all had it not been for my mother's insistence. It was only fair, she said, as other children had invited me to their parties, and when I said that was their lookout, she said I was being silly. So I had a party.

In the event, all went well until Gordon Stacker, who had eaten too much ice-cream, vomited on the carpet. And no one was much bothered by that apart from my mother. Stacker didn't care. He was the class tough, and could say 'fuck' and 'arsehole' with tremendous authority.

When we had finished eating and Stacker had made a complete recovery, we were dispatched to the kitchen while my mother set about cleaning the carpet. At this point, both the friends Linda had been allowed to invite, and two of mine, decided to leave.

'I'm going upstairs to study,' said Linda when they had gone. 'Thomas, see that you and your friends don't make too much noise. I've got my eleven-plus to think about.'

Deciding not to attack her in front of witnesses, I let her depart in peace, and was thus left in the kitchen with Gordon Stacker, Cecil Leach, and the Henderson twins,

Sally and Susie. We were all in favour of watching TV, but this was impossible in the kitchen, and might, I warned, even be vetoed when we were allowed back into the sitting-room. So Gordon Stacker had another idea.

'Let's play doctors and nurses,' he said.

There were no dissenting voices, although I at least was ignorant as to what the game might entail. I could only guess that it might be something like *Emergency – Ward Ten*, one of my parents' favourite television programmes. He said we would have to play it in my bedroom, a condition which both intrigued and alarmed me, as I took it to be an indication that some form of naughtiness, perhaps even wickedness, must be involved.

Stacker was in charge. As soon as we were all in my room with the door closed, he announced that he was the surgeon, and there was an emergency. Sally Henderson had been 'smashed up' in a car accident, and was not expected to live. Leach and I were doctors, and Susie was the nurse.

My apprehension was growing. Stacker was the most depraved human being I had known, and although the prospect of sharing for once in his depravity was exciting, I wished that my room was not the venue. The consequences for me if we were caught were too awful to contemplate. My great fear was that Linda, who, when I was engaged in crime but was not in sight, developed miraculous powers of hearing, would find out what was going on and inform higher authority. At one point I even considered asking Stacker to keep his voice down, but I lacked the nerve.

Sally lay down on the bed, and the surgeon examined her. He grasped her wrist, listened to her heart, and announced in a grave voice that she was in a bad way. He said she would have to take her blouse off to permit a more detailed examination. This, I knew, was not the done

17

thing – I had not lived with my parents nine years for nothing – and I was beginning to understand why it was that we had to play this game in my room. But it was Stacker's next pronouncement that really shocked me.

After a brief examination of her chest, he shook his head and said there was little hope, but he was going to try an operation. 'Take all your clothes off.'

Cecil Leach gasped, and I began to get frightened. What Stacker was suggesting went far beyond naughtiness, and surpassed even wickedness. This was dirty, and dirty was as bad as you could get.

But, to my still greater astonishment, the patient took the rest of her clothes off without demur, and gave Cecil Leach, who was an only child and a notorious mummy's boy, a dreadful shock.

'She hasn't got a willy!' he cried.

The two girls giggled uncontrollably, and my confidence surged back with my feeling of superiority. 'Of course she hasn't,' I said. 'She's a girl. Don't you know anything?' He kept quiet after that.

Stacker told us all to shut up, because this was serious. He then saved the patient's life with a brilliant operation, my part in which was to place my left hand flat on her chest, and knock it at frequent intervals with my right fist. This got me into the spirit of the occasion, and I began to enjoy myself. So much so that, when the operation was over and Sally was getting dressed again, I said I would be the surgeon for the next operation.

But Stacker was having none of it. He said he wanted to do one more himself so that we would all learn properly how it was done, then we could take turns.

'It's got to be a boy who's the patient now,' said Susie. 'You be the patient, Tom.'

'I want to be the doctor again,' I said in some alarm. 'Leach can be the patient.' But I was overruled, and finally gave way, on condition that I could be the surgeon next time, with Susie as the patient.

I lay down on the bed, Stacker listened to my stomach, and announced that I had fever. He said it was the worst fever he had ever seen, and he would have to operate. Of course, I had to take my clothes off, something not even my awe of Stacker would have persuaded me to do had someone else not set the precedent, and the surgeon cut my stomach open with a sixpence. Then Sally Henderson pressed her ear to my chest and announced that my heart had stopped beating. I screwed my eyes shut and held my body rigid, in the belief that this was the behaviour expected of a corpse.

And at that moment, the door opened.

'See, Daddy? I told you.'

I opened my eyes in shock. My father, hands on hips, was standing grim-faced in the doorway, with Linda looking up at him like a dog which has just performed an especially clever trick, and now expects a reward. I was horrified. I would sooner have been caught wetting the bed.

'Thomas,' said my father, 'get dressed. And I think it's time the rest of you went home.'

I feared he might cut my willy off by way of retribution for the extreme dirtiness of my behaviour, but in the event I suffered no physical punishment. Instead, when the others had gone, he talked to me briefly but gravely about what had happened. Other people, girls especially, were not supposed to see me naked, and I was never again to play doctors and nurses, or any other game that involved taking my clothes off. I thought he was right.

~

Matters sexual were thus ruled out of order, but no one made any attempt to delay my political awakening in the general election which took place later that year. Its most notable feature was that school was to be closed for the day, but there was more to it than that. From what my parents said, I gathered that it was to be a contest between a good man called Mister Macmillan, who was the leader of the Conservatives, and a bad man called Gaitskell, who was the leader of the Socialists. (There was also a man called Jo Grimond, the leader of the Liberals. He was neither very good nor very bad, but hardly anyone was going to vote for him.) The country was to be run by the winner, and my parents feared it would be Gaitskell.

'I don't see them winning three in a row, do you?' said my mother after the news on the evening before the election.

My father shook his head. 'No,' he said, 'I can't see it. People still remember Suez, and they blame the Tories for it. They don't understand.'

'I'm sure the Bromheads vote Labour.'

'Oh, they would. Typical socialists, I'd say.'

Following just enough of this to know that my friends were being slandered, I sprang to their defence. 'No they're not!' I said. 'Keith says Macmillan's the only man to run the country. Keith and Jill say he's going to win.'

I was told to be quiet, on the grounds that I was not old enough to understand politics.

But Linda, as usual, took an intelligent interest, and the following day, when our parents had gone to vote, she undertook to explain the issues to me. 'Mister Macmillan wants us all to have our own houses,' she said, 'and that's a good thing.'

'What does Gaitskell want?'

'He wants everybody to live in horrible little council houses, like grandma and grandpa.'

'Why?'

'Oh you silly little boy, stop bothering me. You're too young to understand.'

'You don't understand either. You just pretend all the time.'

She shook her head wearily and left me. I began to get worried about the election. I felt there had to be more to it than I had been told – I didn't much care what sort of house I lived in – and that Gaitskell would surely do some really nasty things if he won. Otherwise, why would all the adults whose views on the matter I knew – my parents, Keith and Jill, and even my grandparents, who already lived in a council house without apparent ill effects – be so anxious that he should lose? There was something they weren't telling me.

I couldn't think why anyone should want to vote for Gaitskell, and yet my parents thought he would get more votes than Mister Macmillan. And then, just as I was about to abandon the problem as being genuinely beyond my comprehension, I had a flash of insight: Gaitskell would get all the votes of bad people, people like Mr Blackett. This was my political awakening.

'Who won?' I said as I went into the kitchen for breakfast the next morning.

'The Tories,' said my father, who was looking pleased with life. 'And a good thing for all of us.'

'Hear hear, Daddy,' said Linda, who was always up before me.

'I'm always going to vote for the Tories when I grow up,' I said.

'Yes, well see you do,' said my father.

My mother poured my cereal for me, and took a sip of coffee. 'John won't be pleased,' she said.

'Is that John Blackett?' I asked, anxious to have my theory about voting patterns confirmed.

'Mister Blackett to you, Thomas,' she said.

'He will not,' said my father. 'But Labour votes are wasted here anyway.'

From then on, I was able to take an intelligent interest in politics, and was as staunch a Tory as could be found anywhere in the country. It was the only thing my sister and I agreed on.

3 Violence

It was a bad day for me when, some months after the election, the Bromheads moved out and the Pendletons moved in. My opinion of Keith and Jill reached new heights the day before their departure when she gave me the biggest piece of chocolate cake I had ever had, and he fulfilled a longstanding promise to 'do the ton' with me on the other side of the village. I could have wept when they left, but my parents weren't sorry. Linda, who disapproved of any friend of mine on principle, was careful to show her indifference. (She, incidentally, now took her famous brain by train every day to Stambridge Grammar School, where she was already considered 'brilliant', cleverness having been left behind in Ashminster.)

I was upstairs in my room when the Pendletons arrived – it was a Saturday morning – and, despite my hostility to anyone seeking to take the place of Keith and Jill, I watched with interest. They had a child, a fat boy of about my height, but to him I paid little attention. My parents, without wanting to admit it, were at least as interested as I was, and took it in turns to watch from the bow window of the sitting-room. Linda helped them.

When I got bored, I went down to the kitchen in search of chocolate biscuits. Not being allowed one until we had coffee at eleven, which was half an hour away, I had it in mind to steal one. Having at last got over the gingerbread disaster of three years previously, I had been pinching chocolate biscuits for some time, but had recently been terrorised into virtue by Mr Blackett, who had warned us that bad deeds were always punished, and that if you didn't catch it from him or from your parents in this life, you would certainly catch it from God in the afterlife, and then you'd be sorry. (He had a gift for making hell sound real, though he could never make much of the other place.)

Just a few days before, though, he had been so careless as to reveal a loophole in this apparently inexorable law of divine retribution. He had said that God never punished people for doing wrong, provided only that they sincerely regretted it afterwards. To sincerely regret, he had explained, was to be very very sorry, and it didn't matter what you did in all your life, if only you were very very sorry about it on your deathbed. So I resumed stealing chocolate biscuits, smuggling them up to my room to eat, then lying on my deathbed in the corner next to the window feeling as sorry as hell about it for a minimum of three minutes afterwards. I knew, you see, that three was a lucky number, and if I only managed two minutes after one crime, I would always make it four after the next.

On this occasion though, I was unlucky, for my mother came in from her stint at the sitting-room window just as I was opening the cupboard.

'What are you looking in there for?'

I nearly jumped out of my skin. 'A mouse,' I said. 'I saw a mouse.' For I had a quick and inventive mind.

'A mouse? Where?'

'Where?'

'Yes, where? Come on, where was the mouse?'

I was frightened. She was trying to fluster me into admitting I had been after the chocolate biscuits. 'There,' I said quickly. 'Going into the cupboard. The door wasn't closed properly.'

'Walter!' she shouted. 'Thomas saw a mouse in the cupboard!'

'Eh?'

'Walter! Come here! There's a mouse in the cupboard!'

When he appeared, Linda was just behind him, and her presence made me even more nervous. She understood me better than our parents did, and I feared that the truth could not long be concealed from her.

'What're you saying, Doris?'

'Walter, are you deaf? There's a mouse in the cupboard.'

I had another stroke of inspiration. 'It was a big one,' I said, with a glance at my sister. 'Maybe it was a rat.' She was, I knew, terrified of rats, and anyway, I felt that the more detail I added to my story, the more convincing it would be.

Linda stopped in the doorway, and simulated a weary sigh. 'Oh well, I suppose there are enough of you to deal with this without my help,' she said, and, to my relief, made a swift retreat to a place of safety.

'Well,' said my father, 'open the cupboard.'

'I started to open it,' I said.

'Be quiet, Thomas. You open it, Walter. I'll catch the mouse if it gets out. The rat.'

My father opened the cupboard while she stood well back. 'I can't see anything,' he said.

'Take everything out, absolutely everything. It must be hiding.'

I began to get worried again. What would happen when they had emptied the cupboard and still found no rodent? 'Maybe I was wrong,' I said. 'I sometimes see things that aren't really there. I get dizzy spells.'

'Thomas, be quiet. Everything out, Walter. I'm not having rats and mice in my kitchen.'

I retired to my room to await retribution, as this struck me as one of those cases in which it was not to be deferred until the afterlife. I felt hard done by because, had I only been granted the few extra seconds necessary to steal and then hide the biscuit – I had only wanted one – I would have got safely away to my room to eat it, and would then have sincerely regretted it on my deathbed, thus heading off the possibility of punishment. But it hadn't worked out, and now I was in trouble.

That at least is what I thought, but I was wrong. All that happened when they failed to find any rodent was that they dug out an old mouse-trap, and put that in the cupboard with a bit of cheese on it. Of course, nothing was ever caught, and the last word on the matter went to my sister: 'Silly little boy, he must have imagined it.'

~

My mother's favourite topic of conversation at this time was Antony Armstrong-Jones, the man who was about to marry Princess Margaret. Judging by the number of times she would mention it in the course of the average day, I would say she enjoyed the sound of his name. She was certainly giving it an extensive airing over coffee that same morning when I, desperate to change the subject to something less boring, raised the matter of the Bromheads.

'What was wrong with the Bromheads?' I said, at a moment when she had temporarily run out of things to say about Armstrong-Jones.

'Nothing was wrong with them,' she said. She spoke sharply, no doubt irritated at having to talk about anything other than Antony Armstrong-Jones.

'You didn't like them,' I said, determined to hold Armstrong-Jones at bay.

'You wouldn't understand,' said my father. 'We'll tell you when you're older.'

I warded off a severe attack of homicidal mania by curling my toes till they hurt. 'Tell me now,' I said doggedly.

'Well,' said my mother, accepting that Antony Armstrong-Jones was for the moment out of the conversational reckoning, 'the Bromheads weren't educated like your father and I. You could tell by the way they talked.'

'How?'

Linda sighed and rolled her eyes heavenwards.

'Well, Mr Bromhead used to say "you was" instead of "you were", and things like that.'

'Bad grammar,' said Linda.

'Yes, and sometimes he used... well, bad words.'

'What bad words?'

My father helped himself to a third chocolate biscuit, something I was never allowed. 'Be quiet, Thomas. We'll tell you when you're older.'

'Is "fuck" a bad word?'

Linda made a noise of startled disgust, pushed her chair violently back and sprang to her feet.

'Thomas!!' My mother was no less shocked. 'You must never never say that word! That's the dirtiest word there is. Never never say it. Never.'

I had, of course, hoped to cause some consternation by using what I knew to be a genuine five-star obscenity, but the violence of her reaction took me aback. All I knew about 'fuck' was that it was a dirty word, which, if Gordon Stacker was to be believed, had something do with dirty things that bad men and women did together.

'Did Keith say it?' I asked. Timidly.

'No. Linda, sit down, will you? Now you must never say that word ever again. Do you understand?'

'Yes... Gordon Stacker says it all the time.'

'Then he's a wicked wicked boy, and you must never never do anything that he does.'

I got the message. 'Fuck' was the most terrible thing you could say. Even Keith Bromhead didn't say 'fuck'. It

27

was probably worse than stealing chocolate biscuits. I promised myself never to say 'fuck' again. Never ever.

~

Unfortunately, 'fuck' was one of the first things Bruce Pendleton said to me when, on my parents' invitation, the newcomers paid us a visit that evening. When the introductions were over, and my father was pouring the drinks, Linda and I were told we could go and play in the garden with Bruce. She declined haughtily, and I wasn't too pleased with the suggestion either, because I didn't much like boys of my age – Bruce turned out to be just three months older than me – but I had little choice in the matter.

'Antony Armstrong-Jones,' I heard my mother say as I closed the door behind us.

'Fuck this,' said Pendleton.

'You mustn't say that!' I said in alarm. 'That's the dirtiest word in the world.' The truth was that, since being caught playing doctors and nurses, I had become a coward and was always afraid that the company of what my mother termed 'rough boys' might get me into trouble I didn't deserve.

'I know all the bad words in the world. I can teach you them if you like.'

'I want to play,' I said, determined to stay out of trouble.

'What do you want to play?'

'I don't know. What do *you* want to play?'

Bruce Pendleton was bigger than me. He had curly fair hair, and I didn't like him. But with our houses standing close together half a mile outside the village, I could see that we had little choice but to become 'best friends'. Children can be trapped into such relationships very easily.

'Let's play chess,' he said. 'I'm good at chess. I always win.'

'I've lent my chess set to somebody,' I said. 'I'll play you when I get it back.'

'I'll beat you.'

'No you won't.' I felt obliged to resist.

'I'll fucking beat you.'

'You mustn't say that!'

'If we can't play chess, we can box. Can you box?'

'Yes.'

'Come on then, let's box. I always win at boxing.' Pendleton put his fists up and began to dance around in front of me.

'I'm not boxing without gloves,' I said.

'You don't need gloves.'

'Yes you do.'

'All right then, we'll wrestle. I'm good at that too.'

I felt I could scarcely turn down another suggestion, so we wrestled. Or rather, Pendleton assaulted me and I did my best to defend myself. Within ten seconds I was face-down on the grass with my left arm in an agonising lock. I began to howl.

'Submit?' shouted Pendleton, but I didn't know what he meant. 'Submit?' he said again, and increased the pressure on my arm. I yelled louder.

There was a fierce staccato tapping on the sitting-room window, and my arm was slowly released. I looked up to see my mother standing at the window, looking disapproving. She waited until we were both vertical and at peace before she disappeared from view.

'You're lucky,' said Pendleton. 'I'd've broken your arm if you hadn't submitted.'

'I was going to win,' I said, resisting with difficulty the urge to feel my left arm to see if there was anything broken.

'No you weren't. Mummy had to save Mummy's boy.'

And at this point I learned one of the most important

lessons of my life: when people tell you they're tough, don't take their word for it.

I flew at my tormentor and beat hell out of him. We were on the grass again in moments, but this time it was Pendleton who was underneath, and his nose was bleeding.

The tattoo on the window was still more urgent than before, but I ignored it in my rage. My father had to dash out and pull me bodily off my shrieking adversary.

I was hauled inside, bent without ceremony over his knee, and spanked hard and long in the presence of the whole Pendleton family, Bruce having followed us inside, still sobbing. His parents put on a show of censoriousness towards him, but his bleeding nose suggested that I had been the aggressor, so he was not punished.

When my father had finished, Pendleton's eyes were dry but I was squawking again. I was to wonder, in later years, if I had ever forgiven my father for that humiliation.

I certainly did not forgive him that day, for within the hour, I made an attempt to gain revenge. Linda and I had both officially gone to bed when I sneaked into our parents' room and helped myself to a hair from my father's pillow and a pin from my mother's sewing box. And when I was safely back in my own room, I took a candle which I had been saving to light a midnight feast, melted some wax, and made of it a tiny figure of a man, embedding the hair inside it. The likeness was not good, but provided it was identifiable as a man, the devil would know it was my father because of the hair. Gordon Stacker had killed five people he didn't like that way.

Once I had managed the essential facial features with the aid of the point of a pencil, I sat down on the bed, held the manikin in my left hand, and thrust the pin through its breast with my right.

Scarcely able to believe what I had done, but not for an

instant regretting it, I crept downstairs to see if the magic had worked. I thought my mother might have screamed as my father died, but then it struck me that he had probably gone so quickly that she hadn't yet noticed.

When I reached the sitting-room door, I stopped and listened. The Pendletons had left shortly before, and the television was on.

'They're a better *type* than the Bromheads,' I heard my mother say.

That was it. When he didn't react, she would say it again, and then, alarmed by his continued silence, she'd go over to him and shake him. His head would flop to one side, tongue protruding, eyes glazed. Then she'd scream all right.

'Oh yes,' said my father, 'much better people to have as neighbours.'

I couldn't believe it hadn't worked. Had Gordon Stacker lied? Then I recalled that he had said you had to curse the figurine as you stabbed it. I returned to my room to try again.

But as I held the thing up, with the pin poised inches from its heart, I realised that I didn't want my father dead after all. Whatever he had done, he was still my father, and I wouldn't know what to do without him. And then Pendleton's jeering voice echoed in my head – 'Mummy had to save Mummy's boy' – and I saw my public humiliation in an action replay.

'Curse my father!' I hissed, and ran the image through.

There could be no doubt about it this time. This time he was dead. I began to cry. I had killed my father, and now there would be nobody to look after me. My mother would hate me for ever, and would throw me out of the house. I would be the only child in the school without a mother or a father. I would have nowhere to live and nobody to love me. Maybe I'd go to prison. Maybe I'd be hanged.

Trying hard to stifle my sobs, I withdrew the pin from the model, and did what I could to heal the two punctures it had made. Then I flopped down at the side of my deathbed and began to pray: 'Please God, let my father come back to life because I didn't mean to kill him and my mother will cry and so will I and so will Linda, so please bring him back, please. I promise I'll never take any chocolate biscuits, and I'll be good for ever, for Thine is the kingdom, the power and the glory, for ever and ever, Amen... pee ess, I'll do anything you want if you just give me a sign.'

I felt slightly better as I stood up and made my way downstairs again, but what if God didn't agree to help me? What if He couldn't bring my father back? I was half way down the stairs when the sitting-room door opened and my father came out.

'Thomas! Why aren't you in bed?'

I nearly died of sheer relief. 'I couldn't sleep. I had dizzy spells.'

'Is that boy still up?' My mother didn't sound pleased either.

'You get to bed this instant,' said my father, 'or I'll give you another thrashing, my boy, d'you hear?'

'Yes,' I said, but as I turned to go back to my room, I closed my eyes for a moment and put a hand to my forehead to show that the dizzy spells weren't just a story.

~

Despite its immediate consequences though, my victory over Pendleton was on the whole a good thing. It was the first fight I had won since leaving Winterby, and the self-confidence I had lost in Ashminster began to come back. I also began to take a serious interest in swearing, determined that my new 'friend' should have no cause to share my own suspicion that I was a cissy.

In fact, the tougher Pendleton had been, the better it

would have been for me, but further evidence that he was more talk than action came on the Monday morning, when Gordon Stacker, in company with a number of hangers-on, approached the two of us in the playground in the middle of the morning break. Pendleton was the target.

'I don't like your face, mister,' said Stacker, who was a devotee of westerns.

'Leave him alone,' I said, not because I didn't want to see Pendleton beaten up – I did – but because I wanted him to know how tough I was. So tough that I could stand up to Gordon Stacker.

I had calculated that the latter would not show much interest in me when there was someone new to bully, and I was right. 'Piss off, Cardwell,' he said.

I shrugged my shoulders as if to indicate that I had decided on reflection that this was not my business.

'I'm talking to you, mister. I said I don't like your face.'

'Go away,' said Pendleton, failing hopelessly to hide his terror. He moved closer to me.

Stacker put a hand on his shoulder and pulled him round until the two were facing each other at a distance of twelve inches. A crowd was beginning to gather, as always when a fight was in the offing.

Pendleton tried to look bored. 'What do you want then?' he said with a sigh.

'Lick that,' said Stacker, pointing to his right foot.

'No.'

Stacker got hold of his ear and began to twist. Pendleton struggled briefly, then gave up and started yelling.

'Lick that.'

'Aaagh!! Yes yes yes! Aagh!!'

He was released, and did as Stacker demanded.

'And before you go, mister, the next time I tell you to lick my boots, don't give me any shit, understand?'

'Yes,' said Pendleton, wiping a tear from his eye.

'Then you and me'll get along just fine.'

~

But even if he wasn't very tough, Bruce Pendleton could always manage to push me around, as could most people. Except when I lost my temper, which was not often, I had as much backbone as a jellyfish.

That very evening, for example, we decided to play British and Jerries in his garden. The game was my suggestion, but Pendleton put forward an interesting variation on the theme of the standard infantry combat which I had in mind. He said that we could use the garden shed as a British bomber, and pretend we were on a night raid over Germany.

He knew a lot about it, because when I agreed and said I would be Field Marshal Montgomery, he said that was daft because Field Marshal Montgomery was a soldier, not an airman. He said that I could be Flight Lieutenant Smith while he would be Captain Douglas Bader, because Douglas Bader was the best pilot there was. I was to be co-pilot.

I objected to this, saying I wanted to be a gunner. Pendleton agreed, but stressed that he would be giving the orders because he was the captain. And when I said we would bomb Berlin, he said no, we would bomb Geneva, because that was where the German weapons were made.

Just before take-off, I discovered that we were short not only of a co-pilot, but also of a navigator, a rear gunner (I was the front gunner) and a bomb aimer, all of whose functions were assumed by the pilot.

In the course of the raid, the co-pilot and bomb aimer were killed, and the pilot and navigator wounded. But Douglas Bader flew on, speaking through gritted teeth in a clipped American accent, and when one of the engines was hit and caught fire, Bader it was who, having put the plane on auto-pilot, crawled out onto the wing to extinguish the blaze.

It was all a bit much even for me, but what really upset me was that Pendleton, in his capacity as rear gunner, shot down many more German planes than I did. Indeed, my presence seemed irrelevant, but when I put this to him he assured me that my contribution was vital to the success of the mission, and I was pacified.

We finally landed on one engine and a damaged undercarriage, and Flight Lieutenant Smith could hardly deny that Douglas Bader, who fainted from loss of blood just after touchdown, had been the hero of the mission. It was fitting that, after he had recovered from his wounds, he should go to Buckingham Palace where I, now cast resentfully in the role of Queen Victoria, conferred on him the Victoria Cross and dubbed him Sir Douglas Bader.

'Why don't I get a medal?' I asked, when the ceremony was over. 'I was on the raid too.'

'You didn't get wounded.'

'I want a medal,' I said. (From my point of view, the only thing to be said for Pendleton's overbearing manner was that at least it was beginning to goad me into some sort of resistance.)

'Oh, all right,' he said with a sigh.

And back at the aerodrome, Flight Lieutenant Smith humbly received the Iron Cross from Sir Douglas Bader.

4 Religion

Bruce Pendleton, this is disgraceful! Do you call this handwriting? If I dipped a hen's feet in ink and made it walk across the page, it couldn't make a worse mess than this! You'd better pull your socks up, my lad, or you'll be in trouble.'

Pendleton cowered, and I gloated. This was only his second day, and already the headmaster had found fault with him. Unless the fat brute could learn to write better, he would be in constant danger of the cane, handwriting being Mr Blackett's greatest obsession. We used to spend extravagant amounts of time on copybooks, in which we laboriously duplicated such worthy maxims as 'Know something of everything.' (copy three times, upper half of page), and 'Know everything of something.' (copy three times, lower half of page). A genuine error in a copybook, such as a wrong spelling or a missed full stop, was always punished with the cane, and so, on occasion, was even an imperfectly formed letter. The first time I was caned was when, in forming the word 'gold', I was so careless as to make the vertical stroke of the letter 'd' equal in length to the loop in the letter 'l', instead of fractionally shorter. A Freudian might have termed Mr Blackett an anal erotic.

It was to my disappointment that Pendleton did manage to produce writing to Mr Blackett's satisfaction in a short space of time, and I waited impatiently for him to fall foul of the headmaster in some other way. But, with his shrewd blend of cowardice and cunning, he succeeded in staying out of serious trouble for the full seven weeks that remained until the summer holidays, a notable achievement. It was nothing, of course, alongside Linda's record of a full year under Mr Blackett without once being caned, but she was not human.

It was in early November that the day came on which Alison Winkle was absent. Absences did not usually cause much stir among us, but there was apprehension that morning as nine o'clock approached and Alison Winkle didn't. The reason for this was that every day began with a choral recitation of the Lord's Prayer, which was in fact led by Alison, who always began each line a split second before the rest of us. Without her, we would be like an orchestra without a conductor and we knew it, for Mr Blackett always remained silent. When Cecil Leach drew attention to her absence, a stormy debate we had been having on the American presidential campaign came to a sudden halt. (This annoyed me, as I, a Nixon supporter, had just made what I considered to be a devastating point in asserting, falsely, that my father said that John Kennedy was a communist.)

'It'll be okay,' I said. 'Blackett'll lead us when he sees Winkle's absent.'

And then Pendleton, who had been on my side in the political debate, decided to assert himself. 'I don't know why you're all so scared,' he said, with a sigh of bored superiority. 'I know the words. I'll lead you.'

Before I could think of a suitably withering riposte, our discussion was cut short by the bell. Every morning, at one minute to nine, Mr Blackett appeared at the door and tolled a great wooden-handled brass bell. His rule was that the moment we heard it, we should run – not walk – to the door, and we never disobeyed him, for the consequences of disobeying Mr Blackett were dire.

In moments we were in front of him, drawn up in three ragged lines, with seven in the shortest and eleven in the longest. (These were the older pupils, the three infants' classes, taught by Mrs Varley, having their own playground on the other side of the school.)

'Class Four,' said Mr Blackett, and the row on the left, made up of the eight smallest children, filed silently past him. 'Class Five.' He followed the last line in, and closed the door.

'All hands clasped. All eyes closed.' This was the signal to start the prayer.

'Our Father,' we began, raggedly, 'Which art in heaven...' And then Pendleton took over. 'Hallowed be thy name,' he said in a firm voice, and we all followed him gratefully.

And then he got it wrong. When we came to 'Give us this day our daily bread,' he began 'Give us our daily bread...' and petered out. We stumbled to a halt.

'Give us this day,' said Mr Blackett, and led us in the rest of the prayer. I was doubly pleased. Not only had Pendleton made a fool of himself, but Mr Blackett had fulfilled my prediction by taking over. He would be telling us what he though of us the moment the prayer was finished, but the only one likely to be in real trouble was Bruce Pendleton... 'Amen.'

'Stand up!' snapped Mr Blackett, as we attempted to follow the normal practice of sitting down after the prayer. 'Cecil Leach, did you hear me tell you to sit down?'

'No sir,' mumbled Leach.

Mr Blackett went to the cupboard behind his desk, and took from it his cane. 'Bruce Pendleton, come out here.'

The fat brute's face was rigid with terror as he walked out to the front, and I could barely conceal my delight. Feeling that this might, in the circumstances, be an unworthy emotion, I told myself that it was a serious matter to get the words of the Lord's Prayer wrong, certainly deserving of the severest punishment. Self-righteousness made me feel even better.

'Bruce Pendleton, did I hear you make a mistake in the Lord's Prayer just now?'

Pendleton treated us to a parody of injured innocence, spreading his hands and widening his eyes as if in disbelief that such an accusation might be made. 'No sir!'

'Hold out your hand.'

I moved a fraction to my right to get a better view. I was close to ecstasy.

Mr Blackett measured his distance by placing the tip of the cane on Pendleton's palm. In the hush of apprehension, the noise of a passing lorry came like thunder through the plate-glass windows, and the barely perceptible trembling of the floor was an earthquake.

The cane rose, and a tear trickled down Pendleton's terrified face. For more than four months, I had looked forward to this moment, but it had been worth the wait.

There was a swish and a crack as the cane came down. Pendleton gasped and his hand crumpled, but before he could withdraw it, Mr Blackett said 'Again.'

I felt like cheering. I hadn't expected him to get more than one.

'That was only for getting the words of the Lord's Prayer wrong.'

Pendleton opened his palm again, and the headmaster delivered a second stroke, appreciably sharper than the first.

'That was for lying about it. Go back to your place. Sit down, all of you.'

I found myself nodding involuntarily in admiration of Mr Blackett's sense of justice. One for getting the words wrong, one for lying about it. I wouldn't have thought of that. But he was so right, because this concerned God as well as Mr Blackett, so punishment had to be severe.

Pendleton was crying silently as he walked past to resume his place behind me, and I was full of contempt. Only girls cried when they were caned. But when I caught his eye, I was ashamed, and looked away.

Mr Blackett put his cane back in the cupboard, folded his arms, and looked down on us with palpable contempt. 'It is quite pathetic,' he began, 'that you children still do not know the words of the Lord's Prayer. It only takes Alison to be absent, and you're lost. Pathetic. Even Class Four should know the words by now, and for Class Six there is no excuse. Now I'm going to give each of you a piece of paper, and on it you will write the Lord's Prayer. You will have ten minutes.' He took a notebook from his drawer, and began tearing out pages. 'And if I see anyone trying to look at anyone else's paper...' (He looked round threateningly.) '... there's going to be trouble.'

'There's going to be trouble,' always delivered in a low voice, full of menace, was Mr Blackett's favourite threat, and for all its vagueness, it was not to be taken lightly.

The tension in the room, which had slackened when Pendleton's punishment was over, was now greater than ever. I knew the words of the Lord's Prayer perfectly – the only reason I hadn't led the recitation was that leading wasn't in my nature – and I was going to enjoy writing them down. And my pleasure would be heightened by the thought of the misery of the likes of Gordon Stacker, who was sure to make an appalling mess of it.

'Sally Henderson, were you talking?'

'No sir.'

'Right, the next person I catch talking will be caned.' Amidst a silence heavy with apprehension, he gave out the paper, then looked purposefully at his watch. 'Start writing. You have ten minutes.'

Pendleton's sobs suddenly became audible, and everyone turned to look at him. It was odd, as he should by this time have been recovering from his pain and humiliation, not feeling it more deeply.

'Bruce Pendleton, what's the matter now?'

'Please sir, I can't write,' said Pendleton, holding up his injured left hand.

To my horror, I experienced a sudden access of sympathy, and felt like crying myself. Poor Pendleton, it wasn't fair! And he was my best friend! I looked away from him, and took a deep breath, terrified that a tear might come.

'Then why,' said Mr Blackett, shaking his head, 'didn't you hold out your right hand, you stupid boy? Do you expect *me* always to remember that you're left-handed? Oh, take out your reading book and revise the last lesson. You've already shown me *you* don't know the Lord's Prayer anyway.'

My composure returned as he spoke, and I began to write. The only real problems I had were with spelling, for I could only guess at the orthography of 'trespasses' and 'temptation', but this didn't bother me, as I doubted that anyone would be able to do better.

Apart from the distant noises which penetrated the room from the world outside, the only sound was of scratchy fountain pens on paper. Mr Blackett sat behind his desk, glancing occasionally at his watch. Whispering or copying were out of the question. I managed one or two surreptitious glances round the room, though, and was delighted to see anxiety and apprehension on almost all faces. At one point, I found myself shaking my head in sage disapproval. Imagine not knowing the Lord's Prayer! A lot of people were going to be in trouble when our ten minutes was up, and rightly so, because this was an insult not only to Mr Blackett, but to God Himself. It struck me that they should be grateful to the headmaster when he punished them, because then they would avoid the much worse fate of being punished by God in the afterlife. They would avoid going to hell. I tried putting myself in their position, and yes, it was clear to me that I would accept the cane gladly, and even thank Mr Blackett for it afterwards. How terrible not to know the Lord's Prayer!

Although I wrote slowly and carefully, determined to make my offering as close to perfection as possible, I still finished with time to spare, and had chance to look over my work twice in full before Mr Blackett said 'Put down your pens. Hand your papers to the front.'

Two places behind me sat Gordon Stacker, and his paper was wonderfully bad. He had got only as far as 'As we for give those', and there were errors even in what little he had written. 'Amen' was scrawled at the foot of the page, alone and forlorn, detached for ever from the truncated prayer. 'Amen'. I was so pleased.

Mr Blackett set us all to do other work while he looked at what we had written, but concentration was impossible. He went through the papers rapidly, making no marks on them, but dividing them into two unequal batches, the smaller of which contained barely a handful. He pushed back his chair, rose to his feet, and placed his hands on his hips.

'Stop what you're doing and pay attention. This is quite disgraceful. There are nearly thirty pupils in this room, and yet only three of you – *three* – know the words of the Lord's Prayer by heart.' He picked up the smaller group of papers, and flourished them in front of us. 'Stand up Mary MacLean, Caroline Tillotson and Thomas Cardwell.'

It was an effort to prevent my features from twisting into a smirk, but I managed it. Mr Blackett had a thing about smirking. Instead I succeeded in holding what I hoped was an expression of piety such as might be fitting at so solemn a moment. I was being held up as an example to the rest, and I was not going to let the headmaster down. What was especially gratifying was that my reputation was at its zenith when Pendleton's was at its nadir. The only thing that clouded my happiness was that quite so many had got it wrong, because Mr Blackett would surely not cane all of them.

'These three, and only these three. Now it's bad enough that nobody in Class Four knows the Lord's Prayer properly, but for the rest of you, it's downright disgraceful.' He turned to his cupboard and took the cane out once more.

My heart leapt with joy. Now I could see what he was going to do. He was going to cane the offenders in Classes Five and Six only. My one regret was that Pendleton wasn't going to be caned again. The sympathy I had felt for him less than fifteen minutes before had now evaporated, and I would have been delighted to see him hurt again. Never mind, I was still going to have plenty to enjoy. I raised my head slightly, and tried to look even more pious.

'You three, come out here.'

For a dreadful moment, I thought he was going to cane *us*. When Mr Blackett had his cane in his hand and ordered someone to the front, that could normally mean only one thing. Then reason asserted itself over instinct. That the two girls and I should be caned was the only thing that *wasn't* possible. No, he wanted us in front where everyone could see us, so that our example might shine the more brightly.

'Now,' he said, when he had us where he wanted, 'you three all knew the words of the Lord's Prayer, but you didn't say them earlier on. Why not?'

I nearly died of shock. This was the most dreadful moment of my life. 'Please sir,' I said in desperation, 'I was going to say the right words, but when Bruce Pendleton made a mistake, I got mixed up.'

'Yes sir!' said Mary MacLean.

'Yes sir!' said Caroline Tillotson.

I was frantic with rage. It was my excuse, I'd thought of it, and it might just have been good enough to get one of us off, but all three? No chance. What right did the little bitches have to take my excuse? I hoped they would both die very soon. Caroline Tillotson began to cry.

'Please sir,' said Mary MacLean, 'I only remembered the words when I was writing them down.'

'Yes sir!' I said.

'But a moment ago you both said you just got mixed up when Bruce Pendleton made a mistake. You've got no excuse, any of you, and I'm going to teach you all a lesson. Caroline Tillotson, you first.'

~

It had been a disappointment to me when Pendleton, who was ahead of me in most things, stopped taking *The Beezer* and *The Dandy*, and started taking *The Eagle* instead. I took *The Beano* and *The Topper*, and always looked forward keenly to our weekly swap, largely because of my fascination with Korky the Cat, who appeared on the front page of *The Dandy*, and whose enormous eyes, coloured bright green in the annuals, gave me a strange thrill.

Now the swap was two to one in Pendleton's favour, and Korky the Cat was gone from my life. Buying *The Dandy* myself wouldn't have been the same, somehow. But I was coming to appreciate *The Eagle* more and more, and Dan Dare had become my hero.

My humiliation of the morning forgotten, I had just had tea, and was now sitting in the kitchen reading his latest adventure while my mother was washing the dishes. The sound of the front door opening indicated that Linda was back from Stambridge.

My sister was the only pupil of Mr Blackett's I knew

who had never been caned by him, and this had the effect of making her gloat all the more when I was punished. Not that this was a frequent occurrence, for the headmaster had me under control, but her attitude made it worse when it did happen. It had been a relief when she and her famous brain left for Stambridge, and I thought as I heard her come in that day that the only good thing about the Lord's Prayer disaster was that at least she did not know about it.

'Who got caned in school today, then?' she said smirking as she entered the kitchen.

Dan Dare's attempt to rescue Digby from the Mekon ceased to matter, and I looked up at her with loathing even greater than usual. She was delighted with herself for having found out.

'Was he?' said our mother. 'You didn't tell me, Thomas.' She did not turn round, or even pause in her dishwashing.

'Yes, he was... I'll help you, Mummy.' She put down her satchel, and grabbed a tea-towel. 'Bet you can't guess how I know.'

'I don't care,' I said sullenly.

'I heard Cecil Leach telling his father about it when I was walking back from the station.'

'Why were you caned, Thomas?'

I clenched both fists and looked down at the table, on which Dan Dare was now a blur.

Linda was enjoying herself. 'He was caned for getting the Lord's Prayer wrong at the start of the day.'

I cracked. 'It wasn't only me!' I burst out. 'It was Bruce Pendleton and Caroline Tillotson and Mary MacLean too! And I was caned for getting it right!'

'Silly little boy,' she said, adopting her most superior tone. 'How could you have been caned for getting something right?'

'You wouldn't understand,' I said, making a dreadful

45

hash of the weary sigh that Linda always used to such effect when delivering that sentence.

'He was crying too. Weren't you?'

'No I wasn't! You're a bloody liar!' I grabbed my comic, and stormed out.

'Thomas!!' Our mother had at last heard something that interested her. 'Thomas, come back here this instant, do you hear me? I will *not* have language like that in this house! Come back here!'

By now though, I was half way up the stairs, and not going to turn back, so she took off after me.

Linda decided to get in on the act too. 'Thomas, come back! You heard Mummy!'

Of course, I should have sought refuge in the bathroom, where I could have locked myself in, but I didn't think of that. Instead, I obeyed my natural instinct and fled to my own room, the door of which could not be locked. My mistake was immediately obvious to me, but with my mother near the top of the stairs in pursuit, I had no option but to make a stand where I was. I braced myself against the door.

'Thomas?... Thomas, you get away from the door! Thomas!'

She made quite an effort, and, frightened though I now was at the unprecedented lengths to which I had taken my resistance, I was surprised and delighted at my success in standing firm.

'Now you listen to me, Thomas. We're having chocolate ice-cream for dinner, and if you don't come downstairs at once, and apologise to your sister, you're getting none... Thomas?'

I said nothing. I had done nothing wrong, and was apologising to no one. And having just had tea, I was temporarily uninterested in food. Even chocolate ice-cream

Another set of footsteps was coming upstairs. 'Oh Mummy, just ignore the silly little boy.'

'Yes, you're quite right, Linda, that's the best thing to do. Do you hear that, Thomas? We're going to ignore you. We're not going to speak to you until you come downstairs and apologise to your sister... Thomas?... And no ice-cream either until you do... All right, we're going back down now. We're ignoring you. Come on, Linda.'

But I stayed where I was. I wasn't fooled that easily, and the exaggeratedly heavy footsteps that retreated from my door served only to confirm my suspicions. I pressed my ear against the wood and, sure enough, after a few hefty thumps on the stairs, I heard the creak of floorboards as she sneaked back.

Her second attempt to force an entry was no less determined than the first, but I was equal to it. 'Now Thomas, you open this door! Immediately! Thomas, do you hear me?... Oh, you're an impossible child at times! Right, no ice-cream. We'll see what your father has to say about this when he comes in.' And this time she really did go back downstairs.

I was pleased with myself. I had called my sister a bloody liar – which she was – and had successfully resisted my mother's strenuous efforts to force me to apologise. As for her chocolate ice-cream, she could keep it. In fact, I would whistle while they were eating theirs, just to show how little I cared. The real problem was my father. He would be upstairs the moment he heard what had happened, and I would never hold the door against him. The solution, I decided, was a barricade.

It took a big effort, but at length I succeeded in placing my chest of drawers side on against the door, and then I laid my chair flat on the carpet with its legs against the chest of drawers, and its head close to the side of the bed. From outside, the door could be pushed open only three

47

or four inches before the chair reached the bed. With a warm sense of security, and an agreeable feeling of competence in the art of siege warfare, I lay down on the bed and turned my attention once more to the plight of Digby.

By the time my father came home, Dan Dare had long since rescued his pal, and I was beginning to get bored. That didn't last. The footsteps on the stairs were strong and purposeful, and the banging on the door was like thunder.

'Thomas! You open up! Now!'

I closed my eyes, and said nothing.

He tried the door, but the chair reached the bed almost instantly. 'Oh for God's sake... Thomas?... The little fool's put something against the door. All right, we'll starve him out.' He went back downstairs, muttering something about Teddy boys.

The success of my barricade for some reason gave me nothing like the satisfaction that its construction had. I was bored now, and my brain was getting signals from my stomach to the effect that chocolate ice-cream should not lightly be forgone. And now the threat was that I would get no dinner at all.

We always ate at seven o'clock. As the time approached and I was not called, I began to get worried. But I had my pride to think of, and I resolved to sit it out. In fact, far from my apologising to anyone, I would demand that *they* apologise to *me*, and if they refused, I would never come out. I would stay in my room, and starve myself to death. Then they'd be sorry. I spent an agreeable few minutes imagining just how sorry they would be, and how horrified the entire world would be at the story of their cruelty. And then I got really hungry.

I stuck it out, though. I stuck it out until nearly five past seven, by which time the pangs of hunger were too much even for my determination. With the profound feeling of a boy more sinned against than sinning, I dismantled my barricade and went downstairs.

The brutes were eating, indifferent as to whether I lived or died. They didn't even look up as I came in. I sat down at my place, and was immensely relieved when, without a word, my mother stood up and took my plate from the oven. It was shepherd's pie.

I let them know what I thought of them by eating in silence, and the meal progressed as if I wasn't there. It was a peculiar and disagreeable sensation, and I felt more sinned against than ever. But I wasn't talking to them until they talked to me.

She didn't give me any ice-cream. My father got ice-cream, Linda got ice-cream, and she got ice-cream herself. But I didn't get any. So I started to whistle. I began with Rule Britannia, but discovered that it was too difficult. I tried The Lincolnshire Poacher, and found I knew only the first few bars. In the end, I settled for the national anthem. At last I got a reaction.

'Thomas,' said my mother, 'if you've finished eating, you may leave the table.'

I stopped whistling, and looked on in silence as they all ate their chocolate ice-cream. I wanted some too. I loved chocolate ice-cream. A wave of self-pity engulfed me, and I had to say something to keep myself from crying. 'I haven't had any ice-cream yet.'

'No, and you won't get any until you apologise to Linda.'

I looked at my sister to see if I could face telling her I was sorry. She was wearing her most pious expression, the one that made her look like a Renaissance saint undergoing martyrdom, and I couldn't do it. Then I looked at her ice-cream. 'Sorry,' I said, in a voice so low that I could scarcely hear it myself.

'What was that?' My mother was not satisfied.

'Sorry,' I said, fractionally louder.

'Say "I'm sorry I was rude to you, Linda."'

I ran up the white flag, and came out with my hands up. 'I'm sorry I was rude to you, Linda.'

I got what I wanted, and with it a useful insight into my own nature. Self-respect was less to me than a bowl of ice-cream.

5 Alcohol

'Look at that dreadful Michael Foot!' said my father.

'Horrible man. Horrible,' said my mother.

This was the third Easter since our move to Ashminster, but we had not previously witnessed an Aldermaston march. As yet, we could see only the head of the procession, but my father had told me there were thousands and thousands of them. The hostility of my parents was unequivocal, and I was beginning to get scared.

'What's it all about?' I asked, trying to sound nonchalant, but surreptitiously moving closer to my father. I was glad we hadn't gone out to the garden to watch, as my mother had suggested.

'These people want to ban the bomb,' said my father, shaking his head. 'They're called CND, and they want to take away our defences, so that the Russians can move in and take over.'

'Boo!' shouted Linda, and I risked a quick shake of the fist when I thought none of the demonstrators were looking. They were making an awful lot of noise, and I was scared.

'Are they socialists?' I said, trying to give myself more confidence than I felt by talking even louder than was necessary.

My father growled and nodded. 'Every one of them, and they might as well be communists.'

'Half of them are!' said my mother, in a tone which challenged anyone to disagree.

Linda gave a self-conscious shudder. 'Well,' she said, with an air of finality, 'I've got better things to do than watch these awful people.' She turned and left the room.

My mind dwelt on the march for days, and I wearied my parents with questions about the bomb, CND, and the Russians. But how else was I to learn? At least I managed in the end to form a clear picture of what was going on.

That America was our friend, and Russia our enemy I already knew, but I now learned *why* this was the case. America and England were both part of the Free World, which was divided from Russia by the Iron Curtain. The Russians were communists, communists being like socialists, only much worse. The Russian people were kept in ignorance of the true nature of the Free World by Propaganda, the lies shouted at them by their leader, Khrushchev, a man more wicked even than the dreadful Nasser, about whom I had once had nightmares. General elections like ours did not take place in Russia, so the people could not get rid of Khrushchev even if they wanted to. They had a huge army and a huge navy and a huge air force, and their aim was to conquer the world. Our best defence against them was the hydrogen bomb, a weapon so terrible that they would never dare attack us as long as we had it, but the moment we got rid of it...

I had never been so terrified. Not even Mr Blackett frightened me as much as the Russians, and my fury against CND was boundless. I discussed the matter with Pendleton, who was in agreement with me. We decided to become pilots as soon as we were old enough, so that we could fly over the Iron Curtain, drop the hydrogen bomb on the Russians, and put a stop once and for all to their dreams of world domination. (Pendleton told me that an aeroplane would be the only safe place in the event of war, but I was careful to give no indication of the importance I attached to this consideration.)

This fantasy didn't last. In the end, I asked so many questions about the Russians that my mother got the idea that I was scared of them. 'Oh Thomas, there's nothing to be frightened of.'

'I'm not frightened!' I cried. 'The Russians don't scare me!'

'They can't hurt us as long as we've got the bomb, and Mister Macmillan will make sure we keep it.'

'I know that. I'm not scared of the Russians... What happens if Gaitskell wins a general election?'

'Even Gaitskell won't give up the bomb.'

I was hugely relieved. This was the best news I had heard since the day of the march, but there was still suspicion at the back of my mind. 'What about CND? What if they win a general election?'

'CND aren't allowed in general elections. Now there's nothing to be frightened of.'

It was only the intensity of the relief I now felt which made clear to me just how scared I had been. 'I'm not frightened!' I said, even more angrily than before. 'Do you think the Russians scare me? Well, they don't.'

It was true. They didn't. Not any more. From that moment, nothing was left of my first period as a cold warrior except my ambition to be a pilot. But now I wanted to fly to New York, the capital of America.

A few days later, even this aspiration was refined, when the news broke that the Russians, as clever as they were evil, had sent a man into space, the first real Dan Dare. I knew what I wanted to be now. I wanted to be a spaceman. But then I was so careless as to let this be known in school, when Mr Blackett was asking us what we wanted to do when we grew up. 'Please sir, I want to be a spaceman.' The place exploded in hilarity. Even Mr Blackett showed signs of amusement. I was surprised and hurt, and later assured everyone, Pendleton especially, that I had been joking, and my ambition was still to be a pilot.

~

On the Sunday of that week, my maternal grandfather arrived to spend a few days with us while my grandmother was in hospital for an operation. Although he was only sixty-five, and healthy with it, my mother and my grandmother both declared that he could not be expected to look after himself, so my father was sent to fetch him.

It was half past six in the evening when they got back, and the first thing that struck me as I looked down from my bedroom window was that the old man had an extraordinary number of bags and cases. He himself had a case in each hand, but my father was scarcely visible through the items of baggage hanging from various parts of him. He looked as if he was camouflaged for surveillance work in a luggage warehouse. All I could see clearly of him was his face, and he did not look happy.

'Come in, come in! Hello Dad, how are you?' My mother always gushed to her parents, a trait which I found embarrassing.

I remained in my room for some time, wondering whether I would be summoned for dinner as usual, or be expected to come down on my own initiative. That things were different when there were other people in the house I knew, but I could never tell in what way they would be different on any given occasion. In the end, I decided to go down and investigate.

My mother was alone in the kitchen. 'Oh Thomas, it's not quite ready yet. Why don't you go and wash your hands? And then you can go through to the sitting-room and say hello to your grandfather.'

'What are we having?'

'You'll find out soon enough. Off you go now.'

I had never understood my mother's obsession with the

washing of hands – Pendleton had suggested it might be a sign of madness – and I never washed mine if I could get away with it. On this occasion I reckoned I could, and went straight through to the sitting-room, where Linda was sitting with the two men. She had a glass of lemonade, and they, if I was not mistaken, were on whisky. Gordon Stacker was a regular whisky drinker.

'Well, young man, how are you?'

'Fine.'

'How's school?'

'Horrible.'

'Oh yes, yes.'

'Well, Thomas, aren't you going to ask your grandpa how he is?'

'How are you?'

'Oh, I'm not bad, not bad. You can't expect much at my age.'

'Is that whisky you're drinking?'

'That's right.'

'It's none of your business, Thomas.'

This annoyed me. Not only was I forbidden to drink whisky, but I wasn't even allowed to talk about it, and was thus being treated like a baby in front of my grandfather, whose great age made him a figure of awe. Well, we would see about that. I went over to the drinks cabinet. 'I think I'll just have a drop of whisky,' I said, this being my father's usual line.

'Oh Thomas, really!' Linda considered that the appropriate grown-up reaction to my statement was one of shocked disapproval.

'Thomas, be quiet and sit down. You're too young to drink whisky.'

'Gordon Stacker drinks whisky.'

'This is one of the young thugs in his class in school, Arthur.'

'Oh yes.'

'He's just making that up, Thomas. Now sit down quietly and wait for your dinner. You can have a lemonade if you like.'

But if I couldn't have a whisky, I wasn't having anything. I sat down, promising myself I would have a whisky sometime, whether my father liked it or not.

My grandfather looked hard at me, pursing his lips. 'So what are you going to be when you grow up, Thomas?'

I almost said I was going to be a spaceman, but I recalled just in time my schoolmates' reaction. 'I'm going to be a pilot,' I said.

His face darkened. 'No, Thomas, don't be a pilot,' he said, shaking his head. 'They nearly all get killed.' He drew the word 'all' out to make it as long as any three other words together, and his voice quavered as he said it. I was horrified.

'No no, Arthur,' said my father, wincing. 'It's not like that any more.'

'Oh yes it is,' my grandfather went on, in a lugubrious voice. 'The pilots I've known are nearly all dead, nearly all of them. Young men they were too, not much older than Thomas.' He shook his head again, and took a sip of whisky.

I was speechless. I had informed both my parents that I was going to be a pilot, and neither of them had said anything to discourage me. Neither of them had bothered to tell me that I was almost certain to be killed. Didn't they *care*?

'Arthur, that's because the only pilots you've known were in the First War. It's not surprising they kept getting killed.'

'Thomas would be sure to crash anyway,' said Linda, 'war or no war.'

My grandfather took another sip of whisky. 'No,

Walter,' he said, ignoring her intervention, 'they weren't all killed because it was a war, no, no. They used to crash as often as they were shot down. Up they went, and down they came. It's the law of gravity.' He shook his head even more mournfully than before.

My father grimaced, and finished his drink. I was watching him closely, anxious for any hint as to why he hadn't told me what a dangerous job a pilot's was. Because there was no questioning the sincerity with which my grandfather spoke. He was a very old man too, and he knew what he was talking about. It wasn't to be doubted.

'Linda!' My mother's voice came through from the kitchen. 'Come and give me a hand, will you? Dinner's nearly ready.'

The meal was, as I had hoped, more elaborate than usual, but, still preoccupied with my grandfather's words, I was unable to enjoy it. We had been eating for ten minutes when he spoke to me again.

'Why don't you become a doctor, Thomas? That's what Linda wants to be.'

'I don't want to be the same thing as her.'

'Well what about being a lawyer, then?'

'What does a lawyer do?'

'He sits in an office and gets a lot of money.'

I thought about this. 'I want to do something exciting, as long as it's not being a pilot.'

'Your father's told Thomas that pilots all get killed, Doris.'

'Very few of them survive, that's God's truth.'

'Oh Dad, that's nonsense!'

'Nonsense, is it? I'll take you to see their graves in France if you think it's nonsense. Hundreds and hundreds of them, all dead. Young men they were too, young men every one, not much older than Thomas.'

'For goodness sake Dad, that was a war! Of course

people got killed. And since all the pilots were young, they died young.'

'No no, I know what happened. They just fell out of the sky. It was up one minute and down the next, that's the law of gravity. Thomas should be a lawyer if he's got the brain for it. You remember that now, Thomas.'

'Yes well, there's plenty of time for him to think about that. He's only eleven.'

~

I went to see Pendleton after dinner, and we went down to the river to skim stones. My decision to become a pilot had owed a great deal to his encouragement, and it was not long before I broached the subject.

'You know what you said about being a pilot?'

'Yes.'

'Well, I've got something to tell you. Pilots all get killed.' I spoke with more rancour than I had intended, because I was irritated by his superior expertise in stone-skimming.

'No they don't.'

'Yes they do. My grandpa's staying with us just now, and he says so. He knows, because he's known hundreds of pilots, and they're all dead.'

'That's balls.'

'It isn't. You ask my grandpa.'

'My dad was a pilot in the war.'

'No he wasn't.' I had no idea what Bruce Pendleton's father had been in the war, but I was determined that he should not have been a pilot.

'Was. He was a pilot in the Home Guard.'

The extra detail defeated me. It sounded depressingly authentic. He was always backing his stories up with additional pieces of information like that, and they always had the same effect on me. But I made a mental note to check up on the Home Guard.

For the time being, I decided to change the subject, and

allude instead to my manifest inferiority in the art of stone-skimming. 'I'm not at my best at the moment,' I said. 'I had a drop of whisky earlier on.'

That made him think. 'What did it taste like?' he said at length.

I was thrown off my stride. Ridicule I had been prepared for, even the blustering assertion that he drank a bottle every night, but how was I supposed to respond to an enquiry about the taste of whisky? I now regretted bringing the subject up, but I was committed, and would have to press on. 'You er... you can't really describe it to somebody who doesn't drink,' I said.

'I drink beer and wine and sherry.'

'Well, it's a bit like wine.'

'You're a bloody liar. You've never touched whisky in your life.'

Somehow we avoided blows, but I was still furious with him for calling me a liar. What evidence could he have on the matter? The injustice rankled, and there was only one thing in my mind when I walked into the sitting-room half an hour later.

'I think I'll have a drop of whisky,' I said, and walked over to the drinks cabinet.

To my surprise, they ignored me. My parents and my grandfather were all there watching *What's My Line* – Linda was upstairs doing her homework – but nobody said a word. This wrecked my calculations. My intention had been to accept with a shrug of indifference their refusal to let me touch the stuff, then grab the first chance I got to take a swig from the decanter when the room was empty. If by any chance I was caught – which with my luck, I probably would be – I would protest that I had twice given notice of my intention to take up whisky-drinking, so they should have been warned.

But what was I to make of their silence? I hesitated for

59

a moment, then chose a small glass and filled it. If they were too absorbed in the TV to take any notice of me, that was their business.

Not until I sat down on the rug in front of the fireplace, from where I could see their faces, did I realise they were all asleep. It was not unusual for either of my parents to nod off in front of the TV in the evenings, but they were seldom both asleep together. My grandfather, though I didn't know it at the time, spent a large part of every evening asleep in his own armchair in front of his own television, which was almost never switched off.

I was nervous. I had felt justified in taking the whisky when I had announced my intention first, but that announcement was invalidated by the fact that no one had heard it. There I was though, with a glass of whisky in front of me, and the opportunity was too good to miss. We'd soon see who was a 'bloody liar'.

I picked up the glass, and sniffed at the tawny liquid. The smell was not appetising – it made me think of hospitals – but I was going through with it now, come what might. I took a sip...

I almost choked. The taste was incredibly strong, and nasty with it. I gulped it back in horror, more to get it away from my taste-buds than into my stomach, and sat there gasping. I wasn't thinking of hospitals now. I was thinking of curry. Because this stuff rivalled curry as the most disgusting thing I had tasted. My mother had let me try some the previous week, when I had refused to accept her assertion that I would loathe it. When I had recovered from the effects of the only mouthful I took, I had accused her of trying to poison me. Well, this stuff was as horrible as curry.

The funny thing was though, that once it was in my stomach, it didn't seem so bad. On the way down, it gave off warm fumes, not unpleasant, that floated into my head, and gave me a strange feeling. My father began to snore.

I was torn between returning the rest of the whisky to the bottle before someone woke up, and drinking some more to see if the strange feeling would increase. For I was in no doubt that it was this sensation that was the reason for not allowing me to drink the stuff. It was exactly the sort of experience they wouldn't want me to have, I knew that instinctively. A quick decision was imperative, because my father's snoring was increasing in volume, and I knew he was capable of snoring so loudly as to wake himself as well as other people. If I wanted to put that whisky back, now was the time. And equally, if I wanted to drink more, I'd better be quick before the opportunity was snatched away.

I looked carefully at all three grown-ups, and established for certain that they were still asleep. Then I took some more whisky, a larger amount this time, more of a small gulp than a sip. I made a mistake though, because, aware this time of how nasty the taste was, I swallowed it as quickly as possible. I choked, and my coughing and spluttering, coinciding with a sudden and dramatic increase in the volume of my father's snoring, woke him up.

It was only as I was recovering that I realised he was looking at me, through half-closed, quizzical eyes. I had no idea what to say. But then I realised that he couldn't see the glass of whisky, because I had put it down when I started coughing, and it was hidden from him by my body. Still, my crime was certain to be discovered if he remained awake, so I sat still and stared at him, trying to hypnotise him. Gordon Stacker was hypnotising people all the time.

It worked. After just a few moments, during which time he said nothing, he closed his eyes and began snoring again, but this time less loudly. It would take several minutes for the volume to reach a critical level again.

I was now beginning to feel peculiar. Whether the sensation was agreeable was not clear, but it was like nothing I had felt before. The attraction in it was that I knew that it was this sensation which was forbidden to children, so I decided to get as large a dose of it as I could, then remove the evidence by washing the glass and putting it back in the cabinet. I was confident that no one would notice there was some whisky missing from the bottle.

Confidence, in fact, was an important part of the sensation which the whisky gave me. Normally, my father's waking, even though it had not led to the discovery of my crime, would have been more than enough to frighten me into getting rid of the evidence without delay, but I wasn't easily scared now, oh no.

It didn't take me long to finish the glass, and although I cannot say that I came to enjoy the taste, I was almost indifferent to it by the time I drained the last drops. By then I was hardly aware that it had a taste.

My father was beginning to snore more loudly again, and I decided that, however confident I felt, it might not be a bad idea to wash the glass and replace it in the cabinet. I was more likely to be able to repeat the crime if my first time went undetected.

I stood up, and navigated a channel between the armchairs occupied by my mother and my grandfather. It was surprisingly tricky, and I retained just enough capacity for rational thought to suspect I might be drunk. My mother had a thing about drunkenness: 'You must never never get drunk, Thomas, because it's the worst thing in the world.' I could remember her saying that more than once. The memory upset me briefly, but then I told myself that grown-ups were always telling children lies, just to stop us enjoying ourselves. The next day, in school, I would let it slip casually. 'I was drunk last night,' I'd say, and see how they reacted. And if Gordon Stacker claimed he had ever been drunk, I'd call him a liar. And give him a good thrashing if need be, oh yes.

I was almost at the door when I heard the footsteps on the stairs, and I hesitated for a fatal moment. If there was a way of telling that I had been drinking whisky, Linda, I knew, would find it. My belief in her capacity to uncover my sins was total. I veered off to the right, and pretended to be studying the wallpaper, so that my back would be turned to her when she came in.

Her entry failed to waken the grown-ups, and when our father's snoring indicated to her that he at least was asleep, she turned on a display of the 'thoughtfulness' that was one of her most admired characteristics, closing the door with infinite care, and walking almost on tiptoe over to the fireplace.

My confidence had now come back, and I turned to face her. She treated me to one of her favourite looks, the one that said she had neither knowledge of what I was up to, nor doubt that it merited the severest censure. Normally, it would not have bothered me, but on this occasion, the effect was to frighten me into believing that she was on to me. 'Funny wallpaper,' I said, to cover my nervousness, and found the words difficult to articulate.

She frowned, and held a rigid index finger before fiercely rounded lips. Then she fixed her eyes on my glass.

Badly frightened, I held it aloft, pointed at the whisky decanter, and gave a silent laugh. My reasoning was that she would surely not expect me to draw attention to an undetected crime I had committed, by making jokes about it.

But I was wrong. Something in my manner made her suspicious, for she came towards me, narrowed eyes darting from the glass to my face, then back again. I made for the door, but she intercepted me, and in the struggle which ensued, the glass splintered against the doorknob. 'Now look what you've done, you little fool!' she hissed.

The noise of shattering glass had woken everyone, but our mother was the first to realise where it had come from, and to look round. 'Thomas, what on earth are you doing? What's that you've got in your hand?'

I looked down, and was mildly surprised to see that I was still grasping the stem of the glass. Linda was now standing back from me, looking saintly.

'Eh?' My father, slowly coming to terms with reality, also turned to look at me, as did my grandfather.

'Have you broken a glass?' said my mother, still well ahead of the other two. 'Oh no, look what he's done! That's one of my best glasses!' She stood up, and made a noise which managed to convey both impatience and resignation. 'Oh, you're a stupid, careless, disobedient little boy, really you are!' She pushed her chair aside, and came towards me.

'I'm not a little boy!' I tried to say, but what came out was more like 'Annorraliboy!'

'Oh God – goodness, I mean – I don't know, I really don't. What were you doing with that glass anyway?' She was standing in front of me now, hands on hips as she looked down at me.

The small part of my mind that remained sober was frightened, and did what it could to retrieve the situation, but it was no match for the drunken part. 'I was drinking water,' I managed to say, preventing with the same heroic effort any slurring of the words, and the addition of 'you old cow'. But then, inspired by this success, I went too far. In attempting to cast the blame on my sister, with the words 'It was Linda's fault. She tried to grab the glass from me,' I came out with a babble of sound impossible to reproduce in print, identifiable only as a drunken slur. My mistake was to press on when I got into difficulties. I should have stopped, taken a deep breath, and had another go at it. But I doubt if I could have managed it anyway.

There was an appalled silence, not broken until my grandfather, an expression of extreme puzzlement on his face, said 'What's he say?' He was always slow to waken up.

A different approach was clearly necessary, but the attempt I made to say that it was all right and that I would clear up the broken glass, was disastrous.

'Good God,' said my father, 'the boy sounds drunk.'

'Oh no!' Linda stepped further back from me, and put her hands to her head.

My mother grabbed me by both shoulders and leant over to sniff my breath. She stared at me, mouth agape. 'Whisky!' she gasped.

My father was up now, and moving purposefully towards us. He also took a sniff, but succeeded in keeping a cooler head than his wife. 'Thomas, have you been drinking whisky?'

'No,' I said, opening my eyes wide, and shaking my head.

He resorted to the intimidating roar which he had found to be the best means of getting the truth out of me: 'DON'T LIE TO ME, BOY! Have you been drinking whisky?'

'Yes,' I said.

They were not pleased. When I attempted to tell them that I'd said I would have a whisky, but no one had heard me, I failed again to make any sense, and was sent to bed, where I was left to dwell on my father's prediction that I'd be sorry in the morning.

And so I was, because I woke up with a headache so dreadful that I feared for a moment that I might have split my head open in the course of the night. A careful investigation with both hands failed, however, to locate any damage, and I could only conclude that my headache was the result of the whisky.

When I dragged myself downstairs for breakfast, I found that my parents and grandfather were of the same opinion – Linda was careful to agree with them – and the two men quickly overruled my mother when she said that she thought I 'really shouldn't miss any school, especially seeing that he's going to be all right later on.'

'*He* can't a*fford* to miss...' Linda began, but got no further.

'Good God, woman, what d'you think's going to happen when John Blackett asks him what's wrong with him, and he says he was pissed out of his head last night?'

'We can do without language like that, Walter!'

My father growled into his coffee.

'Walter's right, Doris. Better keep him off school today, and send him in with a note to his teacher tomorrow.'

'That's right, grandpa,' said Linda.

My mother shook her head. 'Oh well, all right, but I don't like him missing school, I don't like it at all. How's he going to learn if he's never at school, that's what I want to know.'

'Good God, woman, he's never off school, and if you think he's going to have a hangover every other day, you can think again.'

'I'm feeling sick.'

'Shut up, Thomas,' he said, without even looking at me. 'Nobody wants to hear from you.'

'*I* certainly don't!' said Linda.

My mistake had been to try to eat a piece of toast, and I now vomited over the table.

My mother and Linda both made noises expressive of shock and horror, and my father pushed himself back from the table so as to be out of the line of fire. It was too late though, or too late at least for the left leg of his trousers. He looked at me, lip curled in revulsion and scorn. 'You are the most vicious and disgusting child any parents were ever cursed with.'

I began to cry.

~

'What was up with you yesterday, then?' said Pendleton as we walked to school the following morning.

I shrugged. 'Oh, just a hangover,' I said.

'Don't believe you.'

'It's true. I was drinking whisky on Sunday night. I told you.'

'Don't believe you.'

So I gave him all the authenticating details now at my command. I described the taste of the whisky, its effect on speech and movement, the nastiness of the headache the morning after, and so on. And although he went on insisting that I was lying, I could tell he was rattled.

I drove home my advantage. 'It's you that's the bloody liar, not me. You said your father was a pilot in the Home Guard. Well, I asked my dad yesterday. The Home Guard didn't have any pilots, so there.'

Physical conflict was averted when, with both of us smouldering, we arrived at the playground and joined in a game of football, but Pendleton was never one to accept defeat gracefully. This I already knew, and it was not long before I received further confirmation.

Mr Blackett was telling us about Charles the First, and when at one point, still talking, he turned round to write something on the board, I felt a thump on the crown of my head. I turned round furiously. 'Stop that!'

Pendleton bared his teeth in a sadistic grin which left me in no doubt that the connection between his history book and my head was not over for the day.

'Thomas Cardwell, face the front! Repeat what I just said.'

67

I stared at my desk.

'You pay attention, lad, or you'll be in serious trouble, understand?'

'Yes sir.'

But as soon as his back was turned, I was the victim of a second mighty blow. I turned round swiftly. 'Bastard!' I hissed.

'Liar!'

'I am not!'

'You are! You never had a hangover in your life!'

I have no idea how many times he walloped me, but my memory of how the unequal conflict ended remains clear. Mr Blackett, who had the common teacher's habit of pacing up and down as he talked, at one point turned round unexpectedly to face us, and his right hand shot out, index finger straightened in accusation at Bruce Pendleton.

I thought I would die of ecstasy. I always loved it when other people got into trouble, the more so the better I knew them, and to have someone on the carpet for persecuting me – and not just anyone, but Bruce horrible Pendleton – was almost too wonderful.

'Bruce Pendleton, what are you doing?'

I was looking round at him now, and he was a sight, frozen in the act of raising the book to bring it down on my suffering head. Held in both hands, it was now above his own, poised ready to begin its descent. His face displayed consternation.

'I said what are you doing?' Mr Blackett spoke in his quietest, most threatening voice.

Pendleton put the book down and cleared his throat. Barely-suppressed giggles could now be heard from all parts of the room. 'Please sir...'

'Were you going to hit Thomas Cardwell over the head with that book?'

'No sir!' said Pendleton, with the air of outraged innocence which he always assumed when accused of a crime he had in fact committed.

Mr Blackett's voice dropped almost to a whisper, and the giggling stopped. 'Were you going to hit Thomas Cardwell over the head with that book?'

'Yes sir.'

'I didn't hear that.'

'Yes sir. Please sir, he was telling lies!'

Controlling with difficulty the urge to go for him, I stared at Mr Blackett in disbelief, mouth open, head wagging.

'What lies?'

'Please sir, he said he was off school yesterday because he had a hangover.'

'I never did! Please sir, I never did!'

'Yes he did, sir!'

'I did not!'

In my indignation I had barely noticed, but Pendleton's claim that I had said I'd had a hangover had broken the tension. Those who knew what a hangover was, were in fits, and the hilarity proved infectious for the rest. All except Mr Blackett.

'Silence!!... Thomas Cardwell, is this true?'

I wasn't sure what he meant. Was he asking if it was true that I'd had a hangover, or if it was true that I'd told the fat brute I'd had one? It didn't matter, though, because I was denying it either way.

'No sir.'

'Come out here, both of you,' he said, and went to his cupboard.

6 Travel

The eleven-plus was, my parents assured me, the most important exam I would ever take. Mr Blackett agreed, and made us practise by doing old papers for weeks beforehand. These I enjoyed at first, but they soon became tedious.

My parents had a funny way of explaining the issue. They told me that if I passed, I could become a doctor or a lawyer, but if I failed, I would have to be a navvy or a lorry driver. The thought of handling a pneumatic drill, or of driving a lorry all round the country was appealing to me, and I said so. And when my mother said I wouldn't get much money for either activity, I told her that money did not concern me.

My father had the sense to change tack. He said that if I passed the eleven-plus, I could still be a navvy or a lorry driver, but I would also have the possibility of becoming a doctor or a lawyer. If, on the other hand, I failed, then I would *have* to be a navvy or a lorry driver, even if my ambitions should have veered by that time in the direction of a legal or medical career. This made sense, but it was the sort of dreary sense normally made by his pronouncements. I was not impressed.

In the months that had passed since I had conceived – and swiftly abandoned – my ambition to fly in space, I had, mindful of the unfortunate consequences of my avowal of it, told no one of how my thoughts were developing. It was a matter of importance to me though, and I had narrowed the choice down to athlete or cowboy.

My ideal cowboy was the Lone Ranger, and I would have given a lot to be like him. I even tried talking like him, until my mother asked what I'd got in my mouth. In athletics, my hero was Alf Tupper, the Tough of the Track, whose appetite for fish and chips was almost as great as mine, but who, unlike me, could indulge it freely. Alf was a character in *The Victor*, which I now took instead of *The Beano* and *The Topper*. All I wanted to know about the eleven-plus regarding its influence on my future career, was whether the Lone Ranger or Alf Tupper had needed to pass it. I was too secretive about my ambitions to ask, but I thought it unlikely that either had even bothered to take it.

Much more important in determining my attitude to the examination was the new bicycle which was to be my reward for doing well. It had long been a source of frustration that Pendleton's bike was so much better than mine, and I was determined not to miss this opportunity of turning the tables.

Even this, however, had less to do with my desire to perform well than had my fear of having to go to Buggleby. Whatever happened, I would be taking the train to Stambridge every day, something to which I looked forward eagerly, but whereas if I passed the eleven-plus I would turn right from the station and go to the grammar school, if I failed I would turn left and go to the Secondary Modern, known as Buggleby, after the district in which it was situated.

I knew the difference between grammar school boys and Buggleby boys, because one afternoon when I had been to Stambridge with my mother to have an aching tooth seen to, we had emerged from the dentist's just after the schools came out. The grammar school boys – I didn't even recall seeing any girls except Linda – were the ones who wore uniform, and weren't especially tough or noisy. But when a large group of ununiformed boys came towards us, laughing and shouting, my mother said 'Buggleby boys!' in a tone which blended contempt with a hint of trepidation, and we crossed the road.

This little incident had made an impression on me quite out of proportion to its intrinsic significance, and although I was envious of their apparent toughness, the thought of myself becoming a Buggleby boy frightened me. And so when my mother, in despair at my failure to show enthusiasm at the prospect of a career in one of the 'professions', warned me that if I failed the eleven-plus, I would have to go to Buggleby, the threat was more potent than she knew.

In truth though, it did not matter, because I was always top of the class in Ashminster – Pendleton normally came second – and it would never have occurred to me to do less than my best in an examination. I would have passed the eleven-plus without the application of stick or carrot. So indeed would Pendleton, but he, with no reward on offer, was unfortunate enough to be required to prove it.

~

It was a relief to get away from Mr Blackett, but my first day at Stambridge was not a happy experience. Pendleton and I, the only boys from our class who had got into the grammar school, stuck close to each other in the playground when we arrived. Linda refused to have anything to do with us. Having now only dim memories of Winterby, I felt intimidated by the sheer size of the place, and the sheer size of the senior pupils.

The day began with assembly, which Linda had described as a sort of church service. This was more or less accurate, and my familiarity with the hymn Rock of

Ages, helped to calm my nerves. Then we went off to begin lessons.

Pendleton and I were in Class 1A, for whom the class teacher was Mrs Rudge, whose subject was English. We all sprang to our feet when she came in, and she surveyed us sourly for a few moments before ordering us to sit down.

'Old bag,' whispered Pendleton, and I sniggered. The desks were arranged in pairs, and he and I were, of course, together.

Mrs Rudge sat behind her desk, and flourished a thin blue notebook at us. 'This,' she said, 'is the register, with a list of your names. I'm going to read that list, and when you hear your name, you say 'Present!' loudly and clearly. Otherwise, you remain silent. Now... Helen Allingham?'

'Present.'

'Louder.'

'Present!'

'James Apthorpe?'

'Present!'

'Silly old cow,' whispered Pendleton.

'Moo,' I whispered in reply, and we both giggled.

'YOU!!'

I almost died of fright. Mrs Rudge was on her feet now, right arm rigid in front of her, index finger pointing at Pendleton. He did his best to pretend astonishment.

'Stand up! What's your name?'

'Bruce Pendleton sir miss.'

A searing look round the room quelled the giggles. 'You too!'

This time, she was pointing at me. I stood up, on legs which felt ready to give way at any moment.

'Name?'

'Thomas Cardwell miss.'

'Louder.'

'Thomas Cardwell.'

'Well, Bruce Pendleton and Thomas Cardwell, you can take fifty lines each for tomorrow: "I must not talk in class." Sit down.'

I was stunned. Our first day had scarcely begun, and already we were in trouble! I wished I was with Mr Blackett again.

Nothing so dreadful happened for the rest of the day, but I was surprised to find that lunch was, if anything, worse than Linda had reported, and Pendleton and I both left most of ours. At home that evening, I kept my fifty lines secret.

~

The school did improve with familiarity, but it was some time before I was reconciled to the greater quantity of homework expected of me. On warm evenings, I liked to get it done as quickly as possible when I got home so that I could go out and play before dinner. It was always maths that gave me the most trouble, and I was never too proud to ask for help from my mother. I hated it though when she was busy, and the task went to my sister instead. This always prompted a display of the latter's most patronising air. My normal practice was to request assistance only when I felt sure it would not come from Linda.

A couple of weeks into term, though, I felt obliged to humble myself. Mr Wardle, the maths teacher – and a man still more terrifying than Mr Blackett – had caught me doodling that day while he was, according to his normal practice, going through that evening's homework so that no one should be at sea with it. 'Cardwell, you obviously know it all already. Well, I'm pleased if you do, but I give you fair warning, boy. If you make one single error with this, I'm going to cane you tomorrow.'

So when I came to grief on the last problem, down I went to the kitchen, ready to accept help from any quarter.

My mother was busy cooking, and Linda, who always preferred to do her homework after dinner – 'I don't approve of rushing homework the way Thomas does, really I don't' – was having tea.

'Can somebody help me with my maths homework?'

'Oh Linda, you help him, will you, dear? I'm too busy.'

Linda closed her eyes and sighed. 'Oh, I sup*pose* so. I'm sure I won't get any peace until I do.'

Determined not to be provoked, I sat down next to her, and shoved my notebook in front of her.

She looked at it in silence for a moment, then shook her head and sighed. 'I don't know what's going to become of you if you can't do things like this at your age, really I don't.'

I was beginning to get angry, but was careful not to let it show. What mattered was that I should get the thing right, and I was ready on this occasion to put up with a bit of persecution.

'Now listen carefully while I explain this. I don't want to have to do it more than once.'

It took some time, and her explanation was punctuated with frequent reminders, both explicit and implicit, of her superior intellect. Still, I kept my temper in check until, under her patronising guidance, I found the solution.

'Please don't bother to thank me,' she said, while I was still writing the answer, and looked away.

'Thanks, bitch,' I said softly, so that only she could hear me.

'Mummy Mummy! He called me a bee eye tee see aitch!'

'Thomas, you do *not* use words like that in this house!'

'I'm off out.'

'Oh no you are not!' said my mother, and placed herself between me and the door.

'She was annoying me!' I said angrily.

Linda sprang to her feet in indignation, and when she

75

spoke she sounded close to tears. 'So this is all the *thanks* I get for *help*ing him!'

'Thomas, you will apologise to your sister.'

'No.'

'Then you're not going out.'

'Yes I am.'

'Oh no you are not.'

My position was hopeless, and I was forced to apologise, hating myself for it, but hating my sister even more.

'Very well,' said my mother, moving away from the door, 'you can go. But I don't want you playing rough games, and coming back crying with grazed knees again.'

I was breathless with rage. How dare she suggest that I *ever* came home in tears because I'd hurt myself! (My indignation was heightened by the fact that the allegation was true.) 'I hate you, and I hope you die!' I cried, and dashed through the door before she could stop me.

'Thomas, you come back here! Thomas!!'

But I was off at top speed, and I wasn't submitting to a second humiliation. I had meant what I said.

I went next door to see Pendleton, and as we walked into the village to buy an ice-cream, I told him in detail how awful my home life was.

'I'd run away if I were you,' he said.

'I was thinking about that.'

'I'll help you.'

Now I wasn't so stupid as to be unaware of what was going on here. Bruce Pendleton was always having his fun at my expense, always encouraging me to do dangerous, exciting things in which he could assist me without himself running any risk. I decided to have a go at him.

'Haven't *you* ever thought running away?' I said.

'Yeah, hundreds of times. I'll do it sooner or later. But it's you we've got to think about first.'

'If you've thought of it hundreds of times, then why don't you come with me? Now's your chance.'

'Naah, not now. I'd like to come, but you'd have a better chance on your own. It's you I'm thinking about.'

'Well, if it's me you're thinking about, then come along. I'd sooner have you with me.'

'Scared to go on your own, are you?'

'No, but you're scared to go at all, even with two of us together.'

'Am not.'

'Brucie-woosie loves his mumsie-wumsie, boo hoo.'

That was as much as he could take. He swung a punch which caught me in the lower part of the ribcage.

'Cheating bastard! That was below the belt!' I flew at him, and we were soon rolling on the pavement, beating hell out of each other. It was the worst fight we had had since the evening we met.

A passer-by separated us, a real spoilsport. He made us both say we were sorry, then he made us shake hands and promise not to fight again. He said that wasn't how civilised people sorted out their differences.

'You were lucky,' said Pendleton as we walked on, faces burning.

'*I* was lucky!! I could've killed you!'

For once, he did not pursue the argument, and we were silent for some time before I spoke again. 'Well, I'm still going to run away. I've got a plan.'

He turned to look at me. 'I'll come too. What's your plan?'

This was wonderful. He was always the leader, always the one with the ideas, but this time he was going to follow me.

I looked as serious and determined as I could. 'We go down to the river, and make ourselves a boat. It doesn't have to be much. It just has to float and carry us. The river'll take us to the sea, because all rivers go to the sea, and then we row over to France and make a fresh start. They'll never find us there.'

He thought about this. 'Okay, but why France? Why not Germany or Italy?'

'France is nearer,' I said, hoping he would make a fool of himself by contradicting me.

'We'll need things. We'll need food and maps and compasses and things. We can't get everything ready now.'

For a moment, I thought of accusing him of cowardice again, but it came to me that perhaps I wasn't that keen on an early escape either. Maybe a bit of planning wouldn't be such a bad thing. Of course, it would entail giving Pendleton a larger say in the project than I liked, but that was a price I was prepared to pay for an extra few days of security.

In the end, we arranged to make our getaway on the Saturday morning. Pendleton had an encyclopaedia at home, and he would, in the meantime, find out all about France. I said I would see to the boat. On the Saturday morning, we would get a compass, a map, and some food and drink.

~

By the weekend, our enthusiasm for the project was high. Pendleton had already managed to get hold of an old compass and a map of France, and I had located a tree trunk which would, I thought, together with a couple of branches for paddles, serve adequately to ferry us across the Channel.

The language bothered us, as three weeks of lessons had not taken us far, but Pendleton said he had been working on it in the evenings, and reckoned he could acquit himself well enough. I was immediately disposed to question his claim, but he forestalled any expression of doubt by breaking into an impressive burst of French, which he then translated into English. 'Don't worry,' he went on. 'I'll do the talking when we get there. Don't you say anything. We don't want them asking awkward questions.'

Humiliated, but unable to think of an adequate reply, I got my own back by going on about the boat, which was my department. 'There's no trouble about the boat, anyway. It's down there by the river waiting for us. We'll have to shoot a few rapids on the way to the sea, but I can handle that.'

'We can navigate with my compass.' He took the instrument out of his pocket, and tapped it knowingly. 'We just head due south, that's all.'

'Hmm. I'm afraid it'll be dark most of the time, so we might not be able to see it. It won't matter though, because I can navigate by the stars.'

'So can I.'

We managed somehow to avoid a fight, and discussed what provisions we ought to take. Having pooled our savings, we ended up with three bars of chocolate, two bottles of lemonade, four packets of crisps, a jar of peanut butter, and, at Pendleton's insistence, 'medical supplies' in the form of a packet of aspirin. This, we were confident, would last the journey, and when we got to France we would find work, so that money would soon be forthcoming.

All was going well, and we were in high spirits when we got to the riverbank, but then the trouble began. I admit that I was doubtful about our boat the moment I saw it again. It had looked fine when I had chosen it two evenings previously, but it seemed less than satisfactory now. It was part of an old tree trunk, maybe eight feet long, and about two feet in diameter. The rest of the tree, of which there was no trace, had presumably been chopped up and taken away for firewood.

'Where's the boat then?'

79

'That's it.'

'I don't see a boat.'

My awareness that I was in a weak position and likely soon to be under attack, made me aggressive. I strode over to the trunk and stood defiantly beside it. 'This is it.'

'That!' Pendleton put down the bag containing his share of the provisions, and stared contemptuously. 'That's our boat?'

'Any objections?' I moved away from the trunk, and stood facing him, hands on hips, legs apart.

'That thing won't get us to France!'

'Oh yes it will! But not if you don't give me a hand to get it into the water.' I put down my own bag of food and drink, and vented my now considerable anger by attempting to move the great lump of wood towards the water. It wouldn't budge.

'Are you going to help, or do you just want to watch while I do all the work?'

He shook his head, and came towards me. Even the two of us together were only just able to roll the thing, and I was now beginning to have doubts about the whole project. I wasn't letting Pendleton know, though. If anyone was backing out, it was going to be him.

It took ages to get our craft to the water's edge, and exhausted us both, but still he showed no sign of giving up. His tenacity infuriated me.

'Nothing wrong with this,' I said, as we sat on it to get our breath back. 'This'll get us to France no bother.'

He said nothing, but went over to retrieve his bag of provisions. Inwardly fuming at his refusal either to show enthusiasm or to let us both off the hook by announcing that he no longer wanted to see the thing through, I followed suit.

'Who's going to push us off?' he asked, when all was ready.

'I'll do it,' I said in a surly voice. I was now frightened at the thought of leaving home, and was almost ready to swallow my pride and be the one to cry off. I could sense, though, that the same thing was going on in the fat brute's mind, so I decided to hold on a little longer.

We both took off our shoes and socks, and hung them about our necks, socks inside shoes, laces tied together. Then we put both bags of provisions on the front of the boat and rolled up our trouser legs. Still neither of us was ready to give in, so Pendleton climbed astride the log, just behind the provisions.

Of course, I was now unable to move the thing, and he had to get off again and help me get it fairly into the water, so that the effort of the final push would not be beyond me.

And that was how, a few seconds later, Pendleton found himself alone on the tree trunk as it drifted slowly out into the middle of the river. It may be that I did not try as hard as I might have done to take my place behind him, but anyway, I was now standing close to the bank in a foot or so of water, staring at him in fascination.

'Help!' he shouted, in fear and misery.

I felt no sympathy. 'What do you expect me to do? You should've held her steady till I could get on. You've really done it now!'

'Help!!'

I would not have changed places with him for anything. He was now lying forward, grasping the trunk with his arms as well as his legs, but still he looked precarious. 'HELP!!'

My feelings were a mixture of relief that I was not in his position, and gloating over his discomfiture. Not that I wanted him actually to drown, but I didn't mind how wet he got, and I was quite hoping that he would at least *nearly* drown.

81

He did, nearly. I had been watching with the greatest interest for half a minute or so, and was growing concerned about the food and drink, when disaster struck. He now looked a little more secure, and had got over his initial fright to the extent at least of being able to sit more upright and not grip so tightly with his arms, when the log executed a slow clockwise roll. As soon as he grasped what was happening, he managed to yell even louder than before, but he could do nothing to save himself. He, his compass, and the two bags of provisions, all slipped gently into the water.

'Save the food!' I shouted. 'Save the food!' But I was wasting my breath.

Pendleton was a poor swimmer, and once in the water and out of reach of the log, he began to thrash about wildly. I became frightened. If the fat brute drowned while I was with him, I might be in trouble, and that was something I could do without.

'Swim to the bank!' I yelled. 'Swim to the bank!'

'HELP!!' howled Pendleton, whose head was now under the water for part of the time.

Being a strong swimmer, I wondered if I should jump in and attempt to save him. But I was frightened of my parents' reaction if I got back home soaked, so I began searching for a long branch instead.

By the time I had found one, he had drifted some way downstream, and, with his struggles becoming weaker, he was still little closer to the bank. I ran down it until I was some way ahead of him, waded out as far as I could without getting my trouser legs wet, and stretched out the branch towards him.

As I did so, he disappeared completely for the first time. None of him was visible, not even a hand. But he bobbed up again a moment later.

'Grab the branch!' I shouted.

I am still convinced that if he had missed it with his first lunge, he would have drowned, for the bank rose sharply just a little further downstream, and there the branch would have been useless. But he didn't miss. One wildly groping hand clutched it, and he was safe. I pulled one way while the current pulled the other, and he came over to the bank in a wide, slow arc.

'You're all right now. You can stand up.'

He released his grip, crawled out of the water – shoes and socks still, remarkably, round his neck – and lay on his back, gasping. I was tremendously relieved, and tremendously pleased with myself. Not only had I saved my friend from drowning, but I had done so without even getting my clothes wet. I was annoyed with him for losing the food, but things could have been worse. Gritting my teeth, I looked down at him the way I had once seen some TV cowboy look down on a girl he had saved from drowning. 'Learn to swim before you try that again,' I said, remembering his words.

Pendleton did not react. He just lay there gasping, and I became concerned. I had assumed that once he was out of the water, he would be all right, but he didn't look all right. Fortunately for him though, I knew something about life-saving techniques, for I had seen a diagram in a book. I knelt astride him, and, preferring not to administer the kiss of life until all else had failed, pressed down on his chest hard with both hands.

'Aaagh!!' he yelled, and bucked me off him. 'Leave me alone, you bastard!'

'Jerk! I just saved your life!' I lashed out with my right foot, and caught him a useful kick in the ribcage. It was no more than he deserved.

With another howl, he threw himself at me.

When he and I fought, that was my chance to gain some revenge for the humiliations he was so adept at inflicting

83

on me the rest of the time, because I was tougher than he was, physically at least. This time it was different. The power of his rage was overwhelming.

'You bastard! I nearly drowned! And then you try to beat me up when I'm helpless!'

'I saved your life!'

'Bastard!'

I had never seen him so furious, and I was no match for him. This was quickly apparent to me, and when I caught a glimpse of another figure further up the bank, it was all I could do to stop myself screaming for help. Not since our first wrestling bout had I felt the need of outside intervention to save me from his wrath.

Rolling over desperately in an effort to avoid punishment, I found myself in the water, but still he wasn't satisfied. Grabbing me by both ears – yes, by both ears – he dragged me out into deeper water. I was screaming now, splashing frantically after him on hands and knees to prevent my ears being torn off. Finally, he stopped, released me, put both hands on top of my head, and held me under the water until I nearly drowned.

Then we went home.

Both soaked, we were almost back before we spoke to each other again.

'Look,' said Pendleton, 'we're going to have to agree on a story to explain how we got like this.'

My mind had been at work on the same problem, but I had approached it from another angle. 'I've got a better idea,' I said. 'Have you got a heater in your bedroom?'

'Yes.'

'Well, see if you can get to your room without being seen. Get changed, and put your wet clothes in front of the heater to dry. I'll do the same.'

He nodded. 'All right, but we'll still need to have a story ready in case either of us gets caught.'

With my own plan already adopted, I was prepared to accept this small addition, and we agreed to claim, if necessary, that we had been the victims of an attack by a gang of older boys, none of whom we recognised.

Things went smoothly at first. I went in by the back door, took off my shoes, and crept upstairs undetected. Beginning to enjoy the sense of danger, I changed out of my wet clothes and draped them over a chair in front of the electric heater, both bars of which I switched on. I remained in my room until my hair – which, fortunately, was short – was almost dry, then went downstairs to the sitting-room. I was pleased with myself, and hoped that Pendleton done equally well.

My parents were reading newspapers. 'I didn't hear you come in,' said my mother, glancing up.

'I came in quietly,' I said, and took my *Victor* from the top of the television.

It was just minutes later that my father, who had always had a sharp nose, said he could smell something burning. No one else could, but he was not to be put off, and he left the room in search of the conflagration which he believed to be under way in another part of the house.

Not until I heard him climbing the stairs did I realise what was happening. For a few frantic moments, I harrowed my brains to think of a way out, but it was too late. I could only sit there miserably and await retribution.

It was not long in coming. When he reappeared, there were black flecks on his face, and he was panting angrily. 'You little fool! Are you trying to burn the house down?'

I looked as puzzled as I dared under the circumstances.

'What's the boy done?'

'What's he done? What's he done?? He's tried to set the house on fire, that's what he's done! He's ruined a perfectly good set of clothes and a perfectly good chair, and he's blackened the ceiling of his room. The boy's worse than a beatnik!'

My mother, understandably concerned, went up to my room to see for herself, while my father interrogated me about the incident. By the time she got back, he had established that a gang of boys, all older and bigger than Pendleton and me, had tried to drown us in the river. We had fought them off though, and escaped with a soaking. Three of our assailants had also ended up in the water, and I thought I might have broken the arm of one of them.

'Good Lord, Thomas,' said my mother, 'what on earth have you been up to?'

My father repeated my tale to her.

'But goodness, Thomas,' she went on, whatever possessed you to try to dry your clothes yourself?'

'Because you're always so angry if I come in with wet clothes.'

She frowned deeply. 'Thomas, you must never never do that again. You could have burnt the house down. We could all have burnt to death!'

This was too much for me. Coming on top of the dreadful events at the river and the pressure I was under to sustain my story, the thought of burning to death horrified me so much that I burst into tears.

She was not sympathetic. 'Now who were these boys you say were trying to drown you?'

'We'd never seen them before,' I managed to say between sobs.

'Do you think he's telling the truth about this, Walter?'

'Oh God, don't ask me. The boy's an idiot. I don't see why he shouldn't be a liar with it.'

My mother fixed me with her most serious look. 'It's a terrible thing to tell lies, you know, Thomas, a terrible thing. Because a lie always comes back to you, no matter what.'

I continued sobbing, but asserted vehemently that I was telling the truth. I promised myself that I would go upstairs as soon as possible, and regret the lie with particular sincerity on my deathbed. I wasn't having it come back to me.

Linda came in.

'We caught your brother trying to dry his clothes in his room,' said my mother, by way of explaining why I was in tears. 'He nearly set fire to the house. He says he and Bruce were thrown into the river by some older boys.'

'Oh Thomas!' said Linda, 'that's not tr... Oh well, I'm not going to tell tales.'

'What were you about to say, Linda?' Our mother wasn't letting this go.

Linda shook her head. 'I don't approve of tale-telling,' she said.

'Come on,' said our father, 'out with it. This is a serious matter.'

Remembering now the figure I had seen on the riverbank, I could make a fair guess at what was coming next. 'Tell-tale tit!' I managed to chant through my tears, 'Your tongue shall be split...'

'Thomas, be quiet. Well, Linda?'

She shook her head and sighed. 'Oh well, if I must. I was walking down by the river half an hour ago, and I saw Bruce and Thomas having the most dreadful fight in the water. There wasn't anyone else.'

I was walloped, and my only consolation was that when the story became known next door, so was Pendleton. That he sought afterwards to blame me, I though most unfair.

7 Sex and Violence

Maths was my worst subject. I hadn't been good with figures at Ashminster, and at Stambridge I was struggling from the start. Worst of all was geometry. I could never understand what all those shapes were *doing*. This would have mattered less had our teacher been anyone other than Mr Wardle.

Mr Wardle, commonly known as Sunny, was terrifying. He was agelessly ancient – radiocarbon dating might have been worth a try – a force of pedagogical nature rather than a human being, and his grim demeanour cowed everyone. The perfect order which prevailed in his room was attributable solely to this manner, because Sunny hardly ever used the cane – unlike, for example, Mr Willey, the Latin teacher, whose predilection for corporal punishment was legendary, but whose lessons were a riot anyway.

There was, however, one thing which was believed to bring Mr Wardle's cane inevitably into action: rubbing out. 'There was a time when I preferred pupils to write in pencil, but then they would use rubbers all the time when they made mistakes. I can't help you if I don't know what sort of mistakes you make, so I now insist on all work being done in ink. That makes it more difficult to rub out, and I'm warning you now – it's the only warning you'll get – I always cane any pupil I catch using a rubber.'

He told us this the first time we saw him, and no one

put his threat to the test. It would have been too risky, because he kept a close eye on our notebooks, and once a fortnight he would take them all in and mark them. It was not surprising then, that when Pendleton noticed the two erasures in my homework, he informed me in a voice of amazement and horror that I 'must be fucking mad.'

How had a coward like me come to do such an extraordinary thing? Let me explain.

~

Linda. I did not like my sister, and was constantly on the lookout for ways of getting at her. It was unfair that she, who, far from hating me, regarded my existence as a tiresome irrelevance in the serious business of her own, could upset me so easily. And then, when she was thirteen and I was eleven, I noticed something. Linda was interested in boys. Now at last I had a stick to beat her with. It was Richard Chamberlain who put me on to it, because she became addicted to *Doctor Kildare*. I was naive though, and it took Pendleton to tell me what was going on.

'I think my sister's going mad,' I told him one Saturday morning. 'She watches *Doctor Kildare*, and her face keeps going funny when it's on, and she goes berserk if anybody says anything.'

'How does her face go funny?'

'Well... like this.' I did my best to imitate the expression I had in mind. This was not easy, since it was one which managed to combine both vacancy and rapture, with the mouth slightly open and the eyes soft. I did what I could.

'Hmm,' said Pendleton. 'She's on heat. That's what my dad would say.'

'Ah.' I had difficulty coming to terms with this, but I never willingly let Pendleton know he was talking over my head. I managed at last to dredge the expression 'on heat' out of the darker depths of my mind. My father had once used it of a dog whose howling was keeping him awake at night, and when I asked my mother what it meant, she told me with the pained expression which she reserved for the discussion of unpleasant and embarrassing subjects, that it indicated that the troublesome creature was a 'girl-dog' who was interested in the 'boy-dogs'.

I looked hard at Pendleton. 'You mean,' I said cautiously, praying I was not about to make a fool of myself, 'she's getting soppy?'

'That's right. It happens to girls when they're about that age.' Pendleton was in one of his mature moods, in which he was a boy of the world who was not easily shocked or amused, so I was careful to hide my astonishment and delight at his revelation. Linda was going to suffer for this.

Hard though it was to restrain myself, I managed to say nothing until Kildare's next appearance, on Friday evening. Linda was visibly tense as she waited for the programme to begin. As usual, she had switched the television on a good five minutes early, so as to be doubly sure it would have warmed up in time. I was pretending to read a book, and our mother was darning socks. Our father was out. I suppose it was wrong of me to be vindictive, because Linda had just finished helping me with my maths homework, but such considerations did not weigh heavily with me.

Just as Chamberlain was about to appear, I stood up and went over to the television. 'Does anyone really want this?' I said. 'I can't concentrate on my book.'

'You leave that alone!' snapped Linda in a sudden fury. 'Sit down!!'

I was delighted. I knew I had her now.

Our mother looked up, frowning. 'Children, children, please! Neither of you are deaf, so you don't have to shout at each other.'

'I am not a child!' said Linda angrily. '*He*'s a child, not me.'

'I am not, and I'm not shouting either. She's the one who's shouting.' *Doctor Kildare* was starting now, so I was anxious to keep the row going. At the back of my mind was the faint hope that it might even lead to the switching off of the television, and the ordering of us both to our rooms.

Unfortunately, our mother was in one of her more patient moods. 'Now you're to stop arguing, the pair of you. Thomas, if you can't concentrate on your book here, you can take it up to your room.'

With the look of resignation of one who has grown accustomed to injustice, I resumed my seat, and watched the screen. Suddenly the action froze, the theme tune played, and the credits rolled.

'Why do they always stop like that?' I said, looking at Linda.

'It's dramatic,' she said, with admirable self-control.

For the next few minutes I watched in silence, glancing at her from time to time. Pendleton was right – she *was* on heat. She was all soppy about Doctor Kildare.

'Who's that old man?' I said at random.

'Raymond Massie. Be quiet.'

'Raymond Massie Be Quiet. That's a funny name.'

Now she became really angry. 'Shut up, Thomas! Mummy, tell him to be quiet! He's only trying to annoy me!'

Our mother put down her work, rose, and went over to the television. To my delight, she turned the sound down, and stood in front of it, blocking her daughter's view.

'Mummy, please!' Linda wailed in misery.

I adopted my most innocent expression, ready to accept whatever rebuke might be offered, provided only that it should inconvenience my sister.

'Now Linda, first of all, I've told you before not to say shut up. It's a most ugly expression, and I won't have it used in this house.'

'Mummy, please!' Linda cried again, scrambling to her left to try to get a better view of Richard Chamberlain, who had just appeared.

'Linda, be quiet and sit still or I'll turn the thing off completely. Now Thomas, if you annoy your sister once more, I'm going to get your father to give you a good beating when he comes in. If you can't read quietly in here...'

And then Linda did something awful. Unable to contain herself any longer, she leapt to her feet, took one swift pace forward, and tried to push her mother aside. 'Get out of the way, will you!!'

My jaw fell open, and my thoughts went back to that rapturous moment a year previously, when Mr Blackett had caught Pendleton whacking me on the head with his history book. Could this be even better? But while I was amazed and delighted, my mother was shocked and horrified.

The sheer unexpectedness of Linda's action rather than the force of the push did indeed get her out of the way, but her recovery was swift and decisive. She grabbed her daughter's hand just before it could reach the volume control, and turned the set off. 'Don't you dare talk to me like that, and don't you dare push me! Go to your room!'

If there is such a thing as a mental orgasm, I had one.

Tears of frustration and rage started to Linda's eyes. 'Doctor Kildare!' she wailed, as if calling on him to materialise before her, and put right the appalling wrong being done to her.

'Upstairs!' Our mother, immovable in front of the screen, was pointing emphatically to the door, in the attitude of a referee ordering a player from the field.

'Right!' said Linda, and a great sob shook her whole body. 'He's *had* it!' She turned briefly to me with a look of venomous hatred, and rushed weeping from the room, slamming the door behind her.

'Linda!' I called. 'Don't slam doors!'

But the only sound to be heard was that of her footsteps as she ran upstairs.

'What shocking behaviour!' I said.

'Thomas,' said my mother, as she sat down again, 'I don't think you've been very clever.'

Well, she could think what she liked. I had at last fixed my sister good and proper, just as I'd always told myself I would, and my mother's censure made no difference.

~

I was so full of my triumph that I fear I must have bored poor old Pendleton with the details of it over the weekend. I was still talking about it as we took our places in the maths classroom at nine o'clock on the Monday morning. The teacher had yet to appear.

'You must be fucking mad!' he suddenly said, rudely interrupting my thoughtful disquisition on the nature of female adolescent sexuality.

Under normal circumstances, I would have had a real go at him for this display of bad manners, but the shock in his voice was like an icy hand clapped on my shoulder. His left arm was stretched over my desk, and the index finger was pointing at something in the notebook I had just opened. Then it moved and pointed to another spot. There were two rubbings-out in my homework.

At first I was as astonished as I was horrified. I knew I hadn't... And then I remembered Linda saying 'He's *had* it!' and I understood. I was engulfed by a hideous wave of hatred and terror. She had done it so expertly. You *could* see that something had been rubbed out, but it wasn't that obvious. It was just the sort of job that would be made by

93

someone who wanted to erase something without the erasure being noticed.

'It wasn't me!' I managed to gasp. 'It was that bitch Linda, I know it was! She's done it to get her own back over Kildare!'

I was in a panic. Sunny Wardle's method of correcting homework was to ask to see someone's notebook. If it was done wrongly, it was handed or even thrown back, with some sarcastic comment. If, on the other hand, it was done correctly, Sunny would keep the notebook while going through it on the board. From time to time, he would walk up and down the rows, seeing what other people had done, and every couple of weeks he would take in all our notebooks for checking.

'God!' said Pendleton. 'You've really had it now. Sunny'll...'

But I never did find out what Pendleton expected Wardle to do, though I could have made a fair guess, because at that moment, the man in question came in. His simple presence sufficed to kill conversation stonier dead than any amount of enraged histrionics from most teachers.

'Open your notebooks. The weekend's homework. Catherine Middleton.'

Catherine Middleton handed her notebook to him. He looked at it in silence for a few moments, then looked back at her, cold and grim. 'Rubbish,' he said, and gave it back.

I was praying – *praying* – he wouldn't ask me. If only I could survive that period, I was going to tear the offending page out of the notebook, and save my skin that way. Wardle moved to the boys' half of the room. Pendle... No, we had you on Friday. Cardwell.'

Time ceased. There were thirty-four pupils in the room. The chances that he would ask to see my book were one in thirty-four. He was asking to see my book. My number had come up. On the one day when it would mean my death.

Time began again. In an agony of despair and terror, I passed my notebook forward.

'I'm really sorry, Tom,' Pendleton whispered through the side of his mouth.

'Piss off!' I hissed back. I might have been more terrified than any creature has been in the history of the universe, but I wasn't so scared that I couldn't see when the fat brute was enjoying himself at my expense, and hate him for it.

Sunny Wardle glanced at my work, and nodded. 'Right, now pay attention everybody, and especially you, Catherine Middleton.' He moved to the blackboard and took up a piece of chalk. Then he paused, put it down again, and looked more carefully at my notebook.

In the midst of my agony, I felt Pendleton's gloating presence beside me, and managed a kick at him. He kicked back. 'You're going to get murdered!' he hissed.

At last, Wardle looked up. 'Out here, Cardwell.'

Extreme terror has the effect of translating its victim into a different dimension. I got to the front of the room all right, and it must have seemed to all of the thirty-four pairs of eyes on me that I did so by walking. But I say I didn't, and I should know. Jelly does not walk. If I moved from my desk to the front of the room, it was because I was picked up and taken there.

But however the transfer took place, the next thing I recall after the words 'Out here, Cardwell,' is the words 'What's this... and this?' Wardle was holding my notebook open in front of my eyes, and pointing to the two erasures.

I was now back on the same level of consciousness as everyone else, and my mind was racing. I was innocent of the crime with which I was being charged, but did I dare tell this monster what had really happened? What chance was there of being believed? Might it not even make things worse, if only by prolonging my agony?

'You've been using a rubber, Cardwell!' Wardle roared. It was very rare for him to raise his voice, and all the more frightening when he did. 'Well?'

Desperate now, and ready to try anything to save my skin, I opened my mouth to denounce my sister, but no words would come. The monster had got me, and I was speechless with terror.

Compared with Sunny Wardle, Mr Blackett had no notion of how to wield a cane. I got two on each hand, and although I didn't quite break down, the very first blow brought scalding tears to my eyes. Only a ferocious hatred of my sister stopped them spilling out.

~

To my astonishment, she had the nerve to gloat over it at dinner that evening. 'Thomas was caned today, weren't you, Thomas?'

I was too amazed at the sheer effrontery of the allegation to deny it, and anyway I had promised myself that my revenge, when I took it, would be terrible indeed. An accusation that she had framed me would be easily denied, and would only make me look ridiculous. No, I had something more irksome in mind. Like sawing her head off.

My father was delighted with the news. 'Just like old times in Ashminster, eh son?' he said, chortling with satisfaction. 'What was he walloped for anyway?'

Linda's lips were twitching in a smirk of triumph. 'Mr Wardle doesn't allow anybody to rub mistakes out, but Thomas did.'

Deciding to frighten her, I turned on her a stony look of hatred. She smirked still more.

'Well, Thomas,' said my mother, 'you must do as your teachers say, otherwise you're bound to get into trouble, you know.'

My father swallowed a mouthful of food, and pointed his fork at me. 'A good thrashing never did *him* any harm,' he said. 'I'm only glad there's somebody at Stambridge who's taken up where John Blackett left off. He was turning into a right little beatnik.'

What could have made Linda think she could get away with such a thing? It must have been apparent to her that I would be out for revenge. I can only think that she considered me too spineless and ineffectual ever to get round to it. If so, she was right.

8 International Relations

It was during the first term of my second year at Stambridge that my old fears of Russia, buried by my mother a year and a half previously, clambered from the grave like something out of a horror film. But I was bigger and braver now, quite ready to take on the evil Khrushchev if he was so minded.

The finer details of the Cuban Missile Crisis did not interest me, but I knew that America and Russia were moving closer and closer to war, and we were on America's side. And the gravity of the matter was clear from my parents' attitude.

By this time, I was keen on the idea of a war. I thought it would be fun. But the adult world was against it. The problem, as I understood it, was the hydrogen bomb, which was likely to settle the conflict one way or the other without any fighting of the sort in which I hoped to distinguish myself. But my father's opinion gave me heart. If the Russians managed to drop one on us before we could drop one on them, he said, then they would invade to finish us off. They would come by parachute.

I could see it. The sky black with parachutes, and Pendleton and me holed up in the ruins of our houses, picking them off in the air. Of course, there would be too many of them, and in the end we would have to take to the hills where we would organise other boys of our age into a resistance unit. It would all be tremendous fun.

The high point of excitement was reached on the day

the rumour swept the school that the Americans had sunk a Russian ship. It was a story which did not altogether please me, as I preferred to believe 'they' would start it, as 'they' always did in the cinema, and I was able to add my own refinement to this effect.

In its mature form, at the end of the lunch break, the story contained too much detail for any sane person to doubt it. A Russian aircraft carrier on its way to Cuba had launched an attack on an American liner, which had suffered severe damage and heavy loss of life among passengers and crew. The American response had been swift, and the Russian ship was now at the bottom of the Atlantic or the Pacific, sunk by a single torpedo from an American submarine.

There was indignation throughout the school at the dastardly blow struck by the Russians, and wholehearted approval of the American riposte. The only dissenting voice was that of the school intellectual, Eric Crabbe, a professed communist known to all as Lenin. After lunch, Pendleton and I joined the knot of boys who had gathered round him to listen to his views.

'It has been clear since the end of the War that a confrontation between East and West is inevitable. The two systems are irreconcilable, and we cannot have real peace in the world until one or the other is crushed. I sincerely hope that the Soviet Union will be victorious.'

'Don't you know about Stalin?' said one of many dissenting voices.

'Joseph Stalin led the Soviet Union at a difficult and dangerous time, and severe discipline was necessary for important economic targets to be reached. The Soviet Union is attempting to achieve communism without going through the stage of full-blown industrial capitalism which we have in the West today, and which Marx believed was essential before the class struggle could give rise to

99

proletarian revolution. Stalin telescoped the suffering of centuries into less than thirty years, and defeated fascism at the same time, a great achievement.'

I had no idea what Crabbe was on about, but that didn't bother me. My own views were clear, and I wasn't altering them for him or anyone else. Pendleton was the same.

It was a disappointment to discover that none of the teachers knew of any naval engagement off Cuba, but I was pleased to find, on getting home after school, that the crisis had not eased.

The subject came up over tea. 'Oh God,' said my mother, whose language had been affected, 'I hope they find a way out.'

'You don't know what these communists are like,' I said happily. 'They'll stop at nothing.'

'Thomas,' said my sister, in her most mature and serious voice, 'you really don't understand what's happening.'

'I understand it better than you!' I said. 'I don't want the Russians here, even if you do!'

'Be quiet, the pair of you,' said our father. 'We're going to listen to the news.'

It was bad, and I could hardly contain my excitement. As soon as tea was over, I went to discuss the matter with Pendleton.

He too was keeping up to date with developments. His parents had reacted to the news much as mine had, and he said we had better put ourselves on a war footing right away, so as not to be taken by surprise when the fighting began. Whatever happened, we must not be caught unprepared.

I took a deep breath, frowned, and shook my head as I had seen my father do earlier. 'We'd better not kid ourselves,' I said. 'It's going to be hell.'

'You don't have to tell me. And whatever happens, we're sure to be invaded.'

'You think so?'

He nodded. 'My dad says nothing in Europe can stop the Red Army. We've just got to make things difficult for them till the Americans get here.'

My patriotic hackles rose. 'You mean we can't beat the Russians but the Americans can? If we can't beat them, nobody can, I say.'

He shook his head. 'It's manpower, Tom. There are just too many of them, and they've got too many bombs and missiles and things. They'll drop tons of atom bombs on us, then they'll send in the paratroops. It's that simple.'

I was annoyed. As usual, he knew more about it than I did. But I wasn't giving in without a fight. 'So why can't they do the same with the Americans, if it's so easy to beat us?'

'I told you. Manpower. There are trillions of Americans, and anyway, the US is further away. The Russian planes can't get there.'

I kicked a stone.

'But just because we can't stop them coming doesn't mean we can't do anything. We've got to become gorillas. My dad says there'll be gorillas everywhere.'

'Gorillas??'

'Gorillas is the name for people who fight, but they haven't got uniforms.'

'Why are they called gorillas?'

'Because they haven't got uniforms.'

We made extensive plans. We were going to need guns and maps, and a thousand other things. Most important of all, according to Pendleton, was a radio transmitter and receiver, so that we could communicate with the Americans and with other gorillas.

Much as I was enjoying all this, I was delighted when I had my own brainwave. While he was discoursing on the best method of ambushing a military convoy, I suddenly looked distracted and held a hand up for silence.

'What's up?' he said, his irritation both audible and visible.

'Aren't we forgetting something?'

'What?' He could see that I was making a bid to take over the driving seat, and he didn't like it.

'Spies,' I said.

'Spies?'

'Spies. There's no sense in just waiting for the invasion. There must be spies here now, planning for it. We should be going after them.'

As I had hoped, this was too good an idea for him to ignore, even if it wasn't his own.

'You're right,' he said graciously. 'But how do we go about spotting them?'

'Lenin,' I said.

'What?'

'Lenin. Eric Crabbe. I'll bet you anything you like he's a spy.'

Pendleton stroked his chin for a moment, then shook his head. 'Impossible,' he said. 'It'd be too obvious. You're not going to get spies admitting they're communists, are you?'

'Why not?' I said. 'It's the perfect cover for exactly that reason. Who'd suspect him?'

'Well...'

'Can you think of anyone else?' I went on, determined to drive the point home. What I had in mind was that without a spy, life might be as dull as ever – before the invasion, at least – and Pendleton was surely as anxious for a bit of excitement as I was.

He took a deep breath. 'I think you're right,' he said.

This I appreciated. It was an important point, and he was conceding it. I wasn't going to start a row by rubbing his nose in it.

'What do we do then?' I asked. 'Go to the police?' Even as I said it, I thought what a rotten idea it was. If we did that, the fun would be over before it had even begun, and besides, I was not confident that the police would take our word for it.

Pendleton was thinking along the same lines. 'We'll need evidence first, and that'll mean keeping a close eye on him. And we make no move until we're sure we've got him.'

'You reckon he's got a radio transmitter and receiver?'

'Bound to have.'

'And he could be armed.'

'More than likely.'

'Hey!' I said, struck by a sudden brilliant idea. 'You remember that film we saw last week? About the French Resistance?'

'Yes.'

'Well, remember what the Jerries did with the British spy they found? They didn't arrest him, they just fed him false information.'

'Good thinking,' he said, perhaps a little grudgingly – it wasn't so often that I was the one with the ideas.

Before we parted company, we had agreed quite elaborate plans on what to do about the menace posed by Eric Crabbe. First we would find out as much about him as we could, and then, assuming he did indeed turn out to be a spy, we would provide him with spurious facts about troop movements in our area.

We began work the next day. The trick was to find out all we could about the suspected spy without alerting him, and our first task was to test the truth of the claim made by his cousin Joe Vincent, that Eric Crabbe knew Russian. As usual, we ran into the former on our way to school from the station.

'Hey Vince,' said Pendleton as casually as he could. 'Is it true that Lenin speaks Russian?'

'My cousin?'

'Yeah.'

'Course it's true. Everybody knows it. He's a communist, isn't he?'

'Don't believe it,' I said. 'We don't do Russian here.'

'So? He taught himself.'

'All right then,' said Pendleton, 'prove it. When we get to school, you ask him what's hello, goodbye, and thank you in Russian. I bet he can't tell you.'

'Bet he can.'

'Okay,' I said, following our plan of campaign meticulously. 'I'm with Pendleton. In fact, I'll put a bob on it that he won't be able to tell you the words and write them down.'

'Great,' he said. 'I'll go on ahead and I'll have them for you as soon as you reach the playground. Better have your money ready.'

'Good,' said Pendleton as he ran off. 'He doesn't suspect anything.'

'Let's have your tanner then,' I said, and he paid up without a murmur. We were delighted with ourselves.

It worked. Joe Vincent was at the school gate when we got there, brandishing a piece of paper in front of us like Chamberlain after Munich. 'Here it is,' he said. 'Pay up.'

We scrutinised the paper. If what was written on it was not Russian, it was a fair imitation.

'This one's hello,' said Vincent, pointing at the top word. 'Zdrastvootsy. Then goodbye, that's dossvidanny, then thank you, that's spaseeba. Come on Cardwell, pay up.'

I made a show of reluctance. 'How do I know that's good Russian?'

'You're a cheat Cardwell, but if you like, you can check with Ma Mackenzie. She speaks Russian.'

I shrugged, and plunged my hand into my pocket. 'See if I care,' I said, and tossed two sixpences at him.

'Of course,' said Pendleton as we walked on, 'that doesn't actually prove anything, but it's a start. Now we come to the more delicate bit...'

'There he is!' I cried, interrupting him. Eric Crabbe was standing near the main door, talking to one of the prefects.

We looked at each other, nodded, and strolled towards them. Our intention was to listen in to as much of his conversation as we could without making him suspicious. This entailed fine judgment in positioning ourselves as far away from him as was consistent with making out what he was saying.

They were, of course, discussing the Cuban crisis, and Crabbe was certainly taking a bold line for one who was in the pay of the Russians. But Pendleton and I, convinced that an aggressively pro-Russian stance was the perfect cover for a communist agent, only took this as further evidence against him.

~

The news from Cuba got better and better, and we decided that war was inevitable. It thus became a matter of even greater urgency to determine once and for all whether or not Crabbe was a spy, and to begin feeding him false information if he was. To this end we decided at a council of war on the Wednesday evening that we would stay late in Stambridge after school the following day, and keep watch on his house. We would tell our parents that we were involved in a football match. With the intensity of the crisis, we felt sure we would, sooner or later, get an indication of what Crabbe was up to.

We had, in the previous two days, found out a good deal about him, and his address and telephone number were both in a file we had opened on him, one copy of which was held by each of us. It was of course incomplete – we were especially anxious to be able to stick a passport photograph in the little square at the top right-hand corner – but the case against him was already strong. He was a known communist, a Russian speaker, a likely radio ham, seemed to have few close friends, and had a 'suspicious manner'. We didn't need a lot more. (We had each put our copy of the file in a safe place – mine was under my mattress, Pendleton's under his carpet – with a note to our parents, less well hidden, telling them where it was to be found. This was in case anything happened to us.)

It was just gone four when we got to his house, and the immediate difficulty that presented itself was how we were to keep the place under observation without ourselves looking suspicious. He lived in the middle of Nicholson Crescent, a street so quiet that it was hard to see how any unusual occurrence there could escape detection. But with national security at stake, risks would have to be taken.

'Right,' said Pendleton as we strolled past the house for the first time. 'We've got to keep an eye on the place somehow, so here's what I suggest. When we get to the end of the crescent, we'll pretend to say goodbye. Then you go on, and I'll walk back up the crescent again. I'll wait at the other end. Exactly five minutes after we part company, you turn back and retrace your steps. Then we'll compare notes and decide what to do next.'

'But we haven't got notebooks.'

'It doesn't mean that. It just means we exchange our ideas.'

'That's balls. You can't compare notes when you haven't taken any. Anyone can see that.'

He closed his eyes. 'You're so bloody ignorant.'

'Fuck you! I'm not ignorant!'

An outbreak of fighting seemed unavoidable, but Pendleton kept his sense of priorities. He stopped, put his hands on my shoulders, and pulled me round to face him.

I went tense with anticipation, assuming he was lining me up for a physical assault, but I was wrong.

'Listen Tom,' he said, 'this is too serious for us to start fighting among ourselves. How are we going to feel if Crabbe manages to transmit vital information to the Russians because we were too busy fighting each other to bother with him?'

I was impressed. 'You're right,' I said. 'Let's get on with it.'

In accordance with his plan, we parted company at the end of the crescent, and, five minutes later, I turned and walked back again. This time, a woman appeared at the door of Crabbe's house as I was passing, and put out an empty milk bottle. There was a note in it. It had to be significant. Heart thumping with excitement, I walked on. Pendleton was leaning against a tree at the end of the crescent, yawning.

I walked towards him, but he caught my eye, shook his head, glanced down the road to his left, then closed his eyes and began yawning again.

A quick look in the direction he had indicated was all I needed. Twenty yards from him, a policeman was studying a parked car. I turned left at the end of the road, and walked the other way. Then, after what I thought was a respectable interval, I stopped, leaned against a lamp post, and looked at my watch, trying to adopt the air of someone being kept waiting for an appointment. I pretended I was expecting someone to come from the direction of Pendleton and the policeman, so that I could keep an eye on both of them.

It was some time before the latter finished with the car, but when he finally moved on, I strolled back to Pendleton, who did not turn to greet me.

'Don't make it obvious we're talking,' he said in a low voice.

'Right,' I said, without looking at him. 'See anything at Crabbe's place?'

'No.'

'I did. I saw a woman, probably his mother. She put out a milk bottle. With a note in it.' By a careful modulation of tone, I made this sound as sinister as possible.

Pendleton pursed his lips and breathed in. Then, with a decisive nod: 'We must have that note.'

'How do we get it?'

'Wait here and leave it to me. Synchronise watches... Sixteen twenty-five. If I'm not back in ten minutes, it's all up to you.'

I gave the briefest of nods, and took his place against the tree as he went back up the crescent. He was doing the most daring thing so far, but since it was my reconnaissance that had made it possible, I was not dissatisfied. And anyway, the knowledge that it was 'all up to me' if he didn't come back, was enough to compensate me for the fact that I was temporarily in the back seat.

As it happened, his time was nearly up when, to my profound disappointment, he reappeared. But I couldn't help admiring him for having got hold of the note, which he was grasping in his right hand.

Again we spoke in low voices, without looking at each other. 'Station,' he said, 'but stay well behind me.'

'Right.'

I had never felt so daring, and the newspaper vendors' posters, with the latest headlines on the crisis, intensified the excitement.

On the station platform, we continued our pretence of not knowing each other. Then I had a brainwave, and strolled past him to communicate it. 'Different carriages,' I said through the corner of my mouth. He nodded.

Back in Ashminster, we studied Mrs Crabbe's note. It read '2 pints today please'.

'What do you think?' I said.

He shook his head. 'Could be nothing. Even if Lenin *is* a spy, that doesn't mean his mother is.'

'True. Pity we don't know how many pints they usually get. If it's normally one, then two could mean there's an extra person staying, and if it's normally three, it could mean someone's away. It could be significant.'

We subjected the paper to various tests to see if there was invisible writing on it, but found nothing. In the end, we put it in Pendleton's file, a copy going into mine, and agreed that the case against Crabbe was still not proven.

As Pendleton said however, this was no reason for abandoning our campaign of disinformation. If Crabbe was a spy, such a campaign might do a great deal of good, and even if he wasn't, it would do no harm.

By the time we reached school the next morning, we had plotted an elaborate trail of deception for the suspected spy to follow. Our plan was to stand within earshot of him in the playground, and discuss our knowledge of matters affecting national security.

To our annoyance, he did not get to school until almost the stroke of nine o'clock, and our chance did not come until after lunch, when we found him alone near the gate, reading the headline article in the Daily Worker. We took up position several yards away, and put our plan into action.

Our first problem, we had agreed, was posed by the fact that he probably didn't know where we were from, so Pendleton began by getting this information across.

'The trouble with Ashminster,' he said loudly, is that nothing ever happens there.'

'That's true,' I said, sticking to the script. 'I'm sick of living in Ashminster.'

'Of course,' Pendleton went on, 'it's a bit more interesting now, with the soldiers there.'

'Yes it is. My dad says it's a large detachment of troops, probably getting ready for a Russian invasion. It could come any time.'

'Tanks too,' said Pendleton.

'So I've heard. Have you seen any?'

'Yes. I saw one last night. They're keeping them under camouflage during the day.'

Crabbe still seemed absorbed in his newspaper, but I was sure he was listening.

'That'll be in case of spies,' I said. 'It'd be a disaster if the Russians found out where all our forces are. Your brother's in the navy, isn't he?'

'Yes. I'm not supposed to know this, so don't tell anybody, but he says the navy's all been sent to Plymouth ready to fight.'

'God,' I said, 'if the Russians knew that, they could destroy our entire navy in one attack.'

'That's right.'

At this point, Crabbe glanced up at us, folded his newspaper, and walked off.

Pendleton nodded with satisfaction. 'That's one commie spy who won't be doing them much good,' he said.

~

We couldn't think of anything to do with Eric Crabbe over the weekend, so our council of war that evening was concerned with preparations for gorilla warfare.

We agreed that the first thing to do was to establish our HQ, in which we would also have to live. Our original idea was to get a tent, but Pendleton pointed out that this would be too conspicuous, and came up with the idea of a dugout.

It was simple. All we needed to do was dig a large hole in the ground and roof it over with material strong enough to take whatever weight might be put on it. We were hugely excited by the idea, and chose a spot not far from the river, where we could begin work the following day.

'We'll need something to dig with,' I said.

'Right. But we don't want anyone to know what we're up to, or they might tell the Russians. I'll take my dad's spade when he's not looking.'

'I'll do the same. Actually, I don't think mine would talk, even under torture, but my mum might.'

'Same here,' he said, 'so we'll have to be careful.'

I thought of a difficulty. 'What if someone sees us digging?'

Pendleton stroked his chin. 'Good point... Well, only one digs at any one time, while the other keeps watch. We take it in turns.'

'Right.'

It occurred to neither of us that if we were not both digging together, we would not need two implements. Off we went down to the river next morning, each carrying a spade and trying to look inconspicuous. It was only when we got to our chosen spot that we realised that one spade was redundant.

'Never mind,' said Pendleton, 'there's no harm in having a spare. I'll start. You keep watch.'

This struck me as a bit peremptory, but I was too anxious to get on with the business in hand to object, so I took up position some fifty yards off, on a knoll from which I could see anyone approaching on either bank of the river some time before they could see what we were up to.

Several times I had to raise an arm to stop Pendleton digging as people strolled along the river. When I did this, the fat brute would drop his spade and sit down until the danger was past. Fifteen minutes had elapsed when he stopped work and came over.

His face was red, and he was panting. 'Right,' he said, 'your turn.'

I was not impressed with what he had done. He had

only scooped away at the surface, and untidily at that. This irritated me, since we had agreed that the turf would have to be cut out in squares, as it was going to have to be replaced on the roof later for purposes of camouflage. But the damage was done, and at least he could be blamed for it, so I swallowed my annoyance and began digging.

It was tougher than I had expected. The ground was mostly stones, and big ones at that, some the size of my foot. To make things worse, I was continually having to stop when the fat brute raised a warning arm. I soon abandoned the spade he had been using – *his* father's – and tried the other one, assuming that, being *my* father's, it would be better. It was worse. All that kept me going was the determination to do more in my stint than Pendleton had done in his, but I was not convinced I had achieved this objective when I decided my time was up. But I was already weary, so I was happy enough to drop the spade, and change places with him.

My second spell as lookout was well advanced when disaster, in the familiar shape of my sister, overtook us. I signalled to Pendleton to stop digging as soon as I saw her, but had no chance to warn him to make himself and the spades scarce. How was I to keep her at bay?

'Thomas,' she began, in no mood to beat about the bush, 'I thought I'd find you here. What have you done with Daddy's spade? He can't find it, and he's furious.'

'Spade?' I said. 'What spade?'

'Come on, you can't pretend... Oh I see, Bruce is with you. That'll explain why *his* father's spade is missing too.'

I grabbed her by the arm as she tried to walk towards him.

'Let go of me!' She had always hated being touched. 'Look! He's been digging a hole.' She shook me off and walked over to him, with me trailing in her wake.

Pendleton did his best. He moved a little to his left, and

lay down on his back as we approached. I knew what he was doing, and I admired him for it. Lying on top of two spades must have been hellishly uncomfortable.

'Bruce, your father's furious with you for taking his spade without asking. Come on now, hand over. Both of them.'

'Spade?' he said, still flat on his back, but with at least one garden implement incompletely hidden beneath him. 'What spade?'

'The one you're lying on. Or the two you're lying on, rather. Come on.'

Pendleton climbed to his feet, and looked at her earnestly. 'Listen, Linda,' he said, 'I'll tell you what we're doing, and then...'

'No!' I said. 'You don't know her. She won't understand. Don't tell her.'

'We've got no choice.'

I flung my arms in the air, and turned my back on them to indicate that I wanted no part in this. I knew my sister.

'Tom and I are getting ready to fight the Russians when they invade. We're going to be gorillas, so we're making a dugout to be our HQ. You can join us if you like, because we're going to need someone to do the cooking and things.'

'Oh honestly, Bruce,' she said, 'the Russians aren't going to invade, and there's nothing you two could do about it if they did. Now give me the spades and stop being stupid.'

I spun round to face her, shot out my right arm, and straightened my index finger. Like a fanatical priest denouncing a heretic. 'You think you know everything!' I shouted. 'You pretend you're grown-up all the time! It's people like you that are letting the communists take over the world, and it's people like us that are trying to stop them. Well, see how you like it when they come here and there's nobody to fight them. Just don't blame us, that's

113

all. Come on Bruce, give her the spades if she wants them so much. We'll think of something else.'

Pendleton stood for a moment, looking in silence at our antagonist. 'All right, Linda,' he said, in a more-in-sorrow-than-in-anger voice. 'Take the spades, but mark my words. Tom and I will still fight them when they come, we'll still be gorillas. But we won't last long without a dugout, and that'll be your fault. Remember it when the time comes.'

We stalked off, two young heroes prepared to die before we would bow the knee to tyranny. It was no fault of ours that an easing of the crisis over the weekend deprived us of our opportunity.

9 Scandal

My interest in sex began in junior school, but I fought it, believing it to be some form of perversion, and sure to get me into trouble if discovered.

At Stambridge though, things got worse, and I was soon forced to accept that my fascination with girls was not going to go away. I didn't even want it to.

Pendleton's interest was not less keen, and sex became an increasingly common topic of conversation between us. Our discussions would generally take the form of an exchange of puerile dirty jokes, but in truth we took nothing more seriously.

For years I was at the stage of putting girls on pedestals, and the thought of any gross physical intimacy with the ones so honoured would have outraged me. The dirty talk with Pendleton and others was no more than a way of reassuring myself that I was a tough guy in spite of these unmanly feelings. I suppose it was the same with the rest.

Pendleton and I took particular delight in double meanings, and words like 'screw' and 'breast' and 'bottom', especially when used by our teachers, always had us smirking at each other. Best of all was the day when Miss Thurlow, the history teacher, in the course of a lesson on the Industrial Revolution, attempted to demonstrate with the aid of her left hand and her right forearm the action of a piston. And our Latin teacher was

115

a joke without saying or doing anything. His name was Willey.

The biggest sexual thrill I got at this time was from Honor Blackman, who played Cathy Gale in *The Avengers*. I thought she was wonderful, and when she appeared all in leather, I found it hard to keep up the pretence, vital in my sister's presence, that it was the story that interested me.

There was no explicit sex in *The Avengers* though, and when a copy of the notorious dirty book *Lady Chatterley's Lover* circulated around Class 2A, I was appalled by the profundity of my ignorance. The thing was beyond me, and even the bits I could follow didn't give me any thrill, apart from the one I always got from doing something forbidden. But I sniggered with the best of them, and did my share of marking especially dirty bits – those I was capable of recognising as especially dirty, that is – for others to read.

Pendleton, of course, knew more about it than I did. It was by Lawrence of Arabia, and it was banned, as it was the filthiest book ever written. You could go to prison for reading it, although we were too young to go to prison, and would be sent to borstal instead. This frightened me to death – my father was always threatening me with borstal, which I thought of as a sort of boarding Buggleby – and I took pains to see that no one ever caught me reading it.

Nobody was caught as it happened, and this gave Pendleton and me the confidence to take the next important step in our lives, into criminal activity.

We had long coveted the girlie magazines which graced the shelves of Colby's, the big newsagent near the school, but suspected that we would not, at our age, be permitted to buy any. What made this theory the more likely was the title of one of them – *Men Only* – which seemed to be explicit about it. I suggested that the name might simply be a way of appealing to men obsessed with being manly, but Pendleton thought not.

So we decided to steal one. The consequences of discovery being too dreadful to think about, our idea was that one of us should keep watch while the other carried out the theft. If the thief was by some unlucky chance caught, the lookout was also to give himself up. The decision as to who was to adopt which role was to be made by the toss of a coin.

We were in my room at the time, a Sunday evening, and the tension was palpable. It took ages to get the rules of the toss sorted out, but finally we reached agreement. I would spin the coin, he would shout when it was in the air, and we would let it land on the carpet. My suggestion had been that I should catch it in my right palm, and slap it onto the back of my left hand, this being a skill I had recently perfected, but Pendleton wasn't having it. If he called correctly, I would be the thief. If wrongly, he would.

I took from my pocket a George V florin, and, in a tense silence, flipped it high in the air.

'Tails!'

'Heads! It's heads! You're the thief, you're the thief! Don't try to get out of it!' (I knew my Pendleton.)

'Who's trying to get out of it?' What could he do?

The crime was to be committed after lunch the next day, and I found it all tremendously exciting. Pendleton, by contrast, looked more and more depressed and worried as the morning wore on, and he ate almost nothing at lunch time.

'I'm not feeling well,' he said, as we were leaving the canteen.

'Coward!' I had been expecting this. 'All that's wrong with you is the yellow streak down the middle of your back.' I was proud of that. I considered it both accurate and eloquent.

'I'm feeling sick!' he wailed.

'All right, Pendleton, if you're that scared, we'll drop the whole idea. Your hand would be shaking too much anyway.'

So it went on, with him protesting illness, and me insisting it was cowardice. (I can see now that it was a bit of both: he was so terrified that it made him feel sick.) But the great thing was that, as we argued, we were getting ever closer to the newsagent's, and since the theory remained that he was going to carry out the theft, I reckoned that if I could only stop him pulling out before we got there, he would then find himself committed. Once we were at the shop, he might as well carry out his obligation. Why not?

I stopped just before we were within sight of our goal, knowing he would need a bit of prodding, and fearing that we might draw dangerous attention to ourselves if it took place right in front of the shop.

'Ready then?' I asked. It was the first thing either of us had said for a minute or more.

He turned a white, ghastly face on me. 'Honestly Tom, I don't feel well.'

'Jesus Christ, Bruce, we're here now. What's the point of *not* doing it?'

'I don't feel well,' he moaned again.

'All right, coward!' I said, in a voice which oozed contempt. 'We'll go back. But everybody's going to find out about this, I promise you, and I'll never let you forget it!'

His face hardened. 'Coward yourself! Just because you wouldn't have the nerve! Come on.' He strode towards the shop, and I followed, chortling with glee.

According to plan, I entered half a minute after him,

giving a wide berth to the two nasty-looking characters – senior Buggleby boys, I suspected – lounging in the doorway. The girlies were all together on the top shelf, which made them more difficult to steal, but now that Pendleton was in front of them, what could he do but go through with it? I stood three or four yards from him, pretending to browse. While I considered it safe for him to carry out the theft, I was to keep my left fist closed.

A quick look around assured me that no one was watching him, and I bunched the fist as I glanced at the latest issue of *Trout and Salmon*. Through the corner of my eye, I saw him slip a copy of *Playboy* under his jacket.

The plan was that, just as I had entered half a minute after him, so I should leave half a minute before, and so, when I was satisfied that no one had spotted him, I replaced *Trout and Salmon*, and made for the exit. A few yards down the street, I stood waiting for him. He had done nobly and, now feeling generous, I was prepared to forget his earlier timidity, and shower praise on him. Good old Pendleton! What fun we were going to have with his magazine!

They grabbed him as he was walking out the door. The two Buggleby types grabbed him, and hustled him back inside before he knew what was happening. I was horrified.

There was no doubt as to what I had to do. In accordance with our plan, I was duty-bound to give myself up, and take the rap along with him.

I turned and ran like hell. Provided I was out of sight by the time they came after me – for I had no doubt that Pendleton would want to drag me down with him, the bastard – I would be safe. He could make what accusation he liked subsequently. No one else was in on our plan, so it would be his word against mine. People could suspect all they liked, but they would never prove anything.

By the time I reached the playground however, having taken a circuitous route in the hope that walking would soothe my nerves, I wasn't so happy. What if news reached the school that Pendleton had been caught shoplifting? It was horribly likely that Colby's would want the headmaster to know, and Carruthers, who was notorious for his tenacity in getting to the bottom of any wrongdoing by his pupils, would want to investigate any allegation the fat brute might make. What would my protestations of innocence be worth then? What would happen if the two Buggleby types were invited to identify me, and did? I was scared. The more I thought about it, the more likely it seemed that I too was going to be in trouble. I was preoccupied as I went to the toilets to empty my bladder. To my disgust, someone was in a cubicle, throwing up. I couldn't wait for this horrible business to be over, and I now wished we had never got into it. Whatever happened, I was never going on any shoplifting expedition ever again... The door of the cubicle behind me opened.

'Bastard.'

It was Pendleton. I didn't know what to say.

He went over to the sinks to wash his face. 'Why didn't you give yourself up?'

The trouble was that I hadn't got round to thinking of an excuse for my behaviour. I hadn't expected to see him so soon. How had it happened? He must have got back to school even before I did. 'Well, I...' But I could think of nothing.

He looked like a piece of chewed string, and it was lucky for me that he was in no condition to launch a physical assault. 'I'll never trust you again, you fucking coward,' he said dully, a bitter and broken man.

'But... what happened?'

It turned out that he had got away. The two Buggleby

types had taken him to the manager's office, which was behind the counter, and the moment they had left he made a break for it, and didn't stop running till he reached the school. In fact, not till he reached the toilets.

The relief was glorious. 'Where's the mag?' I asked, as we walked out.

'What? What?? Are you serious? You actually expect me to have got away with it? You? *You??*'

He was beginning to look and sound more like his old self, and I decided it might not be safe to provoke him. 'No no,' I said. 'I just thought...'

~

It was a long time before either of us went near Colby's again – I should have been in no danger, but I wasn't taking risks – and we never were brought to book. In the immediate aftermath of his escape, however, Pendleton took the most vindictive attitude. He stopped having anything to do with me.

In school it didn't matter so much, since we could both hang around with other people, but I was not really friendly with anyone else in the village, and the evenings were no fun. I began to wonder if I should apologise.

'Aren't you going to see Bruce?' asked my mother on the second evening as I was mooching around the kitchen.

'No.'

'Have you two fallen out?'

'Yes.'

'Oh well, never mind. I'm sure you'll make it up sooner or later.'

I always hated her for her easy philosophical acceptance of my misfortunes. It was different when things went wrong for her. She couldn't take it any better than I could.

I consoled myself by watching television and thinking about sex. The combination of the near-disastrous attempt to obtain the magazine, and my reading of bits of *Lady*

121

Chatterley's Lover, had thrust the topic further to the forefront of my mind than ever, and without Pendleton to talk to, I thought of little else. I continued to pursue the subject through literature, and made several forays into my dictionary, hoping to find there both information and titillation. Unfortunately, it was one of those which go straight from 'peninsula' to 'penitent', and I abandoned it in disgust. I was more successful with my mother's reading matter. While flicking through a copy of *Woman's Own*, I came across a most stimulating bra advert, and plundered her other magazines in search of similar thrills. She was a collector of the things, one of those people psychologically incapable of throwing things out, and this pursuit kept me busy for some time.

But it was the Profumo Affair that really did it. Before the break with Pendleton, I had scarcely been aware of what was happening, but I now began to take an interest. I gathered that the War Minister, John Profumo, had been caught in bed with a prostitute, Christine Keeler, and had therefore had to resign from the government. There was also a man called Stephen Ward, and some Russian soldier or sailor, but I never grasped what they had to do with the case.

Much more interesting was Christine Keeler's friend Mandy Rice-Davies, whose very name I found titillating. I began to follow the revelations as they appeared in the *Telegraph*, always pretending to be reading a different page. The most exciting phrase I had ever read was 'dressed in underwear and high-heeled shoes', and to this I returned time and again.

It got me into trouble. I was alone in the sitting-room one evening, reading it for about the twentieth time, when Linda came in. As usual, I pretended to be reading the opposite page.

'You never used to read the papers.'

'Nor did you a few years ago.'

'I suppose you're bored because you haven't got Bruce to play with.'

I always sensed, when she started any sort of conversation with me, that she was getting at me, and I felt the irritation growing in me now. But I ignored her, determined not to be riled.

'What are you reading?'

I would have done better to have said nothing, but her question made me nervous. Was she on to me? 'er... the pope, they're er... choosing a new pope.'

She became suspicious. 'You're not interested in that... Oh *I* see. *I* know what you're reading about. Oh you *dirty* little boy!'

I had never felt such loathing for another human being. 'Fuck off, you stupid bitch!'

She was on her feet and heading for the door even before I had finished speaking. 'Mummy! Daddy! He said eff! He said eff! He told me to eff off! Just because I caught him reading about Christine Keeler!'

There were loud expressions of outrage from the kitchen, where our parents were having tea, and my father came through at high speed, determined to sort me out.

'Right, is this true? Come on!'

'She was annoying me!'

My theory that I had become too old to spank was proved wrong. So wrong that I was almost in tears by the time he had finished. Almost, but not quite, because tears were now behind me, even if spanking wasn't. What I felt was a sense of outrage so enormous that nothing less than the deaths of both my father and my sister would have sufficed to assuage it. Linda had returned to witness punishment, and as I resumed a vertical stance, I looked at her with hatred and tried to hypnotise her to death. I failed.

'So he's reading this filth, is he?' said my father, picking up the newspaper with his left hand while vigorously shaking the other. 'At his age!... You're too young to read things like this! We'll keep the papers away from you in future if all you're going to read is filth!'

He went back to the kitchen, taking the paper with him and muttering something about hurting himself more than me, and remembering to keep a slipper handy in future.

This was the fourth successive evening on which I had not seen Pendleton, and I could stand it no longer. My pride kept me going in school the next day, where there were other people to talk to, but the evening was too much. After tea, I went and knocked on his door. His mother answered.

'Oh hello, Tom.'

'Hello. Is Bruce in?'

'Yes, come on in. He's in his room. Are you two speaking to each other again?'

'Yes,' I lied.

'Well, I'm glad to hear it. He's been moping around the house the last few evenings, and it's not doing him any good. Up you go.'

I was relieved to hear that he wasn't having much fun on his own either, but still not sure what sort of welcome to expect. I knocked hesitantly on his door.

'Yes?' He knew it was me – he must have heard me talking to his mother, and might even have seen me coming – and was being careful not to sound too pleased.

'It's me... Tom.'

'Oh. Okay.'

Deciding to interpret this as being more hospitable than it sounded, I went in and closed the door behind me. He was seated at his desk doing his homework, or at least pretending to. He looked up at me in such a way as to make clear that he was not going to be the one to offer the olive branch.

For a moment, I thought I couldn't do it, but the prospect of going back home was too much. I gulped. 'I'm sorry,' I said, and tried to look it. Saying it helped make me feel it.

'Okay,' he said, and shrugged.

I sat down on the bed, embarrassed and desperate for something to talk about. 'Reading about Christine Keeler?' I said.

He gave his dirty grin, and I began to relax. 'And Mandy Rice-Davies!' he said.

'Prostitutes,' I said, in a low voice.

We both sniggered, friends again.

10 Art

A change was taking place in Pendleton. He was becoming almost studious, often getting better marks than me in school, and building up a store of general knowledge that I was unable to match. He was also becoming friendly with Joe Vincent, whose mind was developing along the same lines as that of his cousin. His opinions were becoming unpredictable, and he was the only person in the village who agreed with the decision of a man called Beeching that our railway line to Stambridge should be closed. If this puzzled me, the first indication that he was developing political views of his own, amazed me.

By the time of Mister Macmillan's resignation some months after the Profumo Affair, Harold Wilson, who had been Labour leader for the better part of a year, had become an object of loathing to my father: 'I always thought Gaitskell was a good man in his way, and I didn't mind Bev Inn or Bev Anne, but that bloody man Wilson...' At this point, he would make a noise indicative of intense disgust.

By this time, the only thing that much concerned me apart from sex was pop music, and it was only the desire not to appear more ignorant than Pendleton which prompted the intelligent interest I attempted to take in the Tory leadership contest brought about by Mister Macmillan's departure. It was no good, though. I could make nothing of it. It was like watching a fight between several people concealed under a blanket, and when everyone else was surprised by the result, I decided I was surprised too. The winner was the Earl of Hume, a man who resembled a dog, but was approved of by my parents. 'You can't beat the aristocracy,' said my mother, while 'Hume's the man to put Wilson in his place,' was my father's verdict.

Furnished thus with the correct attitude, I sought Pendleton's opinion the following day.

'I don't care who leads the Tories,' he said. 'I'm a socialist.'

'A socialist?' I said, just managing to avoid screaming the word at him in horror. I didn't understand how *any*one could be a socialist, and that Pendleton should be one staggered me. I was, however, determined not to *sound* shocked, as this would certainly have drawn from him an infuriating display of patronising maturity.

'Well,' I said, recovering my composure as quickly as I was able, 'of course they've had some good people. I didn't mind Bev Inn or Bev Anne, and I always thought Gaitskell was a good man in his way, but that bloody man Wilson...'

'What don't you like about him?'

What didn't I like about Harold Wilson? He had me there. My father had never got round to saying what was wrong with Wilson, so I didn't know. I sought refuge in bluster. 'What don't I like about him? What don't I like about him?? Oh come on, Bruce! What *do you* like about him?'

'He wants to end disparities in wealth,' said Pendleton coolly.

This was meaningless to me. His parents were Tories as staunch as mine, so even if there were arguments in favour of the Labour Party, how could he know them? I shrugged. 'Maybe so, but Hume'll put him in his place.'

'Who's Hume?'

'The Prime Minister. Or didn't anybody tell you?' Perhaps Pendleton wasn't as well informed as I had thought.

'Not Hume,' he said contemptuously. 'His name's Home.'

I knew I had him. I knew I was right. 'Home??' I echoed, ridiculing his pronunciation. 'It's Hume.'

'You're just ignorant. We can check it in a paper if you like.'

We did, and I was mortified to discover that he was right. I *knew* I had heard it pronounced Hume, but old Pendleton's *Express* was not to be doubted. The name was everywhere, Home every time. I returned chastened to my study of sex and pop.

~

With things between us as they were, it was an achievement to get the fat brute to go along with any suggestion of mine, as happened early the following year with the trip to London. We had both been to London many times, but only with our parents, and never together, and it was when Linda was given permission to go there with two friends one Saturday that I got the idea.

Pendleton was enthusiastic, and although we agreed that there would be no harm in asking our parents first, our minds were made up that we would go whatever they said.

'Bruce and I want to go to London on Saturday,' I said over dinner that evening.

Linda rolled her eyes heavenwards. 'Honestly Thomas, you and Bruce can't even be trusted to go to Cranley on your own.'

This was an unfair reference to an incident the previous weekend, when Pendleton and I had set out to visit a friend of ours in a nearby village, and had taken a wrong turning. Only when we got back to Ashminster three hours later, more or less by accident and without ever having found Cranley, was a police search called off.

'That wasn't our fault!' I spluttered. 'There weren't any signposts!'

It may have been that some of the contents of my mouth went over the table. At all events, my father gritted his teeth, growled, and rose to pour himself a fresh glass of water.

'Thomas,' said my mother, closing her eyes, 'please don't talk with your mouth full.'

I swallowed everything in my mouth half chewed, and almost choked on it. Linda was sucking in her cheeks to avoid smirking too openly. 'She was annoying me!' I said. 'I wasn't even talking to her!'

My father sat down again. 'Sorry Thomas,' he said, 'but we're not having you and Bruce going to London on your own, not yet.'

'You let *her* go,' I said, nodding in my sister's direction.

'Linda's two years older than you.'

'Aren't you forgetting, Daddy,' said Linda, 'that what counts is mental age? That makes it four years at least.'

'Linda,' said our mother, 'don't annoy your brother.'

'Oh sorry, I forgot. When he gets angry he spits all over the table, doesn't he?'

Pendleton had no more success with his parents, and at a council of war the following day, we confirmed our decision that if we couldn't go with permission, we would go without it. We had established that we had enough money to get ourselves there and back. What we might do in London we preferred to leave open. In the end, we agreed that it was in fact better – because more exciting – not to have parental permission.

'Sour grapes taste sweeter,' I said.

'Stolen grapes,' he said, 'you ignorant bastard.' He was never very polite.

129

Over the next couple of days, we researched the matter in depth. If we took the 9.47 from Ashminster, then we could get the 10.15 from Stambridge, which was on the line from Reading to Paddington, and be in London before eleven. We might then make our way, for example, to Soho (where the strip clubs were). For the return journey, if we got the 3.30 from Paddington, then we would be back in Ashminster by half past four. There were plenty of other trains we could have taken in either direction, but part of the fun lay in planning the whole thing like a military operation.

The story we told our parents was that we were going to Stambridge to accompany a classmate on a bird watching expedition. The boy we chose was Joe Vincent, who was indeed interested in birds, and whose family, crucially, was unknown to Pendleton's parents or mine.

I came up with the best idea of all: I would ask to borrow my father's binoculars. Any doubts our parents might have that Pendleton and I had suddenly developed an interest in ornithology would surely be dispelled by my asking for them. And the resistance my father was sure to put up would be a useful distraction from the more serious suspicions which my sister was likely to express.

~

'Don't be silly, Thomas, those binoculars of Daddy's are valuable, and everybody knows what you're like. You couldn't be trusted with them.'

'I'm not talking to you. They aren't yours to lend... Joe Vincent's got a pair, but he says we'll need at least two pairs between three, and Bruce can't get any.'

My father scowled at me. 'And what happens when you lose them or break them, eh?'

'I won't. I promise. Please.'

My mother, amazingly, came in on my side. 'Oh, go on,

Walter, he's going to have to take care of valuable things sooner or later.'

'Hmh! And will you buy me a new pair if he comes back without them or comes back with them in smithereens? Would you trust a beatnik or a Beatle or whatever he is with something valuable of yours?' He looked grumpily from her to me, then shook his head with resignation. 'Oh all right, I suppose you can have them if your mother thinks you're to be trusted. But you see and take good care of them. If anything goes wrong, it'll be the last time I lend you anything. Clear? No binoculars, no...' He tried to think of anything else he had ever lent me, and failed. 'No nothing,' he concluded.

That I was destined to lose the bad-tempered old bugger's binoculars goes without saying, but I'll tell you about that in due course.

As we had expected, our mothers supplied us with a flask of coffee and some sandwiches each, and we were happy to give an undertaking that we would be back by five o'clock.

~

We had, as I said, planned it all like a military operation, and it started off smoothly. The trains from Ashminster and from Stambridge both ran to schedule, and we arrived at Paddington in high spirits at ten to eleven. Our big worry had been that there might be someone on the London train who knew us, but we were lucky. We now had more than four hours ahead of us in which we could do anything.

'I vote we go to Madame Tussaud's,' I said. 'I want to see the Chamber of Horrors.'

But Pendleton, as usual, had other ideas. 'It's London we've come to see,' he said, 'not places that just happen to be in London. I think we should go to the West End.'

He had an infuriating way of sounding both more

grown up and more adventurous than me. That we were there to see London, and not just places that happened to be in London, struck me as a devastating point. I would never have thought of it.

'All right,' I said, 'the West End.' (Where the strip clubs were.)

It was wonderful. We took the Tube to Leicester Square, and walked and walked. Charing Cross Road, Shaftesbury Avenue, Greek Street, Piccadilly Circus, The Strand... We agreed that the experience was so different from being there with our parents that it was like being there for the first time. It was one o'clock before we knew it, and we sat down for lunch on a bench in Trafalgar Square. As we ate, I took the binoculars out, and started looking at people.

'Let's have a go,' said Pendleton, who never liked to be left out of things, and we spent some time just staring at people. We focused mostly on girls, and Pendleton said we were thus doing exactly what we had told our parents we would be doing: bird watching. I thought this very witty.

By one thirty we were beginning to feel the cold, and started discussing our next move. I wasn't going to mention Madame Tussaud's again, not after what Pendleton had said about it, and I was astonished when he suggested going to the National Gallery which, unknown to me but not to him, was only a hundred yards from where we were sitting.

'But that's like Tussaud's!' I said. 'It's not London. It just happens to be in London.'

He was, as ever, unabashed. 'It's more important,' he said, 'and anyway, it's full of noods and things.'

Noods? I made a mental note to the effect that my own opinion on the pronunciation of the word had been erroneous, and thanked God that I had never invited ridicule by referring to 'nyoods' in Pendleton's presence.

But however the word was pronounced, if the National Gallery was full of them, that was where I wanted to go. Not even Pendleton could have stopped me.

We walked in past the intimidating uniformed staff – I had feared we might be forbidden entry on the grounds that we were too young to be looking at a lot of dirty pictures – and set off in search of noods. There were plenty of them. We evolved the technique of splitting up when we entered a room, moving round in different directions, and meeting again at the opposite end. We would compare notes, and then return to look more closely at anything we considered particularly interesting. If possible we would sit down and, pretending to be studying the picture hanging next to the real object of our attention – we didn't want to get caught – get an eyeful of nood. It was unfortunate that old masters were strangely unerotic, but no nood could be entirely devoid of interest.

I was the one who first became anxious about the time, but such was my fascination with what we were doing that I was more than ready to accept the fat brute's assurance that we had plenty. But when, at his instigation, we finally left, I noticed that he was walking faster than usual, and only a superstitious dread that naming my fears might cause them to come true, prevented me from accusing him of having miscalculated. Faster and faster we walked, saying nothing, but each made more nervous by his awareness of the anxiety of the other.

It was quite dramatic. We just managed to dive into a tube train at Trafalgar Square as its doors were closing. Pendleton grinned at me, and I could tell that the crisis was over. We were going to make it. I grinned back in sheer relief.

Only when the train pulled out of the next station but one did I notice that he was getting nervous again. He began to study the Underground map above the door with more attention than I liked to see, and then he looked at me. 'Tom,' he said, and I began to feel sick – our convention was to use first names only when there was something serious to be said – 'I think we're going in the wrong direction.'

I could have killed him, and had it not been for my lack of confidence in my ability to get back to Ashminster without him, perhaps I would have. It was now quarter to three, and we were in trouble.

When we got off at the next station, and had to wait more than five minutes for a train to take us back the way we had come, it was clear we weren't going to make it. I was now too miserable even to think, but Pendleton was not so easily crushed.

'We'll be okay,' he said, 'even if we don't get the three thirty. There'll probably be another train that'll get us to Stambridge in time for the four thirty-five, and then we'll be back in Ashminster by five just like we said.'

'Fuck you,' I said, anxious to ensure that he knew I blamed him for our predicament. But I saw his point. The timetable which we had consulted had indeed shown plenty of trains between Paddington and Stambridge, and provided only that we could get to the latter by four thirty-five – our normal train home from school, and the one we had been aiming for, was the 4.15 – we would still be all right. I crossed the first two fingers of both hands, and as I did so, our train stopped in the middle of a tunnel.

If there is anything more infuriating than to be in a desperate rush, and to find yourself on a form of transport which refuses to budge and which you cannot leave, I have been lucky enough never to experience it. In the stillness I became increasingly angry, and my anger focused more and more on Pendleton. Minutes passed until I could no longer contain myself, but nobody in our carriage was talking, and I had to keep my voice down to a whisper to avoid shocking people. 'Why the bloody hell did you get on the wrong train, you idiot?'

He turned to me and drew his lips back over gritted teeth. 'Shut up, you useless bastard!'

'Just because you couldn't tear yourself away from the noods!'

'You were the same!'

There would certainly have been a disgraceful scene if the train had not suddenly started moving. The balance between despair and hope tilted towards the latter, and I forgot, for the time being, about the fat brute. But it was a dreadful journey. There was another long wait at Trafalgar Square, and our train crawled the last couple of hundred yards into Paddington. Pendleton and I shot to the surface like ping-pong balls released under water.

We intercepted the first man we saw in a British Rail uniform. 'When's the next Reading train?' gasped Pendleton.

'Platform six,' said the man, glancing up at a clock. 'You'll need to run though.'

We made it. As we slumped exhausted into our seats, the 4.00 from Paddington to Swansea pulled out of the station. For some time, we just sat there panting, savouring the relief.

Pendleton was the first to speak. 'Tom?'

My first name again. Something was wrong. 'What?'

'Where are the binoculars?'

It is at such moments that you understand how shock can cause heart attacks. It was immediately apparent to me that I hadn't got them. In the midst of my horror and despair, all I could think of was to blame Pendleton. 'Haven't *you* got them?' I said, trying to make it sound as if he had as much responsibility for them as me, and planning already to make my father believe it was Pendleton who had lost them.

'How the hell would I have them? They're not mine.'

It was going to be tricky, I could see. Rather than saying openly that Pendleton was responsible for their disappearance, I would have to say it was my fault, but put it in such a way as to make it seem that I was protecting my friend.

The door of our compartment opened. 'Tickets please... Stambridge? You're on the wrong train, boys. This is an express, first stop Reading.'

~

There would be little point in recounting the remainder of the journey in detail. After a blazing row which ended only when the inspector returned to tell us to keep our voices down and behave ourselves, we sat out the rest of the journey to Reading in quiet misery and mutual hatred. We arrived there at half past four, and when we had established that there was no way of getting back to Ashminster before five even if we could have afforded it, Pendleton rang home, admitted everything, and asked his father to come and pick us up. I was relieved that it was not *my* father who was coming, as I would have found it hard to offload the blame for the loss of the binoculars in Pendleton's presence.

My mother was in the kitchen with Linda, washing dishes, when I got back. 'Go through to the sitting-room, Thomas,' she said. 'Your father wants a word with you.'

Linda neither looked at me nor spoke, but her facial expression was that of an intelligent and serious jury member coming to terms in a dignified manner with the account of an atrocious crime. She had probably been practising.

When I got to the sitting-room, my father was on his feet, hands behind his back. He did not yet know about the binoculars, and I was in no hurry to tell him.

'Binoculars,' he said.

I gulped, and shook my head.

'What?' he said, in the most hushed and menacing tone I had ever heard from him.

'I'm sorry.'

'You little... Doris! Come here!'

My mother appeared from the kitchen, wiping her hands on her apron. Linda was close behind. 'What is it, Walter?'

'It was you who said the little fool could be trusted with my binoculars, wasn't it?'

My mother looked first at him, then at me.

'Oh Thomas!' said Linda.

'Thomas,' said my mother, 'have you lost your father's binoculars?'

'Yes,' I said.

My father sat down and folded his arms, breathing heavily.

'It must have been in Trafalgar Square,' I said. 'We had lunch there, and Bruce asked to borrow them so that he could have a better look at the pigeons... I looked at them too, of course. We were already on the train to Reading when I noticed that he... that I didn't have them.'

I was wasting my breath. The manner of the disappearance of the things was of no interest to him, although Linda told me later that she thought it 'disgraceful' that I should seek to cast the blame onto someone else.

Retribution for both Pendleton and me was savage. For the following two weekends we were confined to our respective houses, and my pocket money was stopped for the same period.

11 Sport

It was old Pendleton's idea that Bruce and I should take up golf. He reckoned that it might help us 'stay out of mischief'. We became junior members of Stambridge Royal. Old Pendleton took us the first time, and did his best to teach us the rudiments.

Neither of us ever reached a high standard, and our early propensity for air shots led to an agreement that no stroke which failed to make contact with the ball should be counted. Even so, it was many weeks before either of us managed a score of under three figures, and that was the cause of all the trouble.

A ten-shilling bet on it gave an edge to our games, but it was some time before the target was in sight, and problems arose as soon as it was. We were both in the habit of cheating, and were each, therefore, tolerant of the other in this respect. But when it became clear that the ten shillings would change hands before long, the matter became serious. We began to have nasty rows when recording the score for each hole, and it was remarkable that we avoided physical conflict as long as we did.

~

It was a warm evening in early August, perfect for golf, and we both had high hopes of winning the wager. Mine probably had more substance, as my previous best score was 103 against his 106, but I was determined not to fall victim to overconfidence. We had agreed that, in the event of our both breaking a hundred in the same round, the lower total would win, while if our scores were equal we would play as many extra holes as might be necessary to resolve the deadlock.

We both started off in high spirits, and mine rose still higher when I had taken only fourteen for the first three holes, par being eleven and Pendleton having taken eighteen. He began to irritate me as we approached the fourth, by launching into a lecture about the Beatles. (Having at last come to share my interest in pop – both of us were, to our parents' distaste, addicted to *Top of the Pops* – he now behaved as if I had no appreciation of it, and it was his task to enlighten me.) I decided he was trying to put me off my game, and kept myself under control.

If that was his intention, he had chosen the right moment, because the fourth is the longest and most difficult hole on the course, a 530-yard par five. It is less the length of the hole that matters than the unusual number of nasty hazards that are packed into it. There is, for example, a vast bunker known as The Magnet 150 yards down the fairway, while the first two hundred yards of the hole run uncomfortably close to the River Shale on the right. This is followed by a vicious dogleg to the left, avoiding Blenheim Wood, then a further three hundred yards of fairway before a raised green defended by two bunkers. If you land in one of them, there is no alternative to playing out backwards.

It was me to drive first, and, in my anxiety to stop my opponent going on about the Beatles, I wasted no time in teeing up. I must have allowed myself to become irritated, because I ostentatiously selected my driver, thinking I would 'show him'. (We both preferred to use irons, and my tendency to slice was always exaggerated when I played a wood.)

I believed in myself though, and I wanted Pendleton to

know it. He wasn't playing badly himself, but I was sure, Beatles or no Beatles, that he must be dismayed by my form, and I reckoned that a good drive now, and hit with a driver at that, might finish him off. With barely a twinge of nervousness, barely a thought of the river on the right or The Magnet in front, I addressed the ball, with every intention of giving it a tremendous wallop.

In the event, I did indeed hit it pretty well, nearly as far as the dogleg, but I sliced it. I watched anxiously as it faded to the right, but the slice was not bad, and it wasn't going to end up in the river. It finally came down not far short of Blenheim Wood, around the margin between the light and the deep rough. It was one of the longest drives I had hit, and I was left with a straight run towards the green. Only the lie was in doubt.

'Not bad,' said Pendleton, which was about the nearest he could get to praise, 'not bad at all.'

I was hoping he might risk a driver too, so as not to be upstaged, and then make a hash of it. But no, he took an iron. His drive was straight enough, but a daisy-cutter, and it was unlucky for him that the ground was so dry, because it would never have reached The Magnet otherwise. It did, though. From the tee it was impossible to see where it had ended up, but we soon found that it had indeed covered an unlikely 150 yards and trickled into the sand.

'Bad luck,' I said, restraining myself with difficulty from leaping up and down, punching the air in triumph. This was going to be my greatest humiliation of the fat brute yet.

His cause was not yet lost though. A good shot from the bunker would take him at least as far as the dogleg, while if my ball had found a bad lie... We walked up to The Magnet in silence, the tension stretched like a wire between us.

'Well... could be worse,' I said, taking stock of the position of his ball. In truth, I reckoned he had been unlucky. The lie was downhill, and I gave him only a fifty-fifty chance of getting out in one.

But Pendleton was never short of tenacity, and, taking a nine iron, his most lofted club, he approached his ball without comment. By this time, my confidence was such that I didn't even grudge him the excellent recovery shot he played. He took a lot of sand, but the ball soared out of the bunker, and landed plumb in the middle of the fairway, giving him a straight run to the green.

'Good shot!' I said, and even applauded, which was more than he had ever done for me – or I for him until that moment, come to think of it.

'Thanks,' he said, nodding with satisfaction.

It brought his confidence back, because, as we walked on, he started another pompous, self-congratulatory monologue, this time about astronomy. (Having discovered that he was an intellectual, he had developed the habit of giving me, at great length, the benefits of his research into various esoteric subjects, none of which was of any interest to me.) This was still going on in the absence of any reaction from me, when we reached the area where my ball had landed. To my dismay, it was nowhere to be seen, which meant that at best it was in the deep rough, while it might even be lost. I could have screamed. I was in fact on the point of giving it up when Pendleton spotted it.

'Here it is!' he cried, and I should have known from the delight in his voice that all was not well.

I had the most evil lie you could imagine, almost unplayable. The ball had not gone far into the deep rough, but had come to rest just in front of a hefty clump of grass, through which I would have to hit if I was to get it out and in the direction I wanted it to go. Had I spotted it first, I would have given it a kick, but that was out of the question now.

141

Pendleton drew in a deep breath and shook his head. 'Bad luck, Tom.'

I could have throttled him. Bad luck it was, and he had no business rubbing it in. I had hit a cracking drive, and a whim of fate had turned it into a disaster... Calm down, I told myself, calm down, you're still well ahead. I had the choice of playing out sideways, for which the lie was at least reasonable, or taking the risk of hacking it out forwards.

Selecting a seven iron, I had almost decided on the former course of action, when my better judgment yielded to the temptation of crushing Pendleton with a recovery shot even better than his. Eyes glued to the ball, or what little I could see of it, I took a long, slow backswing. I was going to show him.

It was the most extraordinary shot I had ever played. I swung so violently that the grass hardly slowed the stroke at all, but it did twist the club in my hand, with the result that only the toe made contact with the ball, which took off, spinning wildly, at an angle of sixty degrees to the right. So fierce was the spin that it sent the ball further away from the hole than it had been before I played it. There was a hollow 'clunk' as it hit a tree, then a splash as it rebounded into the river. My world collapsed.

'Sorry, Tom. Bad luck, really.'

It was a dangerous thing to have said. I was armed with a heavy golf club, there were no witnesses, and killing him would have posed few problems. The temptation was almost too great to resist, but a closing of the eyes and a deep breath sufficed to keep it at bay. All was not yet lost, I tried to tell myself.

According to the rules of the game, I now had to play a new ball from the same position, but the stroke would count as my fourth. Fortunately, my previous swipe had rendered the offending clump of grass less formidable, and, after improving matters still further by surreptitiously adjusting the position of the ball with my foot before addressing it, I was able to give myself a decent lie. I had a right to it.

This time, I took a three iron, and channelled all my rage against Pendleton into the stroke. I gave it a tremendous whack, hitting it as sweetly as I had ever hit a golf ball. It flew straight and true, fading not an inch either to right or to left, and came to rest right in the middle of the fairway, well over half way to the hole. What a shot!

'Hmm. Not bad,' said Pendleton.

How I despised him! But ten shillings would be some compensation for the misery of having to play a round of golf with him. I did some calculating. I had now played four strokes. How many more would I need? With the confidence I now felt, I was sure I could get on the green with my next shot, and might then even get down in one. That would be, in the circumstances, a magnificent six. More realistically, I might two-putt for a seven, in which case I would have taken twenty-one for the first four holes, and still be well set to break a hundred.

I was so engrossed in these calculations that I was hardly aware of Pendleton's presence until I heard his club strike the ball. It was another miserable daisy-cutter, but again the dryness of the ground took effect, and the ball went further than he had any right to expect. It was a good way short of mine, but still well placed for him to reach the green in two. But then, with two putts, that would give him twenty-five for the first four holes, and leave him little chance of winning our bet.

He had by this time taken up his astronomy lecture again, but he was concerned about his position too, because as we walked on up the fairway, he departed briefly from his description of the rings of Saturn, and betrayed his need of comfort.

'How many's that for you, Tom? Only two?'

I said nothing. If he was into cheap points-scoring, that was his business.

'Oh no, of course, your second went out of bounds, didn't it? Into the river. So that makes... what? Four, doesn't it?'

'Right.'

He was cutting his own throat, because the greater my anger, the greater my determination. I kept my mind fixed on the bet.

As you walk up the fourth fairway after the dogleg, the two great bunkers cut into the steep hill on which the green stands are an intimidating sight. There is no position in either of them from which a chip to the green is even a possibility. I would almost have given the ten shillings I would surely win just to see Pendleton hit one of them with his next shot.

In the event, he took the risk of giving it all he had, and this time he struck the ball cleanly. Off it went like a bullet, and I felt my left hand clench with the eagerness of anticipation. Down, down it came, bounced once, bounced again, and ran and ran. As with his tee shot, it was impossible from where we were to say what its ultimate fate had been, but there was the clear possibility that it had found its way into the bunker on the left. 'Please God,' I prayed, 'let the bastard's ball be in the sand.'

But I had my own problems to consider. I was faced with a shot of 120 yards or so, and could afford no mistakes. I was well aware of what was going through the fat brute's mind as I took out my five iron. A careful stance, a deep breath, then a smooth backswing...

It was another dream of a shot, and from the moment it left the club, there was no danger that it would end up in the sand. I thought I might even have overdone it. My only fear was that it might have overshot the green, and gone into the rough behind. But it was impossible to see the green from the fairway, and I decided to forget about it for the time being and enjoy the contemplation of my opponent's problems.

I was disappointed when we found his ball just a couple of yards short of the sand, but at least he was still left with an awkward shot, too close to the steep slope for comfort. A nine iron might do it, but he would have to make sure he got well under it, and if he overhit it in his fear of running back into the sand, he might end up in the rough. Heartened by the problems he faced, I decided to add to them.

'er Bruce... Sorry...' I began, just as he was addressing the ball. 'Want me to go up and hold the flag up for you?'

'No.' He controlled his irritation well, but the word was spoken through gritted teeth. He played the shot.

'Nice one!' Again I demonstrated my superior sportsmanship, but I hadn't liked the look of it. If my estimate of the position of the flag was accurate, he could be well placed to get down in one. That would be a six he scarcely deserved.

We climbed the steps cut into the grass between the two bunkers and surveyed the green. Neither ball was visible. I could guess where mine was, of course, but it was not till I saw Pendleton drop his clubs and run, in shameless excitement, towards the flag, that I realised what had happened to his.

He plucked it from the hole, and flung it gleefully into the air. 'A five!' he cried. 'A five at the fourth! A five!'

Disgusted at this immoderate display, I ignored him as I went in search of my own ball. Why did he have to have all the luck, the fat useless brute?

It could have been worse. I was in the rough, but only a few yards from the fringe of the green and not lying badly. The text-book would prescribe a pitch-and-run, then one

145

putt for a seven, giving me twenty-one for the first four, against Pendleton's twenty-three. The idea of a pitch-and-run made me nervous. It was a shot I found hard to control, and with the green sloping from the flag back to the face of the hill, it was possible that an overhit effort of the type I was contemplating... It was too horrible to think of, and I grabbed my putter.

A firm stroke was needed. I was a good five yards off the green, and perhaps fifteen from the hole. I took my time, praying for a miracle like the one Pendleton had just achieved. That would wipe the smirk off his face.

And it was that thought which tempted me to catastrophe. Determined to get down in one, I hit the shot absurdly hard, and knew it from the moment the ball left the head of the club. I was horrified. My only hope was that it might, if the line was good, hit the flag and go in... The line was perfect.

But Pendleton ensured that no such thing would occur. He was holding the flag for me, but whipped it out the moment he realised what would happen if he did not. And the ball went right over the middle of the hole, that's how accurate it was. But it was going like a guided missile, and, in the flag's absence, there was no chance it would drop. On and on it went, slowing down a little a few yards past the hole, then gathering speed again as the slope took effect. At last, it disappeared from view down the hill and into the right-hand bunker.

There was a moment of silence such as might have been observed by those in the lifeboats when the stern of the Titanic slipped out of sight beneath the waves. Then Pendleton looked round at me, shaking his head in sympathy.

'Rotten luck, Tom. The line was perfect.'

I could hardly breathe. Taking the longest possible grip on my putter, I swung it three times round my head, then hurled it with all my strength up and away, far over Blenheim Wood. Round and round it went, higher and higher, then, turning more slowly, descended towards the trees and was lost from view.

'We can share my putter for the rest of the round,' said Pendleton.

I took eleven for the fourth.

~

As we left the sixteenth green, I was on 101, with Pendleton on 92. Thoroughly demoralised, and grotesquely well informed on the more distant planets of the solar system, I was now dragging my bag instead of carrying it, and the spring in Pendleton's step only increased my dejection. My one comfort was that he was unlikely to break a hundred. The seventeenth was a par three and the eighteenth a par four, so he would have to par them both to do it, and it was long odds against that.

But then he managed a birdie at the seventeenth, the first either of us had ever achieved. I could have wept. He got it with a ten-yard putt from the edge of the green, which only went in because I, in my dejection, was not minding the flag. The ball would have overshot the hole had I been on hand to do for Pendleton what he had done for me at the fourth. I was well used to injustice, but this was too much. My own five left me indifferent. The only thing that mattered was that Pendleton should take at least six for the eighteenth.

I will carry the memory of what happened on that final hole to the grave. It was Pendleton to drive first, and in his quivering determination he missed the ball. This posed a problem. It was a long time since either of us had played an air shot, but we had never formally abandoned our practice of not counting such strokes. I could guess what he had in mind, and he could guess what I had, but neither of us said a word as he addressed the ball again.

I found myself praying to God that he would take at least six more strokes so that there could be no argument, but if he took five, then I was counting the air shot. His next attempt was more successful, and it occurred to me in my misery that I would almost sooner he took four than five.

The rest of the hole was played in a tense silence even more irksome to me than further information on the orbit of Neptune would have been. I would have given twenty shillings for Pendleton to lose the bet rather than the ten which his winning it would cost me.

His fifth undeniable stroke was a three-yard putt which curled half-way round the hole before dropping. He raised his putter high in triumph, and turned on me a face which beamed with more than earthly joy. 'Ten shillings please!'

He wasn't getting away with this. 'Sorry Bruce, but ninety-four plus six makes one hundred. My ten bob says you won't *break* a hundred.' (A clever touch. By pretending that I thought he had misunderstood the terms of the wager, I was implying that we both accepted he had taken six for the eighteenth.) I replaced my own ball, which I had taken out of the way for him. 'Can I have the putter?'

He lowered the club, as hatred froze his features. 'I took five, not six. Pay up.'

I assumed a look of puzzlement, and pretended to try to recall the strokes he had played. 'No, Bruce,' I said at length, 'six, definitely six.'

Withholding the putter from my outstretched hand, he adopted a posture of aggression, hands on hips, legs apart, mouth turned down. 'Misses don't count. Remember?'

I dropped my hands to my side, let my jaw hang open, and stared at him, head shaking in what might, I hoped, resemble disbelief. 'Oh come on! That was ages ago. You can't pretend that old rule still applies!'

'We never abandoned it.'

'Okay,' I said, discarding my parody of incredulity in favour of one of reason, 'let's ask in the clubhouse.'

'It's our rule,' Pendleton growled, 'not the club's. Pay up.'

'No.'

'You bastard.'

'Give me the putter.'

'Pay up!'

'Piss off.' I curled my lip, and turned away.

He was on me in an instant, trying to get my wallet out of my back pocket. Of course, I had to defend myself, and soon we were rolling around on the green, a mass of flailing limbs, yelling obscenities at the tops of our voices.

This was bad enough, but what made it catastrophic was that we were only twenty yards from the open windows of the clubhouse. I was barely aware of the outraged voices in the background however, and would have ignored them anyway. Pendleton was trying to cheat me out of ten shillings, and, his bluff having been called, was intent on wresting it from me by force. I had no doubt that I was the injured party, and he was no less convinced of the justice of *his* cause, and the intensity of moral conviction on both sides rendered the conflict the more savage.

But just as I was beginning to prevail – I was on top anyway, and contemplating the possibility of a head-butt if I couldn't get a hand free – I was dragged off my prey. Pendleton was up and at me again the instant we were disentangled, but before he could press home another attack, he too was seized, and his arms pinioned.

Who had hold of me I had no idea, but behind him was the formidable figure of Ray Greenham, the club professional.

'This is disgraceful!' said the voice of my captor, whom

149

I was thus able to identify as Major Harrington, the club captain, and a great pal of my father and old Pendleton. I didn't care. My eyes blazed at my enemy, and his blazed back.

'He owes me ten bob... shillings. He won't pay!'

'He's a cheat and a liar!'

'I broke a hundred, you bastard!'

'Fuck you!'

'That's enough foul language! The pair of you are a disgrace.' Major Harrington was laying it on the line. 'We'll just hold on to them till they cool off, Ray.'

It took some time, but cool off we eventually did, and our captors released us. 'Now you listen, both of you,' said the Major, as we stood straightening our clothes and dusting ourselves down. 'Nothing justifies a scene like that on a golf course, so I'm not going to go into the rights and wrongs of the matter. You can sort it out for yourselves. But the next time you're caught behaving like that at this club is the last time you'll be allowed in. Understand?

We muttered our agreement.

'Now go home, and see if you can't learn to behave like civilised human beings.' He turned his back on us, and accompanied the professional back into the clubhouse.

Before we left, we agreed to a compromise on the wager, by which I gave Pendleton five shillings, the remaining five to go to the first of us to achieve an undisputed two-figure score. On the train home – almost the last ever to run between Stambridge and Ashminster – we maintained an unbroken silence.

Neither of us believed the matter had ended with our humiliation at the club, and there was indeed more in store for us when we arrived home. We had said a surly goodbye, and I was on my way up the garden path, when the front door opened and Linda appeared. She was wearing her most severe expression.

'Thomas, you're to go next door with Bruce. Daddy and Mr Pendleton want to speak to both of you. They're furious.' She shut the door.

Pendleton waited for me, and we went to our doom together. We found old Pendleton and my father, grim-faced, in the sitting-room.

'Another one, Walter?' said the former, ignoring us and pointing to my father's empty glass.

'Just a small one this time, Stan.'

There was a silence as old Pendleton poured whisky for both of them, and it was clear that his son and I were not to be offered anything. 'Sit down, you two,' he said, without looking at us.

We sat. I looked at Pendleton, he looked at me, and we experienced that rare sense of camaraderie that only common adversity can bring.

'Cheers.'

'Cheers.'

The two men sipped their drinks in silence for a moment, then Stan Pendleton cleared his throat.

'An hour ago,' he began, I had a phone call from Major Harrington at the club. He said you two were involved in a disgraceful scene on the eighteenth green this evening. Well?'

Pendleton and I exchanged another look, all our earlier hostility towards each other now directed against the adult world in general, and against our fathers in particular. But we said nothing.

My father's patience, if he can be said to have possessed such a quality, snapped. 'You can't answer, can you, either of you? Rolling around on the green right in front of the clubhouse like a pair of wild animals, kicking and scratching and God knows what, and using language not fit for a bro... an army barracks!' He shook his fist at me. 'I should have knocked you on the head at birth!'

Old Pendleton sighed and shook his head. 'I don't know what gets into you two when you're together, but it can't go on like this. You both know that, don't you?'

'And what's all this about a ten-shilling bet?' said my father, determined to play a full part in the proceedings. 'Betting at your age? Ten shillings?? My God, Thomas, when I think what your grandfather would have done to me...' He shrugged his shoulders in helpless despair and shook his head.

'Well, Walter, they've obviously got nothing to say for themselves, so we may as well get on with it.' Old Pendleton rose, grabbed his son's golf bag and mine, and announced that he would be taking charge of them for the next week at least. He and my father would then make a decision on whether or not they might be returned. 'Now both of you listen carefully. We've given Major Harrington a guarantee that if we ever allow you to go to the club again, there will be no repetition of your appalling behaviour today. If there is...' He left the threat unspecified, perhaps believing it would frighten us more that way.

12 Exploration

Pendleton had never been much good at sports, and the debacle on the golf course confirmed him in his hatred of all games. So intense was this loathing that he was not even prostrated by infatuation with Mary Rand at the Tokyo Olympics, and although he had been interested enough in their first meeting, the return fight between Cassius Clay and Sonny Liston prompted in him only the observation that boxing was barbaric, and ought to be banned. It had, he claimed, fascist overtones. He and I agreed on little, but we did at least have similar tastes in music, in particular a love for that of the Beatles, whose Hard Day's Night I considered to be the finest record ever made. *Top of the Pops* remained one of the high points of the week.

My sister had gone straight from Cliff Richard to Mozart, to whose music she would listen with an expression of intense absorption which made me want to punch her face. She referred to Radio Luxembourg, the background against which I chose to do my homework, as 'Thomas's din'. ('Mummy, since he never listens to me, can you ask Thomas how he expects me to concentrate on French subjunctives with his din at that volume?')

It was a bad day for her when I asked for, and to my astonishment was given, a record player for my fifteenth birthday.

I imagine it was a common love of appalling music that

drew together her and her first boyfriend, Pimple Simon, who was studying the violin in London, and whose family had recently moved into the area. He and Linda met at some party over Easter 1965, and Pendleton and I christened him Pimple Simon because he happened to have a prominent blemish in the middle of his chin at that time.

He had nothing going for him. Not only were his two great loves, my sister and classical music, two of my great hates, but his attitude to me drove me wild. Although he was only eighteen to my fifteen, he used to patronise me in the way that an insensitive adult might a child. He even had the nerve to address me as 'young Thomas'.

'Well, young Thomas, how's school these days?'

'Fine.'

'And what are you going to be when you grow up, eh? Engine driver?'

I avoided him whenever possible, but had to put up with substantial doses of him because he took to coming home every weekend in his old and crestfallen blue Ford Popular just to be with Linda. Certifiable behaviour, I thought.

By this time, Pendleton and I had become more dirty-minded than ever, and we used to speculate obscenely on how far Linda and Simon went together. And as the weeks passed, our conjectures became ever more lurid.

'Honestly, I've never even seen them kissing.'

'I don't believe it.'

'Swear to God.'

Pendleton thought about this. 'I suppose she might be frigid,' he said at length. 'It would fit with the rest of her personality.'

'How do you explain Richard Chamberlain then?'

'That's true. But they've been together since Easter. That's *weeks*. By this time he should be sucking her tits at the very least.'

'She hasn't got any to suck.'

'Absolutely sure you've never seen him with his head up her skirt?'

'I'd have noticed.'

With my loathing of Pimple Simon, such conversations were useful as a means of letting off steam, pressure from which might otherwise have caused me to do something dreadful. In the event, the closest I came to using physical violence against him was on the only occasion on which he ever made himself useful to me.

One Saturday morning at the end of May my record player refused to work. I plugged in and switched on, but nothing happened. This would have been bad enough at any time, but the Pendletons were away that weekend, and I had persuaded the fat brute to lend me his records for entertainment. I gave the machine a few thumps, banged the plug harder into the wall, and so on. Nothing happened. I went downstairs to the kitchen, where the rest of the family were being mature and sensible over the newspapers.

'My record player's not working,' I said, preferring a simple statement of fact to an explicit and humiliating request for assistance.

'Good,' said Linda.

I ignored her, and stood there, trying to look miserable in the hope that someone would take pity on me.

'Don't look at me,' said my father. 'I don't know anything about them.'

Linda sighed. 'I don't know why I should help Thomas to get his din back,' she said, 'but Simon should be here soon, and he could probably repair it. If he wanted to, that is.'

'There you are, Thomas,' said my mother. 'When Simon gets here, you ask him nicely if he'll have a look at it.'

'Mm,' I said, and retreated to my room. It wasn't surprising that Linda thought her boyfriend could do the job, since she believed he could do anything, but I was far from sharing her confidence, and the thought of demeaning myself by *asking* Pimple Simon for anything, let alone asking him nicely... But he was my only chance. I was still wriggling on the horns of this dilemma when the old Popular pulled up outside the house ten minutes later. I decided to toss a coin – heads I'd ask him, tails I wouldn't. It was tails, but while I was considering whether or not to make it best of three, footsteps came up the stairs, and I could guess what had happened. Linda had taken it on herself to invite the Pimple to show off at my expense. My door opened, and in they came.

'Well, young Thomas, mum says the record player's not working.'

I grunted, thinking it better not to point out to him that he and I did not share the same mother.

'And his friend Bruce is away this weekend,' said Linda, 'so he's got nobody to play with.'

'Oh!' said Pimple Simon, widening his eyes like a pantomime actor who must exaggerate every expression of feeling. 'We can't have that, can we?' Uninvited, he crouched down by the record player and switched on. Nothing happened. 'Well, the nasty thing just doesn't want to work, so we'll jolly well have to make it.'

The most irritating thing about the next few minutes was that he did clearly know what he was doing. Linda played nurse to his surgeon, bringing him the small screwdriver he demanded, and holding whatever he gave her until it was needed. He quickly established that a loose connection in the plug had caused the fuse to blow. With deft confidence he removed the fuse, put in a new one and tightened the faulty connection. And when he plugged in and switched on again, all was well.

Linda beamed. 'Well, Thomas, what do you say to Simon?'

'Thanks, Simon.'

'That's all right, young man. And now you've seen how it's done, maybe you could think about becoming an electrician instead of an engine driver, eh?'

When you find yourself under an obligation to someone you didn't like in the first place, the effect is to make you loathe them all the more. I was delighted to have my record player working again, but I promised myself I would die rather than accept help from the Pimple ever again.

~

Pendleton and I were now in the habit of going on long cycling trips on Saturdays, and it was a week later that we undertook an especially ambitious one. We used to plan our journeys with the aid of an Ordinance Survey map belonging to old Pendleton, and on this occasion we decided on a fifteen-mile round trip to Lake Grafton. We got there at half past twelve, and it was Pendleton who first noticed something interesting up ahead.

'Just a minute,' he said, breaking into my reflections on the sexiness of Una Stubbs in *Till Death Us Do Part.* 'Isn't that Pimple's car?'

We had just come round a sharp left-handed bend, and on the grass verge less than a hundred yards from us, an unlovely blue car was now visible.

'Looks like it. Shh!'

We dismounted, left our bicycles, and crept up on the old Popular. 'Why isn't it bouncing up and down?' whispered Pendleton, and we both sniggered.

The car was, to our disappointment, empty.

'They must be somewhere,' I said vacuously.

'He's probably screwing the arse off her even at this moment.'

'He wouldn't dare... Hang on, that might be them over there!' Far out on the placid waters of the lake was a rowing boat. It was difficult to be sure from such a distance, but we thought there were two people in it.

Pendleton became excited. 'If that's them they must've hired the boat somewhere. And if they can do it...'

'We might catch them doing something disgusting at last. Maybe blackmail them. Come on!'

There was indeed a boathouse just a little further on, and, having convinced a sour-faced old man that we were both over sixteen, we hired a rowing boat for an hour. The idea of the boat now excited us as much as the anticipated thrills of voyeurism, and we were in high spirits as we climbed in.

'I'll row for the first half hour,' said Pendleton, and I lay back in the stern. 'I won't make it too obvious we're after them. We've got plenty of time.'

Everything would have been fine if only he had rowed better. I was prepared to give him time to get the hang of it – which was just as well, since his efforts for the first few minutes were as grotesque as they were ineffectual. But even when we were out into the open water and moving smoothly, he kept splashing me. I think I behaved reasonably. I asked him not to and, though with no good grace, he said he would try. But I went on getting wet, and asked him again. He told me angrily that he was doing his best, but it wasn't possible to row without splashing at all. Contenting myself with suggesting he try harder, I lay back and closed my eyes. Linda and Simon no longer concerned me. I was enjoying the sensation of gliding across the calm waters of the lake, and if Pendleton would only stop flicking water... SPLASH! My anger was, I think, pardonable.

'You did it again!' I shouted, sitting up and exaggeratedly brushing water off myself.

'I told you it was impossible to row a boat without splashing! Go on, you try!'

'Oh no, you're not getting out of it that easily. You finish your half hour, then I'll show you h...' This time, a substantial quantity of water got me full in the face. 'You're doing it deliberately!'

Pendleton lost control. Without a word, he let go of both oars, and dived at me. I was almost knocked overboard. It wasn't much of a fight, because the boat was such a confined space and was rocking about so much. Only a few seconds had passed before we were obliged to disengage for fear of going overboard or even capsizing. We sat down again, breathing heavily, fists bunched, glaring at each other.

And then, with a look of horror and despair, Pendleton stretched out his right arm, and pointed to something in the water behind us. 'The oars!' he wailed. 'We've lost the oars!'

I looked round in shock. Our impetus had carried us far beyond them now, and we were still moving.

When I turned again to look at him, his face was contorted with rage and anguish. 'It's your fault, you stupid bastard! If you hadn't been moaning all the time.'

'My fault? My fault? I like that! Who was rowing then? Who had the oars? *My* fault??'

Another outbreak of fighting seemed likely, but we were restrained by the knowledge that it might result in disaster even greater than we had already suffered. We continued to glare murderously at each other, but the crisis passed.

'Look,' said Pendleton at length, putting on his mature act, 'we're going to have to get the oars back somehow.'

'Oh brilliant. Brilliant! We *can't* get the fucking oars back because we haven't got the fucking oars to move the fucking boat with! Or maybe you hadn't noticed.'

'Well,' he said, 'we're going to have to try.' He leaned out and started using his right hand as a paddle. I sat and watched.

'Look,' he said after a few moments, 'if we can't get the oars back ourselves, then we're going to have to get Linda and Simon to help us.'

I had forgotten all about our original reason for hiring the boat. Suddenly terrified by the prospect held out to me, I spun round to see where the other boat was. Still, to my relief, a long way off. Our humiliation would not be apparent to them from that range. Taking Pendleton's point though, I leaned out over the other side and made my own contribution. The water was surprisingly cold.

He stopped paddling and sat up. 'What do you think you're doing?'

I gritted my teeth and continued my efforts. 'Helping to move the bloody boat,' I said.

'You really are stupid, aren't you?'

Trying hard to control my anger, I took my frozen hand out of the water and turned to face him. 'Maybe you'd like to explain that.'

'If you paddle on that side and I paddle on this side, we're just going to carry on going forward, aren't we? What we've got to do is both paddle on the same side so we come round in a circle. Then when we're actually facing the oars we can start paddling on different sides.'

I had never been an unreasonable boy. When Pendleton could make out a logical case for doing things his way rather than mine, I was ready to admit that he was right. As he was on this occasion. We did it his way.

It was a pity the water was so cold, because we were making some progress. Paddled by hand, the boat moved very slowly, but it did at least move. The trouble was that our paddling hands soon became so cold as to be unusable. We both changed to the other hand, but by the time it too was out of action, we had still not quite got the bows pointing towards the oars, which were close together but only just in sight.

'What about swimming to them?' said Pendleton as we sat on our hands to try to bring the circulation back.

'Who?'

'You're a better swimmer than me.'

'How did I guess? Well, I'm not risking swimming in water that cold. You can do what you like.'

I turned to look again at the other boat. It was now moving in the direction of the boathouse, and, though moving at no great speed, was thus coming closer to us.

'Looks like their time's up,' said Pendleton. 'We're going to have to decide what to do.'

Pendleton knew I was resolved never again to accept help from Pimple Simon, however desperate my needs. I had gone on so much about my humiliation of the previous weekend that he had become bored and told me to shut up about it. What was I to do now? I closed my eyes, and images floated before me: Jack Cornwell, mortally wounded, remaining at his post at Jutland; the Dutch boy, spending the night with his finger in the dyke; Grace Darling, rowing through the crashing waves to the wreck of the Forfarshire...

I opened my eyes and took a deep breath. 'I'm going for those oars,' I said, and began to undo my shirt. Pendleton was going to get a lesson in guts, and Pimple Simon was going to get nothing.

I struck out boldly, but the water was icy. Only profound admiration of my own heroism kept me going. By the time I knew I was in trouble, I was nearer to the oars than to the boat, and I went on only because I needed to grab hold of the nearest thing that floated. Reaching the first one, I tried to grasp it, but my hand was numb. I looped an arm round it instead.

'Help!' I shouted, terrified that Pendleton might see this as an opportunity to take revenge for my unsympathetic attitude to him in a similar situation four years previously.

He didn't. Standing up, he waved my discarded shirt above his head and yelled to the other boat.

It was the nearest I had come to death. I lost awareness of whether or not I was still treading water, and by the time help arrived – it can only have taken a few minutes – I was not fully conscious.

'All right, got you... end of his tether... young Thomas... circulation... something hot... silly little boy...'

Fortunately, Pendleton and I had taken a flask of coffee each, and with the help of this and much rubbing and slapping, I was revived. It was painful as the circulation came back, and I almost wanted to return to the dreamworld in which I had been floating at the moment I was rescued, but they wouldn't let me.

Even when I was fully conscious again and recovering, it took me all my time to persuade Simon and Linda that I did not need to be taken to hospital.

'Yes,' said Linda at length, 'I suppose hospitals shouldn't have to bother with silly little boys like you. Come on, Simon, we're over our time already. Now if you two lose those oars again, don't expect us to help you.'

13 More Sex

My interest in sex had become still more intense. Lustful thoughts invaded my mind when it should have been concentrating on other things, and the topic was now an obsession. My days were devoted to attempts, normally unsuccessful, though growing less so as skirts became shorter, to look up girls' skirts or down their blouses, and my nights to doing for myself what I feared no girl would ever do for me. I used a handkerchief, which I would wash myself lest my mother should suspect.

For a time, Pendleton seemed to have lost interest in the subject, but this was an affectation caused by his desire to be considered an intellectual. He had taken to reading Aldous Huxley, whose work, he assured me, I would be unable to appreciate. I took his word for it. His political views were beyond me. He had only contempt for Edward Heath, the new leader of the Conservative Party, and no sympathy with the Rhodesian prime minister Ian Smith, who, I understood from my parents, was an unalloyed Good Thing. And he professed himself well pleased with Harold Wilson's second, and overwhelming, general election victory, an event described by my father as 'an unmitigated disaster for this country and for the whole of the Free World.'

But his main interest was the music of Bob Dylan (that of the Beatles he now considered 'attractive but superficial'), whose songs I found as ugly as they were incomprehensible. Not knowing any better, I had long since accepted that he had, in the previous couple of years, turned into an intellectual much as a caterpillar turns into a butterfly, and I was at first prepared to believe that intellectuals were above sex. This was probably the view he took as well. Certainly he now performed better than me in school in spite of affecting to despise everything we did there.

It couldn't last. He could not forever blind himself to the fact that neither Aldous Huxley nor Bob Dylan had anything against sex, and he soon gave up trying to pretend that his mind was any less dirty than mine. In fact, he swung to the opposite extreme, now apparently believing that an obsession with sex was the hallmark of an intellectual. It was confusing.

We had both just turned sixteen when he bet me ten shillings that he would be first to lose his virginity. This was the first bet either of us had proposed since the disaster on the golf course, and a sense of honour compelled me to accept. It seems odd that we made no arrangement whereby a claim to the money might be substantiated, but I suspect that we were both happier that way. I was not pleased with the wager, seeing little possibility that I would ever break my duck, let alone break it before Pendleton broke his. The trouble was that I was pathologically shy with girls, and the more attractive the girl, the shyer I was.

What Pendleton's chances of seducing anyone might be, I had no idea – the truth was that I couldn't imagine how anyone ever accomplished a successful seduction – but I put nothing past him. For myself, I decided that the only hope, and that a remote one, lay in a gradual progression from theory to practice, and to this end, I turned to literature. A thorough search revealed nothing of any use in the house, which meant I had to try the library.

My parents often went into Stambridge on Saturday mornings, and on this occasion, when I heard Linda say she would 'give it a miss – I haven't got time for light reading with my A-Levels coming up' – I announced that I would go with them to change my library books. This was true after all, if not the whole story. (I would never have risked a dirty book search without being sure that my sister, who had, to my relief, broken her first heart by leaving Pimple Simon a couple of months previously, was not in the vicinity.)

I had two fields of enquiry. I wanted to know the facts of sexual intercourse in maximum detail, and I wanted to know how a seduction should be carried out – how I might get a girl into a position in which my theoretical knowledge could be of practical use. I was not entirely ignorant of what intercourse involved, but there were still questions to which I needed answers, chief amongst them being that of the sexual geography of women. My great fear – so great that I scarcely admitted it even to myself – was that I might choose the wrong orifice. The consequences of such a blunder I could not bring myself to contemplate, and I was determined to make sure it should not happen.

But it was in the matter of charming a girl out of her clothes and into bed that I expected to encounter the gravest problems. How to perform the sex act was something I could learn from theory, but I had serious doubts as to my capacity to get through the earlier stages of the process no matter how much I read about it beforehand. Still, that wasn't going to stop me trying.

Getting hold of the necessary book, or books, was, I knew, going to cause problems. For a start, I didn't know where in the library to look, and I certainly wasn't asking. Then there was the matter of checking the books out. Did I have the nerve to reveal to the librarian, who knew my mother well, that I was mugging up on sex? I had gone so far as to practise this part of it in front of a mirror (walking casually to the desk, putting the books down casually, saying casually 'Just some stuff I need for biology', picking them up, strolling casually out), but I knew it would be difficult. To minimise my embarrassment, I was going to use up my full ration of four books, but two of these at most would be on sex. The other two or three would be almost grotesquely innocent – I thought that geology or archaeology might be suitable.

My parents were also a problem, since my father would probably be in the library with me – he usually killed time there on Saturday shopping trips – and my mother had the infuriating habit of wanting to know what I was reading. I decided I could deal with the presence in the library of the former by keeping a close eye on him, making sure I checked my books out well before him, or well after him. As for my mother, whom we normally picked up in her favourite coffee shop on the way back, I would conceal the book, or books, on sex, and only let her see the others.

Things began smoothly, since my father quickly became engrossed in the periodicals section, and I was not long in locating a volume that answered my needs. It was entitled *Sex for Beginners*, and was full of illustrations. I was disappointed to find, after a detailed study, that these were not very arousing, but reminded myself that arousal was not what I was after – and anyway, I got plenty of that from the underwear adverts in my mother's magazines.

Satisfied with my progress, I put the book back, noted its position, and went off in search of books on geology or archaeology. This proved far more difficult than finding the sex book had been. I could see no book on either subject which would not make anyone who knew me suspicious as to why I had borrowed it, and it was some

166

time before it struck me that there was no point in pretending to have acquired suddenly an interest in topics which I had ignored hitherto. When I came to this realisation, I went to the fiction shelves instead, and started looking for something less improbable and more entertaining. This took ages, and I was still searching for a third novel when my father appeared.

'You nearly ready? Time we were off to pick your mother up.'

I nodded, and kept an eye on him as he checked his books out. Then I swiftly made my own final choice, and went over to pick up *Sex for Beginners*. I had abandoned my intention of claiming that it was to aid my study of biology, reckoning that, with the number of dates already stamped in it, Miss Vetch must be well used to seeing people borrow it. The old bag could think what she liked.

I got past her no bother, and it was with a feeling of triumph that I crossed the road to the car. My father was already at the wheel and the engine was running. All I had to do was to get in and conceal the sex book somewhere, which was not likely to be difficult. Failing all else I could slide it under one of the front seats.

But as I was opening my door, the books slipped from my grasp and onto the pavement. This would not have mattered if my mother had not suddenly appeared.

'Oh Thomas, you are careless! Yes, I finished my shopping early today, and decided not to bother with coffee... Well, let's see what you've got then. Four books, I see... Walter, my door's still locked.'

What could I do? She now knew how many books I had, and her curiosity was boundless. As we drove off, she turned round and asked again to see what I had borrowed. If I tried to keep one back, she would demand to know why I was hiding it, and then the thing would become even more awful. I gave her the books without a word, but I hated her as much as any son can ever have hated his mother.

'Now what's this? P.G. Wodehouse, oh yes... Jack London... *Tales of Terror*, oh nasty, and er... *Sex for Beginners?*'

'That's for biology,' I said desperately. 'We're doing reproduction. It'll come up in the O-Level.'

'Oh yes,' said my mother. 'Well...'

'Your sister used to do biology, and she never read filth like that.'

'Maybe that's why she was so bad at it.'

He growled. 'She was good at it, you little devil, because she read the right stuff, and not dirty books like that.'

'It's not a dirty book.'

My mother decided to be reasonable. 'Yes, well,' she said, handing the books back, 'of course it's up to you what you read. And you have to know about these things, I suppose.'

'It's for biology!' I cried indignantly. (I had now convinced myself that this really was the truth.)

'Yes, Thomas, I'm sure it is,' she said, 'and anyway it's up to you what it's for.'

My father growled again, and I maintained a sullen silence for the rest of the journey.

~

My mother's discovery of the book made things easier for me, because there was now no need to conceal it. So I put it in my room with my two biology textbooks, which seemed a good way of driving my point home.

It was highly informative on the physical details of sexual intercourse – indeed, it told me more than I needed to know – but it was a dead loss as a source of information on the art of seduction. It began with the business of stripping for action, and although this was in some ways the most stimulating section, I desperately needed to know a reliable route by which I might arrive at that point. Still, I read with interest about the desirability of being adept at removing one's partner's clothes, and wondered if I might be any good at it.

And as I thought about it, it came to me that it might be tricky to take off a bra while facing its wearer. I was aware, through my study of the advertisements in my mother's magazines, that bras had a clip at the back, so how...? And if it came to that, how did women get into them in the first place? It was on the Saturday afternoon that I began thinking about this, and in a spirit of scientific enquiry, I decided to borrow one of Linda's bras to find out.

Excusing myself from dinner before everyone else, I pinched a bra from her room, and took it to my own to experiment. The thing struck me as extraordinarily complicated at first, but I soon worked out what the various bits were for, and began to feel a certain respect for its inventor – in its way, it was quite ingenious. I decided to try it on.

I took off my shirt, slipped the thing over my shoulders and attempted to do it up. It was impossible. How did they manage it? I took it off again, studied it further, and had a brainwave. The thing was to do it up first, and then put it on. This solved the problem, and I began to feel I was getting somewhere. I could now turn my attention to the central issue – that of how, putting myself in the position of a person facing me, I might go about taking it off.

First of all though, I wanted to see how I looked in it, but I had no mirror in my room. So I pulled my shirt on, did up a couple of buttons and made for the bathroom. It was unfortunate that Linda was now on her way up the stairs, and that I had not gone to more trouble to conceal what was under my shirt. She saw it straight away.

'Thomas!! Thomas, what *have* you got on under that shirt? Oh no, I don't be*lieve* it!'

169

I froze, and made no resistance as she stretched out a horrified arm, and gave my shirt a violent tug, which took off both the buttons I had done up. 'Thomas! That's mine!'

'You've ripped my shirt!'

'I'm telling Mummy!' she said, and turned to go back downstairs.

I panicked. 'Linda, for God's sake no! I can explain. Just listen a minute...'

She turned to face me again. 'Thomas, you're a pervert and you need psychiatric help. Mummy and Daddy will see you get it.'

'I'm not, really I'm not! I just wanted to see how I looked. It's a joke, something to tell Bruce about, that's all.' I was in a blue funk. What might happen if she told our parents, I could not even imagine, and for a dreadful moment, I thought she was going to ignore me.

But she relented. 'Just take it off and give it to me,' she said. 'This time – just this once – I'm going to say nothing, but if anything like this happens again, I'll have to tell Mummy and Daddy. It'll be for your own good.'

I practically died of relief, but then I found I couldn't get the thing off. Forgetting how I had put it on, I got into a tangle, and my terror lest either of our parents should make an appearance made things even worse.

'Oh for goodness sake, you *stupid* boy! Stop struggling or you'll tear it. Turn round and let me do it... Right, that's it. Now give it to me. And remember, if anything like this happens in future, I'm telling Mummy and Daddy.'

~

The fright she had given me put me off my research, and I did not resume it until a week later, when Pendleton took his turn at humiliating me. A dreadful experience.

Cathy Figgs had arrived from London at the beginning of that term, and had wasted no time in making her mark.

She was not especially attractive, but she had developed a way of moving and of looking at older boys which made her school uniform, which still looked demure on most girls despite rising hemlines, seem almost indecent. She was a year below us, and Pendleton and I were in the habit of concocting lurid fantasies about her even before she earned her reputation as the school tart.

It was Jerry Dean, an unsavoury member of the fifth year, who first claimed to have 'had' her, but Pendleton and I chose not to believe him – he was just the sort to make up stories like that. It troubled us, though, and when his pal Simon Barstow said that he too had 'had' her, we began to have doubts. Soon the claim was being made by other people and, even allowing for a certain amount of exaggeration, the weight of anecdotal evidence became overwhelming. Horribly jealous, I was increasingly unsuccessful in my attempts to convince myself that no girl worth having could be that easy.

Of course, I always had masturbation to fall back on, but it was growing less and less satisfying, and knowledge of the availability of Cathy Figgs was causing me the first focused sexual frustration of my life. Everyone knew the drill. Cathy Figgs would go out with anyone, or at least with anyone older than her, and for the price of an ice cream and a cinema ticket, a goodnight kiss and feel were guaranteed when you walked her home. And if she really liked you, then she would take you 'round the back', where you 'had' her up against the wall. It was painful. The greater the number of people who had 'had' her, the more obvious was her availability, and the more mortifying my frustration.

I could take it though, if only because I accepted without question my own inability to ask her out. My virginity was with me forever, like a hunchback's hump, and I would have to live with it. I was thus able to listen in

171

stoical misery to the tales of conquest told by others, but each story made my own frustration the greater. They had all 'had' her, even George Pordle, whose combination of spots and blubber made him revolting.

When Pendleton made the bet with me, my thoughts had turned instantly to Cathy Figgs – not in the hope that I might succeed with her, but in the fear that he might. The money was the least of my worries. What I could not take was the thought that Cathy Figgs, whatever her other transgressions, should have been 'had' by Bruce Pendleton.

He made sure I knew all about it too, the bastard. It was Saturday afternoon, exactly a week since Linda thought she had discovered that her brother was a transvestite. I was in my room, wondering whether or not I could be bothered whiling the time away with a wank, when the doorbell rang. I ignored it, and began to unzip my trousers.

'Thomas! Thomas, it's Bruce!'

'Right. Coming.'

We had had an argument the day before over the date of the Battle of Poitiers, and had not spoken to each other since. It was a matter of pride that one should not be the first to speak after a quarrel, and I had been sure I would not see him at least until Sunday. But I was bored, and prepared to be conciliatory if he weakened first.

When I got to the door though, I received one of the nastiest shocks of my life. Cathy Figgs was with him. 'Hello,' said my voice.

'Hi Tom.'

'Hello.'

'Can't stop, but here's the book you lent me. Sorry I kept it so long.'

I took it from him dumbly. He had had it just five days, and I had told him I was in no hurry for its return.

'Just wanted to make sure I gave it back while I remembered. We're on our way to the flicks.'

'Ah.'

'Bye.'

'See you.' I told myself that excessive self-stimulation had affected my brain, and this was a hallucination. I watched in silence as they retreated down the path, and I recall thinking that he must have gone to some trouble to dream up a pretext for dragging her all the way out to Ashminster just so that I should see her with him.

Then he turned. 'Oh Tom, by the way, you were right. It *was* 1356. Sorry.'

I felt like pursuing and strangling him. That he should call round on a ridiculous pretext, only to show me that he was going out with Cathy Figgs was bad enough (why couldn't he just have given the book to my mother, for God's sake?), but that he should then, triumphant over me in the thing that mattered most to both of us, show himself to be a good loser in an affair of triviality, was too much. His normal practice of kicking me when I was down was merciful compared with this pretence that he was helping me to my feet. I returned to my room and wanked until it hurt.

~

The rest of the weekend was agony. I would have given anything – *anything* – to learn that the tart had rebuffed the advances I knew he must have made, but I was willing to bet she hadn't.

Nothing would have made me ask him about it, and I avoided him on the Sunday rather than risk an account of his triumph. On the Monday morning, I talked almost non-stop throughout the forty minutes between the time we left home and the start of assembly, but I was only postponing the dreadful moment. Jerry Dean asked the question as we stood waiting for assembly to begin.

173

'Hey Pendleton!' he hissed, from his position immediately behind us. 'How'd you get on with Figgsie on Saturday night?'

'Oh not bad,' said the fat brute, pretending to suppress a yawn. 'She's not such a bad lay.' There were knowing sniggers all round.

'Then he turned to me and lowered his voice: 'Oh, that reminds me, Cardwell, that's ten bob you owe me.'

I swear to God that only the entry of the headmaster prevented me from launching a murderous assault.

In the end, I beat him down to five shillings, saying he could hardly expect the full amount if he could offer no proof of his achievement. And when he asked how that would have been possible, I told him as casually as I could that, in his position, I would at least have come away with the knickers she'd been wearing. To my surprise, he finally accepted the coins, albeit with a bad grace, saying it was a safe bet that *I* would never get inside any girl's knickers. Although privately agreeing with him, I gave him a superior look which was intended to implant in his mind a germ of suspicion that maybe, just maybe, I had already 'had' a girl, but had, for some reason, chosen not to tell him. I was wasting my time.

~

I was pleased to have averted total disaster, but I still had to accept that he had come out on top, and, desperate now to register a success of my own, I returned to my research with renewed commitment. The following day, I gave lunch a miss and went to the library in the hope of finding a book which might give me some advice on how to begin a seduction. I drew a blank. And then, on my way back to school, I decided to buy a bar of chocolate to compensate for my missed lunch. I went into a newsagent's and, as usual, my eye strayed to the girlie magazines which I hadn't the nerve to buy or, after

Pendleton's disaster three years previously, to steal. The cover of *Men Only* hit me right between the eyes: 'HOW TO GET THAT GAL RIGHT WHERE YOU WANT HER!!' There were a number of people in the shop, and I reckoned I might risk a glance at it without drawing too much attention to myself.

It was the first time I had dared touch a girlie magazine, and I found it most exciting. Not only that, but the article on seduction turned out to be just what I was after...

'Cardwell.' The voice was not loud – scarcely above a whisper – but it cut like a whiplash.

Beside me stood Jocelyn Carruthers, the headmaster. I was incapable of speech or movement. He took the magazine from me, glanced at it with a curl of the lip, and returned it to its place on the shelf. 'Not entirely suitable reading matter at your age, Cardwell, take my word for it. O-Levels in a few weeks. You might do better to read for them.' He had not raised his voice, and no one else in the shop was paying us any attention. 'I think' he went on, looking at his watch, 'that you should consider getting back to school.'

~

It was all a bit much. I borrowed a sex book from the library and my mother found me with it. I tried to find out about women's underwear and my sister caught me in one of her bras. I glanced at a dirty magazine and my headmaster materialised beside me. Fate, I concluded, was determined to frustrate my research, and who was I to resist the irresistible? If theory was out, practice would have to be in.

And I did it. I actually managed to ask Cathy Figgs out the following Saturday night. It took a huge effort of will, and her acceptance astonished me, even it was a truism that she would go out with any boy who was older than her. I had been convinced that my role in Cathy Figgs's sex life would be that of the rule-proving exception.

But she said yes, and thus it was that I took her to the cinema just fourteen days after Pendleton had done so. My parents were not happy about it, being of the opinion that I was too young to be taking girls to the cinema, that I should be studying for O-Levels instead, and ought not, in any case, to be allowed to enjoy myself. I didn't. What the film was I do not recall – she said she had seen it before, though it didn't matter – but I will never forget what happened afterwards. I wish I could.

I had prepared it all beforehand, determined that nothing should be left to chance. I would try holding her hand as I walked her home from the cinema. If that worked, I would put my arm round her. If all was still going well, I would kiss her when we got to her front door. And then, in the continued absence of resistance, I would ask if there was 'anywhere we could go'. That matters should progress beyond that point I was unable to believe, but in case she took me 'round the back' I had invested in a packet of three contraceptives. Still in the interests of thorough preparation, I had used one of them for practice, and was pretty confident that if, just if, the unthinkable happened, I would not make a fool of myself.

In the event it was remarkable how smoothly things went. Up to a point. Or perhaps I should say it was remarkable how smoothly they went on the surface, for my nerves were in an appalling state. The awful thing was that my success in carrying out each meticulously planned stage in the assault made me more, not less, anxious, and even before we had reached her front door I was having doubts as to whether I would be capable of storming the last bastion.

So far, my inner turmoil had allowed me to enjoy nothing, and the same went for the prolonged kiss which she so readily gave when we reached her house. Things were, in fact, only getting worse, and when I asked hoarsely, 'Is there... anywhere we could go?' I was praying she would say no.

But she didn't. She didn't say anything. All she did was to slip out of my clumsy embrace, take me by the hand, and lead me round the house.

So this was it. The prize was now within my grasp, and all I could feel was misery. My conviction that I would be unable to seize it was so complete that I didn't even feel nervous any more, only wretched. You know that bit in the Bible where Jesus is in Gethsemane, and he says to God that if it's all the same to Him, he'd just as soon not be crucified after all? Well, I uttered a similar prayer as I followed Cathy Figgs round the house, and I got the same result. God let Jesus be crucified, and He let me be crucified too, because God's like that. Read the Bible.

Of course, I could still have got away with it if only I'd kept my wits about me, but they had departed even before the evening began. I could have pretended that all I wanted was a bit of heavy petting, why not? All I had to do was leave her pants on and all would have been well, but oh no, no such possibility even occurred to me. The whole purpose of the evening was that I should 'have' her, as Pendleton had 'had' her. That was all there was to it.

That I couldn't make it, couldn't even begin to, was soon as clear to her as it was to me. 'You haven't done it before, have you?'

'Course I have. Lots of times.'

'What's wrong then?'

'Just don't seem to be in the mood, that's all.' My only desire was to get away from her as quickly as I could.

'Your pal was the same.'

'*WHAT??*'

~

177

The Pendletons were away that weekend, but I wasted no time on the Monday.

'I want my five bob back,' I said as we walked to the bus stop. The man called Beeching had long since deprived us of our rail link with Stambridge.

'What??' He was predictably outraged.

'You heard. I want my money back. You never made it with Figgs.'

'Oh yes I did! Who says I didn't?'

This was the moment I had been waiting for, because he was unaware that I had been out with her too – I had preferred not to give him advance notification. 'She does. I had her myself Saturday night. She says you couldn't make it. Come on, pay up. I want my five bob back, and ten bob for winning the bet.'

'Piss off! Either you're lying or she is. I won fair and square.'

'Lying bastard! If you don't pay up, it'll be round the whole school that you couldn't make it with Figgs. She won't deny it.'

'Jerk! All right then, let's see her knickers. Come on, let's see them.'

He was lucky it was daylight and there were witnesses, or I would certainly have killed him. But I was aware of the weakness of my own position. 'I just didn't think about it, that's all.'

'You didn't have her then. You couldn't make it. You're a bloody liar.'

'Listen, jerk, I'll let you off the ten bob if you feel that strongly about it, but if I don't get my five bob back, it's going round the school that you can't do it.'

He was admitting nothing, but he agreed in the end to let me have the money back, saying he didn't have much choice in the matter if I was threatening to slander him, knowing he couldn't prove I was lying.

14 The Supernatural

Linda went away to university. She went to Oxford, which wasn't nearly far enough for my liking, but at least it kept her out of the way most of the time. This was always gratifying, and occasionally made possible behaviour I would never have contemplated with her around.

It was during her first term there that Pendleton and I became interested in the occult. In addition to Bob Dylan, Aldous Huxley and left wing politics, he was now into religion – Zen Buddhism, to be precise. I, as usual, had no idea what he was on about, but, having recently taken the daring step of informing my parents that I was an agnostic, I felt my usual combination of awe and suspicion.

The fat brute was game for anything, and I suppose I should not have been surprised when he expressed an interest in the supernatural. A casual remark he made to me one lunchtime started things off.

'Did you hear about Graham Lidden?'

'No,' I said, without much interest. Lidden was in the year below us, and noted chiefly for his extraordinary display of acne.

'Just a few days back, him and his sister and Jackie Bell were messing about with an ouija board – you know, the spirit in the glass thing. Seems to have scared them.'

I gave a patronising laugh, which I thought would reflect his own attitude.

179

'Want to try it?'

'What?' I assumed I had misheard him.

'Do you want to try it?'

Pendleton's thought processes were beyond me. Having flicked through a book on Zen which he, probably more with the intention of boasting than of proselytising, had lent me, I felt pretty sure that Zen philosophy would consider western occult dabbling a joke. I nearly told him this, but two considerations dissuaded me: first, I would certainly be the victim of a barrage of abuse if I did so, and second, the idea of the ouija board fascinated me too

'Might be interesting,' I said.

'Great. We'll need at least three.'

We found to our annoyance that Lidden had indeed been frightened by the experience, and had sworn, as had the two girls, never to touch the thing again. He would not say precisely what had happened except that the séance had ended when the glass, with no hand touching it, began to describe violent circles round the table before hurling itself against the wall and smashing.

Pendleton and I couldn't wait to try it out, and forced Lidden, much against his will, to tell us how we might acquire and use an ouija board. But he told us we were making a 'terrible mistake', and made us promise not to reveal to him anything the spirit in the glass might tell us. 'I just don't want to know, that's all.'

We were both by now bursting to try it out for ourselves. All we needed was a glass, a table with a smooth surface, twenty-six cards with one letter of the alphabet on each, and two cards for yes and no. And, of course, at least one more person. My parents were to be out that Saturday evening, so an ideal opportunity was before us, and we wasted no time in getting the third man. We kept it as quiet as possible, so that we would not have scores of imitators, but managed to arrange with Cliff

Tarling, who lived in Ashminster and who was in Lidden's year, to come round to my place on the Saturday evening.

I undertook to make the necessary preparations, and we agreed that it would be appropriate to dress predominantly in black and red. (Pendleton had read somewhere that these were the colours of black magic, and we felt pretty sure that what we were going to do was more evil than good.)

This was on the Wednesday, and I thought of little else between then and the Saturday. We were going to venture into realms of the unknown, and this would be the greatest adventure of my life. I was also terrified, and made sure there was a bible in a cupboard in the sitting room, where the séance was to take place, just in case things got out of hand.

I spent the whole of the Saturday afternoon getting things organised, making sure the table was suitable, choosing a likely glass (with one or two in reserve in case the spirits proved capricious), getting chairs ready, preparing the cards, buying red candles – I couldn't see evil spirits taking to electric lights – and a hundred other things.

What made it all so awkward and time-consuming was that these preparations had to be hidden from my parents. Of course, I told them that Pendleton and Tarling were coming round, but said we would just be listening to records and so on.

'Yes, well I don't want any horseplay,' said my mother. 'From now on, you pay for any breakages.' This was a reference to an evening that had, admittedly, got a little out of hand the previous month. A cup and two glasses had been broken, though she had never noticed the torn cushion, on which I had performed a cunning repair.

I treated her to my eyes-closed-nodding-inner-sigh-of-weariness-all-right-all-right-anything-you-say look. This always infuriated my father.

'And don't you look at your mother like that! It's about time you grew up, boy, and stopped all this superior cynical stuff. At your age! My God, I wouldn't have liked to try that on my parents, I can tell you. You've been spoilt of course, that's your trouble.'

'Whose fault is that, then?' I asked, as he picked up a newspaper, behind which he could more ostentatiously ignore me.

'Oh yes,' said my mother, 'it must be our fault. Everything always is as far as you're concerned, Thomas, isn't it?'

'No, of course not, but I can't have spoilt myself, can I?'

My father was stung into rejoining the fray. 'Can't you? I wouldn't put it past you. I wouldn't put anything past you.' He growled, and disappeared behind his paper again.

'Just see that nothing gets broken this time, that's all,' said my mother. 'I don't want to get back tonight and find the house in smithereens again.'

They had told me they would be going out at seven, and I became more and more impatient with them as the deadline receded further into the past. Pendleton and Tarling were to come round at half past, and I was anxious that my parents should be gone by then. I never liked to witness them talking to my friends, and anyway, I feared that the appearance of the latter, if they were entering into the spirit of the thing, might cause comment and suspicion. The atmosphere of the séance was vital, and for my parents to behave patronisingly to the participants before it had even got under way might, I thought, prove ruinous.

'Oh no, I've lost my purse now!'

'What the hell have you done with my green tie? I can *never* find things once you've put them away.'

It was now ten past seven and I was in the sitting-room. My father's voice came from their bedroom, and my mother's from the kitchen, where she was rummaging noisily in drawers and cupboards.

'You put your purse in here two minutes ago!' I called in exasperation. Were these people never going to leave? The suspicion came to me that spirits, good or evil, might find the atmosphere of our house uncongenial, impregnated as it was with the trivial concerns of these two walking banalities. My mother came in.

'Where is it then?'

'On your chair where you left it.'

'Oh yes. Good.'

From upstairs, the sounds of drawers and doors being opened and closed were increasing in frequency and volume, a sign that my father's temper was being tried by his continued inability to locate his tie.

'Doris! Doris, are you there?'

'Yes!' My mother had now sat down and was checking her make-up in a compact mirror.

'Where the hell is that green tie?'

'Well, I don't know, Walter, do I? Where did you put it?' She smoothed an eyebrow with an index finger and replaced the mirror in her handbag.

'God damn it, woman, it's you who hides things, not me!'

'Oh Walter, Walter! Language!' My mother had become less concerned about swearing since Linda's departure, but there was a limit to her tolerance. 'You'd better hurry up, you know. We're late as it is.'

The sound of slamming drawers and doors stopped, and when he spoke again, his voice came from the top of the stairs. 'All right then, I'll come out without a tie. Is that what you want, hmm? *I* don't care if I wear a tie or not – it's only the Harringtons we're going to. I'll just wear an open neck, okay?'

'Don't be silly, Walter. You just find...'

'Oh I'm silly now, am I? Silly because I want to wear the right tie. And you tell me I must be colour-blind if I wear things that don't match. Okay, fine, I'm colour-blind, I'm silly, anything you say.'

My exasperation was making it difficult for me to breathe. How could *any*one get so worked up over such a thing? And to think that while they were out at their appalling bourgeois dinner party, Pendleton, Tarling and I would be wrestling with demons! How I despised these people!

It was twenty past seven when, to my immense relief, the tie was found and they were ready to go. By that time the house was in silence, as they had stopped speaking to each other, and I had shut myself in my room to prevent them from practising their occasional trick of communicating through me.

I sighed with relief as the car finally moved off – it was not uncommon for one of them to have to come back again having forgotten something, but they rarely turned back once they were in the car and on their way.

Anxious to have everything ready for when the other two arrived, I changed quickly into the outfit I had chosen and went downstairs to prepare the room. By the time the doorbell rang fifteen minutes later, all was in readiness. Tarling was wearing black jeans and a red sweater, but Pendleton appeared to have made no sartorial arrangements.

'You're supposed to be in red and black!' I said in annoyance. 'At least Tarling and I have made an effort!'

'Keep your hair on, keep your hair on. My stuff's in here.' He held up a bag he was carrying.

'Okay, good, but get changed before you come into the sitting-room, otherwise you'll spoil the atmosphere.'

'Right,' he said, and went off to the cloakroom. Tarling and I went into the candlelit lounge to await him.

'Actually,' said Tarling, and cleared his throat, 'I'm beginning to get pretty scared about this.'

'But you're not backing out?' I said.

'Are you kidding? I wouldn't miss this for the world!... I wonder what did happen when the others tried it?'

'I was thinking that that's something we could ask *our* spirit. We might even get the same one.' We both looked apprehensively at the wineglass which stood upended on the table, in the middle of the circle of letters. 'I hope we do get a spirit,' I said.

The door opened, and Pendleton came in. Even by candlelight he looked extraordinary. He was wearing a black towelling dressing-gown tied with a red belt, and a bright red hat, presumably his mother's. Tarling took one look at him and burst out laughing.

I was angry. 'Stop that!' I said. 'You'll spoil the atmosphere, and then the spirits won't come. He looks fine.'

Tarling did his best to control himself, and Pendleton walked over to us with what dignity he could muster. Only then did I notice that his legs were sheathed in black nylon.

'Christ, Pendleton, what have you got on your legs?'

'Stockings,' he said. 'Otherwise the effect would be ruined.' He lifted his dressing-gown to reveal that they were held up by a black suspender belt. This was too much even for me, and for the next few moments Tarling and I were helpless.

Pendleton covered his legs again, and adjusted his hat. 'Perhaps,' he said with self-conscious coolness, 'when the hilarity is over we can get down to more serious matters.'

'You're right,' I said, controlling myself with difficulty. 'Actually, you look the best of all of us. Tarling, please!'

'I decided on the hat because of my fair hair,' said Pendleton.

Tarling gave a final snort and was silent.

'Good. Well then...' I nodded at the table. 'Shall we begin?'

We looked in silence in the direction I had indicated, and I gulped. I placed my index finger on the glass and made sure it could move freely.

'Should be okay,' I said, 'but we can always change it if it's no good.'

'Please God,' said Pendleton, 'send us a spirit.'

'Shh! That'll put the spirits right off,' said Tarling.

'How do you know? We might get a good spirit, not an evil one.'

'We won't,' I said, attempting a sepulchral voice. 'I can feel it in the atmosphere.'

'I'm not sure I like this.' Pendleton moved back from the table.

'Cissy! You're not backing out now!' Tarling was as keen as I was.

'Did I say I was? Did I say I was? I just think we might get more than we bargained for, that's all.'

'Well,' I said, 'I suppose we could ask the spirit if it's good or evil, and then sort of, you know, decide if we... if we really want to talk to it or not.'

The other two muttered their agreement.

'I mean, we might think a good spirit's too boring!' I attempted a laugh.

'Let's begin,' said Tarling.

Pendleton moved closer to the table. 'How *do* we begin?'

'Right index fingers on the glass,' I said, and I could feel my heart beating with the thrill of anticipation. 'Is there a spirit present?'

I practically died of fright as the glass moved smoothly to 'YES'. Whatever I had expected, it was nothing as instantaneous as this. The glass moved back to the middle of the circle and was still.

'Jesus Christ!' Pendleton breathed, in the midst of an awestruck silence.

'Gentlemen,' said Tarling, in a voice which cracked slightly, 'I did not push that glass.'

'Nor me,' Pendleton and I said in unison.

'Well,' said Tarling, 'let's go on.'

'Ask if it's a good spirit or an evil spirit,' said Pendleton.

'Tell you what,' I said. 'I'll just ask if it's a good spirit, then it won't have to spell out an answer.'

'Just get on with it!' said Tarling.

I coughed. 'Are you a good spirit?'

'NO'

Pendleton took his finger off the glass. 'Look, I really don't like this.'

Neither did I.

Tarling looked at me. 'What do you think?'

I nodded towards the drinks cabinet in the corner. 'I've got a bible in there in case things turn nasty.'

He nodded, but I doubt if he had any more idea than I had as to what we might do with it.

'Listen,' said Pendleton, now so scared that he was not ashamed to let it be known that he was the biggest coward among us. 'We're getting into something we don't understand. We're dealing with the powers of darkness, and I vote we stop now before we unleash forces we can't control... Well?'

'Hang on a moment,' said Tarling after an awkward pause. 'We don't actually know it's an evil spirit we're dealing with, do we? I mean, why shouldn't spirits be like us – part good, part bad?'

'Good point,' I said, 'Let's find out.'

'Okay,' said Pendleton, 'but if it's evil, I vote we stop and talk about whether we should go on or not.' Tarling and I voiced our agreement, and we put our fingers back on the glass.

'Are you an evil spirit?'

'YES'

'I knew it,' said Pendleton, withdrawing his finger. 'I can *feel* it. Let's sit by the fire and talk about this before we go any further.'

'Spirit,' I said, in what I hoped was a commanding voice, 'remain in the glass until we summon you again.' This, I felt, was an appropriate way to address such an entity.

'And do no evil!' said Pendleton loudly. 'In the name of God!'

'Amen,' said Tarling.

'Amen,' I said.

We spent a long time discussing the matter, but the more we talked, the less afraid we felt. Or perhaps it was only that we became used to our fear. But anyway, we agreed in the end that we would at least see what the spirit had to say. We returned to the table and I broached a subject that had been on my mind since we left it. 'er... Anyone else like to have a bash at talking to it?' (I felt that if the spirit was going to have a real go at any of us, it was most likely to be the one whose voice it knew.)

'No, you're doing fine, Tom.'

'You just carry on – it's best that you do the talking in your own house.'

I wished them both in hell, but could hardly say so without admitting that cowardice had prompted my suggestion. So I carried on.

'Fingers,' I said. 'Are you still there, spirit?'

'YES.'

'It could hardly say no if it wasn't!' said Tarling, and laughed.

'Shut up!' said Pendleton.

'Are you the spirit who was at the Liddens' house last week?'

'YES.'

'Why won't they talk about you?'

'F-E-A-R'

I cleared my throat. 'What d'you want me to ask?'

'Ask why they're scared.'

'Why are they afraid?'

'D-E-A-T-H'

Pendleton took a deep breath. 'Jesus Christ.'

What gave us the nerve to go on, I cannot say, but we did. And the longer we talked to the spirit, the less frightened we became. If familiarity did not exactly breed contempt, it did at least diminish terror. Tarling and Pendleton even agreed to take turns as medium. It proved difficult to get a straight answer to any question that did not demand a simple yes or no, but we agreed that this was how an evil spirit might be expected to communicate, and were well satisfied.

We even got on to sex, and to our delight, the spirit, being evil, was as interested in the subject as we were. Pendleton was putting the questions.

'Ask it how much shorter skirts are going to get,' I said.

'Evil spirit,' said Pendleton, 'how short will mini-skirts become?'

'A-R-S-E' said the spirit, and we all roared.

Tarling quietened down first. 'I want to know what my sex life's going to be like!'

Pendleton nodded. 'What will Cliff Tarling's sex life be like?'

'G-O-N-O-R-R-I-A'

'That's not how you spell it!' cried Pendleton.

'Shut up!' I snapped. 'Don't offend it. Anyway, who says evil spirits can spell?'

Tarling took his finger from the glass and put his hand to his forehead. 'But that's serious!' he wailed.

'No it isn't,' said Pendleton. 'Syphilis is the bad one. Gonorrhoea's nothing.'

I almost said that in any case the veracity of an evil spirit was no more to be trusted than its orthography, but checked myself when I realised that this might spoil the fun. 'Cheer up, Tarling,' I said instead. 'They can always cut your willy off if it's really bad. Get your finger back on the glass and let's hear about *my* sex life.'

'Evil spirit,' said Pendleton, when the third finger was back in place, 'tell us about Tom Cardwell's sex life.'

There was an uncharacteristic pause before the spirit replied with 'I-N-C-E-S-T'.

I was horrified, and now wished I *had* told Tarling that our evil spirit might be a liar. Incest? Me?? The other two thought it a tremendous joke, but the ringing of the phone stilled their laughter.

We turned to look at it. There was something unnerving about this, as if the spirit had found another means of communicating with us, and was getting closer. I took a deep breath, then went over and picked up the receiver. 'Hello?'

'Thomas?'

'LINDA!!' I screamed, and gave a jump which caused my left elbow to knock a hideous old vase from the mantelpiece. It shattered on the tiles of the fireplace below, and Pendleton uttered a frightened yelp.

'Thomas, what's going on? What are you up to?'

I didn't care about the vase – my mother was always threatening to throw it out – but that Linda should phone at this moment was too much of a coincidence. The others thought so too.

'I've just got a couple of friends in. Mum and Dad are out,' I said, as calmly as I could. 'They're at the Harringtons.'

'Is Bruce there?'

'Yes.'

'I heard something break just now.'

'No you didn't.'

'Hmm... Oh, never mind. I'll ring again tomorrow. Bye.'

'Bye.'

I put the phone down and resumed my place at the table. 'Clever spirit,' I said with an uneasy laugh, and shrugged.

Tarling cleared his throat. 'What about the vase?'

'Doesn't matter,' I said. 'Everybody hated it. I'll clear it up later.'

'Well,' said Pendleton, looking down at the circle of letters, 'shall we get on with it?'

'Why not?' I said. It was with renewed respect for the sinister glass that we put our fingers on it once more.

For the next ten minutes, we conversed with the spirit on less personal matters, chiefly current affairs. This was safer, but lacked the earlier fascination. The exchanges began to flag.

And then, as we were trying to think of something interesting to ask, the glass began to move again. Our belief in the spirit was by now unquestioning, but it was eerie that it should choose to offer an opinion without even being asked. 'R-E-S-T-I-N-P-E-A-C-E'

'Oh my God!' gasped Pendleton, and took his finger away.

Tarling turned to look at him. 'It meant you!' he said. 'You were asking the questions. It was talking to you!'

'I think it was all of us,' said Pendleton in an unsteady voice. 'Why should it only be me?'

I stood up. 'I'm putting a stop to this right now,' I said, and went over to the bookcase. What bothered me was that there was an evil spirit in my house, and I wanted it out. I strode over to the drinks cabinet, took the bible out and held it aloft. 'I'm going to perform a service of exorcism.'

'Yes!' said Pendleton.

'What do you want us to do?' said Tarling.

I considered this. 'I think you should pray,' I said at length. 'Both kneel down and keep praying aloud until I've finished.'

They knelt. 'Our Father,' Pendleton began, and Tarling joined in.

'Not so loud,' I said. 'Try to put some feeling into it, but keep your voices down. It's me the spirit's got to hear.' They began again, this time in an undertone.

How a service of exorcism should be performed I had no notion, but was not going to let anything so trivial as total ignorance stand in my way. 'I exorcise you,' I began in my loudest voice that was not actually a shout, and described a huge vertical cross with my right hand. 'In the name of the Father, in the name of the Son, and in the name of the Holy Ghost!' Another cross.

'Keep going,' I said, as the chorus began to falter, and I repeated the invocation in all four corners of the room, believing these to be the likeliest hiding places for an evil spirit who was being given a hard time. (I did alter the incantation slightly by saying thee instead of you, on the supposition that the language of the King James Bible was best suited to putting the wind up the malevolent entity we had been so foolhardy as to summon from the pit of hell.) All this went on to the background of the Lord's Prayer, softly but fervently intoned from the floor.

Finally, I returned to the centre of the room to complete the operation. I raised both arms high and wide. 'Evil spirit!' I cried in a voice of thunder. 'Begone from this house!'

The door flew open. Pendleton screamed, and I held the bible desperately between me and whatever horror might enter. The light came on, to reveal my father framed in the doorway, eyes wide with astonishment. I lowered the book and cleared my throat.

He was now staring at my two colleagues rather than at me, and when I turned to follow his gaze, I understood why. Tarling and I no longer even noticed Pendleton's appearance, but I could see the effect he must have on my father, as he cowered behind the table, his mother's hat awry on his head, and his dressing-gown having fallen open far enough to reveal his mother's suspenders. Behind him in the fireplace and here and there on the carpet were the remains of the vase I had broken.

'Good God,' said my father, in a voice that was little more than a whisper. 'Linda was right.'

I knew what had happened. As soon as she had put the phone down after talking to me, Linda had rung our parents at the Harringtons, and said that someone should come back to see what we were up to. Sneaking bitch.

'Look,' I said, determined to be taken seriously, 'we've just driven an evil spirit from this house, so you should be grateful. You don't know what we've been through tonight.'

My father began slowly to shake his head. 'Mad,' he said. 'Certifiably and incurably insane.'

15 Transport

By the time I was seventeen I was, I fear, a 'normal, healthy adolescent'. I was selfish, self-conscious, sulky, spotty, pretentious, rebellious, and sex-obsessed. So was Pendleton. Having found by now that Aldous Huxley was not beyond me at all, and nor was Bob Dylan – I reckoned that the harsh, vengeful Like a Rolling Stone was nearly as good as the Beatles' gentle, wistful Penny Lane – I was now less intimidated by him intellectually. He, however, had no difficulty in staying ahead, claiming now to indulge in regular meditation sessions, and to be thus far undecided as to whether he should devote his life to the communist or to the anarchist cause. Intense political discussions with Joe Vincent now punctuated most of his days in school. I had at least become an atheist and a socialist, but the fat brute just looked down on me from his lofty philosophical peak and sneered. We got on better if we avoided discussing such things.

We preferred talking about more superficial matters, like sex. We were now capable of discussing it more seriously and had long since admitted to each other the truth about our dreadful experiences with Cathy Figgs a year before, since when neither of us had been out with a girl even once. It was all so difficult. We agreed that long hair and cigarette smoking were attractive to girls, but, as these were both opposed by the adult world, the first was impossible and the second possible only surreptitiously, which nullified the effect. And we didn't even like smoking.

Then Pendleton, the day after he passed his driving test, gave it as his opinion that a car was a bed on wheels, and said he was thinking of buying one. Being three months older than me, he had had a head's start in learning to drive, and my efforts were still at an early stage.

~

'Thomas, stop!' yelled Linda, clapping her hands to her temples.

I must have got the brake-clutch coordination wrong, because I stalled. We were at the top of Waterloo Road, at its junction with the High Street, and I had been hoping to get straight across so as to avoid Stambridge's most notorious hill start, but then a damn great lorry had appeared from nowhere.

Linda took a deep breath and lowered her hands. 'Thomas,' she said, in the voice a frightened person might use in addressing an armed robber, 'please slow down more at Give Ways.'

'I didn't see that lorry,' I said. There was a car not far behind it, then one from the other direction, so I, like a condemned man before his execution, was given time to contemplate the horror before me. This was only my fourth time behind the wheel, my earlier attempts at hill starts had all been on straight roads with gentle rises and no other traffic in sight. And I couldn't do them anyway.

My three previous lessons had been with my father, my mother having made clear before my seventeenth birthday that she did not believe her nerve was steady enough. He, after one or two admittedly near things in and around Ashminster, had sworn never to be a passenger of mine again until and unless I passed my driving test. 'Teaching *him* to drive,' as he put it after our last outing, 'is a job for the professionals... God help them.'

But that weekend, Linda came back from Oxford, aglow with her triumph in getting her latest boyfriend through his test. She assured our parents that such was her prowess as a driving instructor that she could teach even me, and this was the result.

The road was clear again. Accelerator down a little, clutch up a bit, handbrake off... We moved forward in a series of bumps and thuds, and as I clung to the steering wheel, I was aware of Linda beside me being jerked to and fro like a dummy in an accident simulation. When we were straddling the High Street's white line, blocking the traffic in both directions, we stalled.

'Thomas, please!' cried Linda, now openly despairing.

'Well,' I said, myself flustered, 'I told you I was no good at hill starts.'

'You're blocking the road. Unblock it and let's get home. I've had enough.'

At home it was considered a great joke.

'Honestly Daddy, I thought my end had come!'

'Oh I know the feeling. My hands are still shaking from the last time I took him out. I'll be changing your kangaroo petrol before I drive the car again, Thomas.'

Linda looked at me archly. 'If I were you, Thomas, I shouldn't apply for my test *quite* yet.'

I was fuming. 'You should know. You failed your first test, didn't you?'

'That is not funny!'

~

It was two days after this debacle that Pendleton passed his test (for which achievement I hated him more than ever), and said he was considering buying a car. After he had mentioned the topic wistfully a few times, I began to see what he was getting at.

'Look,' I said, 'I'll go halves with you if you teach me how to drive.'

'Oh I see, you're after free lessons now, are you? Mean bastard.'

I shrugged. 'Okay, forget it, but I reckon it's fair, 'cos you'd have it any time, but I'd only have it when I was with you – till I passed my test anyway.'

He thought about this for a moment. 'All right,' he said. 'You're on.'

His parents weren't pleased though, and neither were mine, as I found out that evening. I had been wondering how, or even whether, to let them know, when a telephone call took the matter out of my hands. My father picked up the receiver.

'Hello... Stan?...' It was old Pendleton. 'Yes...' There was a long pause, during which his brow clouded, and I guessed what was going on. 'Good God, Stan, can you imagine those two on wheels? With an engine? It doesn't bear thinking about.' He turned to fix me with a look which made clear that we would be 'discussing' this once he and old Pendleton had worked each other up into sufficient of a lather.

As the conversation continued, my mother leaned over to me. 'This isn't you and Bruce, is it?'

I nodded.

'Well, we'll have to discuss this,' she said, in a tone that made 'discuss' more or less synonymous with 'prevent'. 'We'll have to decide...'

My father covered the mouthpiece of the phone with his hand and turned to her in irritation. 'Quiet, woman, I'm trying to listen.'

She sat back and folded her arms. I could see what was going to happen. As soon as he was off the phone, they would launch a joint assault on me, making clear that they did not consider me a fit person to be part owner of any form of motorised vehicle. Well, I was old enough to make my own decisions on such matters, and I was going to tell them so, with as much emphasis as was necessary to get the point across.

'... What?? Bruce? Teach Thomas to drive?... Ha ha ha... Not something I'd risk again... ha ha...'

Oh so it was funny now, was it? I was beginning to get annoyed. I could take it when they tried to be strict with me, even when they got angry, but what I really hated was being laughed at. Not even being taken seriously. I indulged in an agreeable fantasy about their hearing of my death in a horrific accident which was entirely the fault of the other driver. That'd sort them out.

'All right, Stan, thanks for calling. We'll see what we can do, and I'll get back to you... Yes... Yes... Right, Stan, bye for now.'

He turned to face me, hands on hips.

'Now then, Thomas,' said my mother, in her most irritating voice, the one that blended reason with censoriousness. 'What's this about you and Bruce getting a car?'

'They're thinking of going halves on some old banger,' said my father. 'Can you imagine it? Those two let loose on the roads of this country? There ought to be a law against it. I thought you had to be sane to drive a car, for God's sake.'

'We'll just leave God out of it for once, if you don't mind, Walter.'

'Bruce's got a licence,' I said. 'He can have a car if he wants to.'

'But you've only got a provisional one, dear,' said my mother. (I always hated it when she called me 'dear'.)

'Well, the car'll be in Bruce's name, and he'll be in charge of it. There's no law against that, even if you think there should be.' I looked challengingly at my father. 'And then he's going to give me lessons.'

'Oh Walter!' said my mother, in a for-goodness-sake-let's-be-reasonable voice. 'Surely there's a law against *that*? I mean, Bruce has only just passed his own test.'

'His licence is as good as yours,' I said. 'Cleaner too.' This was way below the belt, a reference to the one endorsement on my mother's licence, for doing thirty-five on the outskirts of Stambridge once.

'That's enough of that,' said my father, giving me the satisfaction of knowing that the shaft had reached its mark. 'I don't see you keeping a clean licence for long, even if you found an examiner daft enough to let you have one.'

'Bruce found one,' I said.

'I wouldn't see Thomas keeping a licence at all for long,' said my mother, who had been stung by my reference to her endorsement.

'Right,' said my father. 'Banned for life before long, I'd be prepared to bet.' He gave a snort and resumed his seat. 'The question is, though, what are we going to do about the car the two young fools want to buy?'

'You don't have to do anything,' I said, 'though you're welcome to chip in if you want to.'

'Don't try to be funny. Your mother and I won't think it very amusing if you're involved in an accident.'

'That's right. It's you we're thinking about.'

There was a silence. I was now enjoying myself, secure in the knowledge that there was, in the end, nothing they could do to stop me.

But my father was determined to do a bit more grumbling before he would concede the point. 'Do you suppose there's an insurance company daft enough to insure a car driven by you and young Pendleton? Even if there is, they'd have to invent a new premium for the purpose.'

'Yes,' said my mother.

'How'd you pay it? Rob a bank?'

'For goodness sake don't give him ideas.'

I looked serenely at them and waited for the storm to blow itself out. As it happened, the thought of insurance hadn't entered my head, but I was not going to show that it bothered me.

'Oh well,' said my mother with a sigh, 'I suppose we can't actually stop him.'

'We could have him certified,' said my father, with what I hoped he intended as irony.

~

What especially annoyed us (Pendleton told me he had been through a similar scene with his parents) was that our fathers, even when forced to accept that we could not in the end be prevented from buying a car, insisted that we were not competent to choose one without assistance. We would have to have at least one of them along, preferably both.

If they had only been a bit more tactful they might have got away with it, but as it was, we were stung into rebellion. After school on the Friday we went along to Jarman's, the used car dealer. Having sold our bicycles and a few other things, we had mustered sixty pounds between us. A glance around Jarman's that morning had assured us that there were indeed cars to be had for that price.

If my experience is anything to go by, used car dealers have the extraordinary policy of employing salesmen who look and sound exactly like the sharks they are, and this one was no exception. The word spiv might have been invented for him. Every car we looked at was a bargain, the more so the higher the price, and the one thing of which we could be sure was that we couldn't go wrong with Jarman's.

'Twenty years we've been established, gents, twenty years, and how have we managed to survive and grow in that time?' He spread his hands and widened his eyes.

'Quality, that's how. We sell quality cars. Always have, always will.'

He overwhelmed and terrified us. Naive as we both were, we were not so blind as to be unable to recognise a wolf in wolf's clothing, but what could we do? From the moment he got his teeth into us, he would not let go until he had sold us a car, and we both knew it. I was wishing to God that we had listened to our fathers, and I feel sure that Pendleton was too, but neither of us was going to admit it.

He showed us several cars ('models' he called them) that were outside our price range, before Pendleton succeeded in blurting out that actually, sixty pounds was our limit.

'Sixty? Right you are, gents. Now sixty's not much, and plenty of car dealers couldn't give you nothing at that price – nothing worth having anyway. But Jarman's? No problem. Come and have a look at this…'

The irony was that this person clearly believed he was winning our confidence, and that this was the way to make a sale, whereas in reality the best tactic was to intimidate us, and this was exactly what he was doing. Finally, he packed us off on a test drive of an ancient green Morris Minor. Pendleton took the wheel.

'God, he was coming on a bit strong, wasn't he?' I said as we moved out onto the road.

'That's salesmanship, I suppose,' said Pendleton, and we were both silent for a while as we savoured our sense of freedom in getting away from him.

'How does it feel?' I said at length.

'Not bad. not bad at all.'

We were beginning to get our confidence back, and could already imagine ourselves as owners of this vehicle, which would leave us one pound change out of our sixty.

'Maybe we should check the lights,' said Pendleton.

'Right. And the indicators.'

When we drove back into Jarman's yard ten minutes later, our minds were made up, and when we had concluded the deal we took off for home in high spirits. The car was ours, we had acquired it without parental assistance, and no one could take it from us.

Old Pendleton was out of the house before his son had switched off the engine. Ignoring us, he went to fetch my father. As they approached us grim-faced, my mother appeared in the doorway, wiping her hands on her apron.

Stan Pendleton was in blunt mood. 'I thought we told you not to buy anything without taking one of us along.'

We said nothing.

My father jabbed an index finger at me. 'I'd expect it of you, of course,' he said, 'but I thought Bruce might show more sense.'

'Not a chance, Walter. You don't know him like I do.'

'Oh, for God's sake!' My father was making no secret of his exasperation.

Old Pendleton was now on his hands and knees, inspecting one of the front wheels. My father followed suit at the other one, then they moved to the back.

They told us we would have to invest immediately in one new tyre, the other three being retreads which might or might not explode in the near future. Our mothers had now joined us too.

'It's not very pretty,' said mine.

'Hideous,' said my father.

'So they chose it on their own, did they?' said Mrs Pendleton.

'Yes,' I said, determined that we should not be spoken about as if we were not even present.

'Where?' said my mother.

'Jarman's' said Pendleton.

'Crooks,' said my father.

'And I bet they saw these two coming,' said old Pendleton.

'I suppose,' my father went on with heavy irony, 'you checked the lights as carefully as you checked the tyres.'

'We checked them,' said Pendleton, 'and they're all fine.'

I nodded emphatically. This at least was a point to us.

'Let's see them anyway,' said old Pendleton.

I opened the driver's door, but before I could get in, my father grabbed me by the collar and pulled me back. 'Not you. You're not allowed to be in charge of a car. And please God you never will be. Bruce, you do it.'

Old Pendleton stood at the front, my father at the back.

'Sidelights,' said the former. 'Headlights... Dip... Right indicator... Left indicator...'

'Brakes,' said my father. 'Again... Well, whoever checked the brake lights must have been blind. The left one's not working.'

Pendleton looked up at me and made wanking movements with his right hand. We were forever making jokes about masturbation leading to blindness.

'Stop that, you dirty little brute,' growled his father, and I stood aside as he opened the door. 'Out.'

'Oh, it's too bad,' said Mrs Pendleton. 'A bald tyre and a brake light not working. Shouldn't Jarman's fix these things?'

'Walter!' called old Pendleton. 'Come and have a look at the steering. I suppose it's just about okay.'

~

My father was right about the insurance, and the new tyre didn't come cheap either, but we did eventually succeed in making the thing legal and roadworthy. We should have thought about petrol before we bought it, though, because it demanded far more than such a small car had any right to, and no car ever consumed oil so fast without having a leak.

We loved it, though, and Pendleton, with numbing predictability, revelled in his role of driving instructor. For once, however, I was happy to indulge his ego, because I knew when I was on to a good thing. Of course, neither his parents nor mine were happy with the thought of Pendleton as instructor and me as learner, but we showed them when I passed my test at the first attempt five weeks later.

We christened our car the Bomb, because we kept assuring each other, in the nervous early days, that it went like one. Later, when we were more confident that it was not always on the point of exploding, we liked to maintain that its name indicated our conviction that it might blow up at any moment.

Pendleton, although we had agreed he had the right, seldom used it on his own, because he couldn't afford the fuel, and the Bomb brought us closer together. The great thing was that it gave us a freedom we had never known before. Cycling is hard work, and you can't go very far in the course of an evening, or even a day. But in the Bomb, we covered vast distances, despite the cost of running the thing.

The one thing we never even tried to use it for was sex. This may seem odd, but, in making us feel more adult and important, the Bomb was a substitute for sex rather than a place for it. It did almost as much for our self-esteem as a successful seduction would have done.

One of our favourite pastimes, when we could be bothered getting up early enough, was to drive through the countryside on a Sunday morning, open all the windows, and set up a hideous caterwauling whenever we drove past a church. Why we did not soon tire of this unambitious pursuit, I cannot say.

More interesting from almost any point of view was our motorised pub-crawling on Friday and Saturday nights. In truth, I loathed beer, and I feel sure Pendleton did too, but, because we had the freedom of the Bomb and because we were under age, we would go to three different pubs every Friday and Saturday evening, and have a half pint of shandy and a cigarette in each. And if we felt really daring, we might even make it a half of bitter. The alcohol wasn't the point though. The point was that we were breaking the law.

We avoided the two pubs in Ashminster, where we were known, but were prepared to chance any other bar within a twenty-mile radius, with the exception of those near school in Stambridge. We were frequently asked whether we were over eighteen, but soon learned to brazen it out. And we were never actually refused service on suspicion of being under age.

~

It was rare for us to go out in the Bomb on any evening other than a Friday or Saturday, and things went wrong when we tried it one Thursday in June a couple of weeks after I had passed my test. It was Pendleton's fault.

The church clock had just struck eight, and I was in my room, officially studying for exams, when he came to the door. He said he couldn't face doing any more work that evening, and suggested that we both relax with a walk by the river. Without actually saying so, my parents made it clear they did not approve of my going out on a weekday evening so close to exams, but that wasn't going to stop me.

The walk was marred for me by a Pendleton lecture, even more tedious than usual, on the war then in progress between Israel and the Arabs. I was an admirer of gallant little Israel, but knew I shouldn't be, because that was how my parents felt. The fat brute explained to me that Israel was only the catspaw of the US, and that a Zionist victory would be a catastrophe. I was bored, and it was in desperation that I suggested a visit to a pub. Back we went to get the Bomb.

'Shouldn't we tell our parents?' I said, as he opened the driver's door.

'Why?'

'Well, they think we're out walking. When they notice the car's gone, they might think it's been pinched.'

The fat brute sighed. 'All right,' he said. 'Tommy go tell Mummy and Daddy.'

'Fuck you!' I climbed in and slammed the door.

We drove to a pub we knew a few miles away, and ordered our usual halves of shandy. Fifteen minutes later, we were considering having our glasses refilled when the door behind us opened and two policemen came in. It gave us a nasty turn.

'Is the owner of car GTL 256 in here?'

I nearly jumped out of my skin. He was talking about the Bomb.

'Yes,' said Pendleton.

The policemen turned to look at us, and the same one spoke again. 'Is it your car?'

'Yes.'

'Well, we've had a report that it's been stolen.'

'No.'

The other policeman spoke. 'Are you two lads over eighteen?'

'Yes,' we said in unison.

'Then you're not the owner of that car. The owner of that car is one Bruce Pendleton, and he's seventeen.'

They had us there.

They were very decent about it. Pendleton proved his identity, they told us to stay out of pubs until we were eighteen, and to report to our nearest police station with documentation proving ownership of the car. We'd got off lightly.

The trouble was that it was old Pendleton who, believing the fat brute and I were out for a walk, had reported the car missing, so we had to be careful about what we told our parents. It wasn't a serious difficulty though. They would have no way of knowing where we had been, so any old story would do. Or so we thought.

We decided the best thing to do was to stop off at home on the way to the police station and set our parents' minds at rest. We would claim we had been at a café in Stambridge. They would be none the wiser.

Although they were all of the opinion that we had no right to go out in our own car without telling them first, things went smoothly enough, and we then drove to the police station, where a surly desk officer checked Pendleton's documentation. On the return journey, we agreed that it hadn't, on the whole, been such a bad evening. But it wasn't over yet.

'I don't know,' said my father, lowering his newspaper as I walked into the sitting-room. 'You two have had half the police in the county out looking for that old banger. Typical.'

'It's our car,' I said. 'We've got a right to...'

'And don't answer back!'

Now my father was always short-tempered, but I thought this was a bit over the top, and wondered if something else was wrong.

'Thomas,' said my mother. Her quiet reasonable voice set my teeth on edge. It was her way of indicating that I was in trouble.

'Yes?' I said aggressively.

'We'd like you to tell us again where you were this evening.'

'Out. In the Bomb.'

'Yes, but where?'

'Stambridge. The Sunny Snack Bar. I told you.'

'The Sunny Snack Bar closed down yesterday.'

'Oh.'

My father crumpled his paper. 'So where the hell were you then? Come on, out with it!'

'Walter, language, please.'

He growled.

'Actually,' I said, picking up a magazine, 'I'm not sure it's any of your business.'

He reached over and grabbed it out of my hands. 'I said where were you?'

My attempt at a weary sigh was drowned out by the ringing of the telephone. My father answered it.

'Yes?' he barked. If I had heard anyone shout at me like that in answering the phone, I think I would have banged the receiver down in terror. My mother used to say that some people did, but it didn't happen this time.

'Oh... No, we haven't got it out of him yet, but... Oh they were, were they? Well well well... Yes, that's right, and if you ask me, it'd do no harm if the police flung the book at them. Might bring them to their senses... Yes... Okay, thanks, Stan, I'll have it out with him now.'

While he was talking, I had retrieved my magazine, and was now engaged in the pretence that I was reading it. He grabbed it from me again before he sat down. 'You know where they were?'

'Where?'

He folded his arms and spoke in a sort of well-where-would-you-think-I-mean-isn't-it-obvious tone. 'In the pub.'

I felt a vague satisfaction in the knowledge that Pendleton had cracked before me – appropriate enough in view of the fact that this whole mess was his fault – but I was still in a bit of a spot, and would rather not have been. I looked out of the window.

'Thomas,' said my mother, 'what were you doing in the pub?'

'Knitting socks,' I said.

'Don't you talk to your mother like that! If you carry on like this, my lad, you'll come to a bad end one of these fine days.'

I always hated it when he called me 'my lad', and I hated it when he prophesied disaster for me. Linda was never called 'my lad', and all that was ever predicted for her was 'great things'.

~

Of course, neither Pendleton's parents nor mine could actually stop us going into pubs, but we became more careful about it, and did most of our drinking from then on in the dingier parts of Stambridge.

But we were not streetwise. We didn't know where not to go. If we had, we wouldn't have wandered one night a month or so later into one of Buggleby's most notorious dives, The East Wind, known to the locals as The Red Fart. Representatives of the middle class were not welcome there, as we soon discovered.

We weren't completely stupid, and we did sneak an anxious look at each other as we walked in. But we were in the habit of entering pubs with exaggerated boldness, like wild west outlaws flinging open saloon doors in the hope of finding someone worth shooting, and this meant that we were always half way to the bar before we had the measure of the place. Our earlier practice of entering with the greatest timidity after a fierce whispered argument at the door as to who should go in first, and a good deal of pushing and shoving, had ensured that we managed a good look at the place in question before we felt committed. Not any more.

There was something threatening about the place. It wasn't the tattiest we'd been in, but the clientèle of the really shabby pubs we'd visited tended to be old and quiet. They might be depressing, but they were not frightening.

Most of the people in this place were young – some of them looked as young as we were – and the term 'Buggleby boys' sprang unbidden to my mind.

'My turn,' said Pendleton with exaggerated determination. 'You find somewhere to sit.'

Making an inadequate attempt to appear casual, I looked round for a free table. There were several, and it must have been bravado that made me choose one next to a rough looking group of four boys of about our age. Or perhaps it was my way of seeking reassurance that these people were in reality harmless. But whatever was going on in my mind, it was a bad move.

The four of them looked at me with interest as I sat down, and my face burned. I could not have been more aware of how out of place I looked. I wished we had had the sense to turn round and walk out while we had still had chance. Suddenly they all started sniggering, and I heard one of them say, in a fair imitation of Pendleton's voice, 'Two halves of shandy, please.' Trust the fat brute to order halves of shandy in a place like this. I only just managed to restrain myself from shouting to him 'Get a couple of whiskies with them!' We couldn't have afforded it.

He sat down opposite me, and pushed my drink over to me. I tried to indicate, with a slight inclination of the head, that I was wary of our four neighbours.

He gave a just-perceptible nod. 'Better hurry up,' he said looking at his watch. 'We haven't got much time.'

'Right.'

The largest member of the group at the other table now took to taunting us openly. 'We haven't got much time,' he said in a parody of an upper-class twit accent.

'I say chaps,' said one of his companions. 'Anyone for tennis?'

They all roared.

I took a gulp of my drink and leant over to whisper to Pendleton, 'Let's get out of here.'

There was a tap on my shoulder. 'Sorry, old chap, but I didn't jolly well catch that.'

I turned and tried to look calmly at the speaker. It was the big one. He was wearing a leather jacket, and his upper lip was pulled down to its farthest extent in a music hall parody of an aristocratic expression.

'Actually,' I said, 'I wasn't talking to you.'

The four of them roared louder than before. 'Eow,' said leather jacket, 'wahn't yaw ectually?'

But help was on its way. The barman, a massive creature, came over from his post behind the counter. He towered over all six of us, and would have done even if we had all been standing. 'Finish your drinks and get out. I'm not having trouble in here.'

This quietened them down. 'We wasn't causing trouble, George,' said leather jacket. 'Just trying to be friendly like.'

'Finish your drinks and get out. Now.'

I wouldn't have fancied arguing with George, and neither did they. With a last subdued request that he should keep his hair on, leather jacket drank up and led his gang out.

'Thanks,' said Pendleton as they left, but George, already on his way back to the bar, ignored him.

'Christ,' I said, 'I thought those guys were going to have a go at us.'

'Naah,' said Pendleton. 'Big mouths, if you ask me.'

Nobody else bothered us, but we were still not anxious to spend any more time in The East Wind than we had to. We stayed only long enough to finish our drinks and give our four tormentors time to get well away.

'Home?' I said as we left. I had been frightened, and felt like spending the remainder of the evening in reassuring surroundings.

'Okay... It's not that guys like that actually scare you, is it? It's just that you get so bloody angry that you can't even enjoy your drink.'

'That's right. I suppose you can feel sorry for them in a way. I don't want to sound bourgeois, but they really haven't got much of a future, have they?'

Pendleton sighed and shook his head. We walked on in silence.

We were green. Neither of us had the sense to guess what might happen. Unobserved, they must have followed us the hundred yards or so to the quiet side street where the Bomb was parked. Pendleton was fumbling in his pocket for his keys when we heard a great yell behind us, and turned to see all four of them galloping towards us.

'Open up! Open up!' I cried in terror. They were perhaps forty yards off, and we still had time to escape if he moved fast.

It could only have been a matter of seconds, but these were not the seconds of everyday insignificance. Everything was happening in slow motion – Pendleton scrabbling in his pocket, the four thugs bearing down on us, the black cat fleeing before them. I can see, hear, and feel it all now, and it took forever. Closer and closer they came. Pendleton at last produced the keys. Closer. He tried the wrong key, and they were twenty yards off. He got the right key, but now they were closer still. He flung his door open, leapt in, slammed it and reached across to unlock mine.

But they were on me. Two of them knocked me over with the impetus of their charge, and my yell of terror was stifled as the fall winded me. Curling myself into a ball, I wrapped my arms round my head to protect myself from the kicks and punches that were raining in on me. It was horrible, but I was aware of what was happening throughout, and I felt my wallet being pulled from the back pocket of my jeans.

I was in no position to see how Pendleton was faring, but he filled me in on the details later. They had opened his door, dragged him out onto the road, and given him the same treatment as me.

Our ordeal ended when, whooping with triumph, our attackers piled into the Bomb and drove off at high speed. People must have heard what had happened. They must have come to their windows and seen it all. But no one even emerged from a house to see if we were all right.

I crawled over to the pavement, sat down on it, and tried to work out whether or not I had any broken bones. More slowly, Pendleton got to his feet, dusted himself down, and put a handkerchief to his nose, which was bleeding. Satisfied that I was still more or less in working order, I stood up. Pendleton came over to me.

'They got my wallet,' I said.

'And mine.'

The sound of his stupid voice infuriated me. It was, I decided, all his fault. I tried to control myself. 'I thought you said they were just big mouths.'

'You didn't say any different.' He put his head back to stop the blood.

'Why the hell did it take you so long to open up?'

'Piss off,' he said in a choking voice.

'Useless jerk.'

'Useless jerk yourself!' He brought his head down to look at me again, and put his handkerchief back to his nose. 'You didn't do much to help.'

'What the hell was I supposed to do?'

He put his head back again without replying.

I resumed my seat on the kerb. Quarrelling would get us nowhere. 'We'd better go to the police,' I said.

'Yeah.'

'But what do we tell them? We'd better not say we were in the pub. Wouldn't do any good anyway. It hardly matters where it started.'

He sat down beside me, having now got the bleeding under control. 'What if we need witnesses?'

'There aren't any. Not to what happened here anyway.'

'I bet there are. But nobody'll want to get involved.'

The black cat was now, in a more leisurely manner, retracing its steps, tail erect. Pendleton flicked a pebble at it. It ignored him.

I shook my head. 'This is really stupid, you know.'

'What?'

'We've got to tell them where we were. Their best chance of finding the thing is to know who took it, and George the barman would know who those guys are.'

He grimaced. 'Yes.'

'They probably won't bother with how old we are anyway.'

'Okay.'

'Let's go to the cop shop then. Ferndale Road must be the nearest.'

The true delicacy of our position however, impressed itself on us on the way there. If the police did establish that we were under age, and decided to make an issue of it, they might find out that this was not our first such offence. We could almost hear the clang of the borstal door behind us.

'We can't risk it,' said Pendleton at length.

'No.'

'Anyway, a stolen car can't be that hard to find. I mean, if the police have the number and everything, so we can just...'

'But look,' I said, 'if they find it, and find out who pinched it, won't it come out that we'd been in the bloody pub anyway? So why not tell them now?'

'No. Chances are they'll find the car abandoned somewhere. It's a hundred to one against them finding who took it.'

It wasn't long before we were agreed. As official owner of the vehicle, Pendleton was to tell our story, and by the time we arrived at our destination, he was well drilled in it.

Ferndale Road Police Station was dismal. A lone sergeant, sitting behind a desk, ostentatiously ignored our entry. A lengthy clearance of my throat, however, attracted his grudging attention, and Pendleton informed him that we had come to report a case of assault and battery, and the theft of a car. A book was opened, and a pen taken up.

Pendleton's name and telephone number were noted, as were a description of the Bomb and its registration number. The story was that we had parked the car in Lockwood Lane at half past eight, and had been on our way to the fish and chip shop round the corner when we were the victims of a sudden and unprovoked attack by four youths, who had beaten us up, taken our wallets, then driven off in the car. All this the glum sergeant noted in silence, except for a few brief requests for more information or for clarification. He then said that it wasn't much to go on, but Pendleton would be informed of any developments.

He was. Two days later, he learned by phone that the Bomb had been found, but that it was 'not in a roadworthy condition'. We went to see it the following day. The windscreen was smashed, as were the rear lights, two of the tyres were cut, and the body was scratched and dented. More imaginatively, both front seats had been used as toilets, and on the boot, in white spray paint, was the bold legend 'FUCK OFF'.

16 Politics

It was never any good sulking with my parents. One would just observe to the other that I was going through a phase. This used to drive me wild, but there was nothing I could do about it. I just wished they would keep their opinions to themselves.

Between the ages of sixteen and eighteen, I had every reason for going through a phase. I was scrawny, I bit my nails to the quick, I had acne, and I carried my virginity like an albatross about my neck – an albatross which grew heavier as time passed.

The acne gave me endless trouble, and nothing affected it. What made it worse was that I could never resist the temptation of looking at my face in the magnifying mirror which my mother kept in the bathroom. This gave the impression that my chin was covered by a range of volcanoes, some extinct, some dormant, and some active, complete with lava flow. The details of the landscape would change from time to time, but the general impression remained the same. My physical appearance was repulsive.

My greatest source of enjoyment was music: Dylan, the Beatles, Donovan, the Rolling Stones, Pink Floyd, the Beach Boys, and, above all, one record by Procol Harum, A Whiter Shade of Pale. This I would listen to in my room in the evenings time and again, curtains drawn and lights off, at the maximum volume I could get away with.

Pendleton was getting on my nerves more than ever. In his capacity as one of the school's intellectuals, he had now become keen on Samuel Beckett, whose work, he told me, I 'probably wouldn't understand.' Zen remained another of his affectations, as did left wing politics, in which, although he might still be a communist or an anarchist depending on his mood, he never lost sight of his ultimate aim: 'the total destruction of this disgusting bourgeois society.' His greatest hero was Che Guevara, the news of whose death prompted him to wear a black armband for a day.

It was, he said, media coverage of student demonstrations, especially American ones against the war in Vietnam, which transformed him from 'just another left wing intellectual' into an activist. For the time being however, he was content to splash red over a smaller canvas, and his most passionate rhetoric was reserved for Stambridge Grammar School, 'a perfect microcosm of a moribund bourgeois capitalist system.'

One of the peculiar features of the school was an unwritten rule to the effect that, at break times, girls should walk round the building clockwise, and boys anti-clockwise. There were other things one could do, of course, such as playing rounders in the playground. But the most popular form of activity was walking round the school – girls clockwise, boys anti-clockwise.

Towards the end of our penultimate term, Pendleton decided he had had enough of it. The surprising thing is less that he rebelled than that he even noticed the absurdity of the convention. The rest of us took it for granted, much as we took for granted the rising of the sun every morning and its setting every evening. But not Pendleton. Pendleton, whatever else might have been said about him, had more imagination than the rest of us put together.

'Has it ever struck you how daft it is, the way we all spend break times walking round the school?' he said one Monday afternoon as we were walking to the bus stop.

I shrugged. 'I hadn't thought about it.'

'Well, think about it now. Girls walking in one direction, boys in the other. It's mad.'

'So what are you going to do about it?'

'Walk in the wrong direction.'

I said nothing, astonished at the sheer effrontery of it.

There was a surprise for us the following morning, when assembly was conducted by Saunders, the deputy head. He informed us that Carruthers had gone down with a bout of flu, but he was confident that we all wished him a speedy recovery.

'Personally,' whispered Pendleton, to whom the headmaster was the Beast of the Apocalypse, 'I wish him a slow death.'

As we came out of assembly, he claimed to be disappointed by this turn of events, because he considered Saunders a less formidable bastion of The System than Carruthers, but the rebellion, in which I had agreed to join him, was to go ahead.

By the time break came round, we had spoken to a number of other sixth-year boys, and all was ready for the revolt. On the assumption that there is safety in numbers, out we went together, all fourteen of us, and began walking *in the wrong direction*.

People were astonished. The boys, as we passed them, stared at us in incredulity while the girls squealed their delight. Blank faces appeared at the window of the staffroom. Nineteen sixty-eight had come to Stambridge.

Other boys, first only the seniors, but then younger pupils too, turned and walked in the wrong direction, and by the time the bell rang for lessons to resume, there were at least as many boys walking clockwise as there were walking anti-clockwise. It was a triumph, and I felt scarcely less of a hero than Pendleton.

But nothing happened. We spent the rest of the day in breathless anticipation – part agony, part ecstasy – of retribution. As everyone in the pioneer group of rebels had wanted to appear as prominent as possible, Pendleton and I had not found it difficult to obscure our leading role in the affair, so we felt we had no more to fear than any of the others. We just wanted something to happen, some acknowledgment of our rebellion. But there was nothing.

Pendleton's opinion was that Saunders, a notoriously irresolute man, was hoping that the swift return of Carruthers would take the matter out of his hands. If the head were not back the next day, however, he would have to deal with it himself, presumably by bringing it up at assembly.

We were disappointed. The head was still absent, and Saunders ignored our rebellion. I was almost as annoyed as Pendleton. What is any revolutionary gesture worth, if the society against which it is aimed shrugs its shoulders and looks the other way? Although we went on with our clockwise circulation, and reassured ourselves that we had won a famous victory, it was difficult not to feel that we had been made to look foolish.

But Pendleton was out for revenge. He had now decided that The Revolution mattered even more than Samuel Beckett or Zen Buddhism, and he was going to force straight society to take notice of him whether it wanted to or not. He decided to demonstrate against the Vietnam War. I was not much interested, having reacted to our debacle by returning to my preoccupations with acne and sexual frustration, but I was prepared to join in.

The difficulty lay in deciding what form the demonstration should take. There would have to be a march to some focal point at which speeches could be made, but it was difficult to think of anywhere that might qualify. I was happy to help Pendleton arrange the thing though, and untroubled by the fact that I never expected it to take place. It was only when he invited Joe Vincent to be the third member of a committee which would plan the event, that I began to take it seriously. We first discussed the matter after lunch the next day.

'The question,' said Pendleton, 'is where to begin the march and where to end it. The rest will fall into place.'

'Haven't we got to tell the police?' I asked, pleased with myself for having established this important fact.

They turned on me. 'You know, Cardwell,' said Pendleton, in a voice that oozed contempt, 'that's typical of you.' He twisted his face, and began to whine in a parody of extreme timidity: 'Haven't we got to tell the police?'

'An utterly irrelevant consideration,' said Vincent. 'Our argument is with bourgeois capitalism as a whole. The last thing we should be doing is playing the game by their rules.'

'For Christ's sake,' I said, badly frightened, 'it's the success of the demonstration I'm thinking about, not keeping any stupid law. What I'm saying is that we've got to be careful not to give the police any excuse to move in and break up the march. Surely you can see that?'

'Well we're not telling the police anyway,' said Pendleton, and turned to Vincent.

It was awful. Pendleton clearly regarded Vincent as the more important ally, and my presence seemed irrelevant. There wasn't much I could do about it though, since I knew little and cared less about Vietnam. All I could say for certain was that the Americans were there fighting against the communists, who were trying to take the place over. If anything, my sympathy was with the former, but at least I was able to see the main point held by the other two members of the unequal triumvirate, namely that it should be the Vietnamese who decided what to do with their country, not the Americans.

As a means of regaining some of the limelight, I tried being even more militant than the other two, but they were unimpressed. I began to sulk.

'Tell you what,' said Vincent, when it became clear that the discussion on the route of the march was getting nowhere. 'If we have it a week on Saturday, my cousin'll be back from London. He could be our main speaker. I mean everybody knows him. They'd come to listen to him.'

'Good idea,' said Pendleton, but the lack of eagerness in his tone gave the game away. I wanted to avenge myself on him for ignoring me, by bursting out that he was now pissed off because that would mean that *he* couldn't be the main speaker. But I held my tongue, thinking I might taunt him with this later, when it would only be him against me.

And then the bell rang and the meeting was adjourned. I spent the afternoon nursing my grievance, and when Pendleton started talking about the demonstration on the bus after school – we had not been able to afford another car after the Bomb – I was ready to attack.

'Look Bruce,' I said, thinking I would do this with subtlety. 'About the date of this thing. I don't see why you should have to move out of the limelight to make way for Eric Crabbe. I could see you weren't happy when Vincent suggested it. Have it on some other date when you can be the main speaker.'

I was delighted to see how furious this made him. 'What the hell do you think you're talking about? Limelight? *Me??* I just want the best speaker possible, and if you thought I wasn't happy with Vincent's suggestion, that's because I thought we might get an MP or a trade union

221

leader or something, but I didn't want to hurt his feelings. Limelight? Ha ha. All I want is to get the Yanks out of Vietnam.'

I cleared my throat to indicate that I was sorry if I had said the wrong thing, but I wasn't finished with him yet. 'Sorry,' I said. 'I really shouldn't have said that.'

The rest of the journey passed in silence, and our conversation on the way home from the bus stop was stilted to the point of formality, with no mention of the demonstration. I had hit the fat brute where it hurt, and I wasn't sorry.

But I was in a foul mood, and made myself as difficult as I could at home, prompting my parents to reassure each other that it was just a phase I was going through. With one thing and another, I was beginning to grow a chip on my shoulder, and it was on this evening that the thing became apparent to them.

The news showed pictures of an anti-Vietnam War protest in Washington, and my mother began tut-tutting. 'Isn't that dreadful? I mean, you would think they could express their opinions without shouting and screaming and burning things.'

'Yes,' said my father, shaking his head sadly. 'It's the way of the world now, though. It doesn't matter how much these young people have. They never seem to be happy these days.'

I turned to them with lofty contempt. 'So you think it's all right for the Yanks to be in Vietnam, do you? You think that's all right?'

I had not previously expressed political disagreement to them so strongly, and they looked at me with mild surprise, much as they might have done if I had announced that I was going to bed an hour early.

'I suppose Bruce told him to say that,' said my mother. 'Janice tells me he's getting very left wing these days.'

My father harrumphed, and both turned their attention back to the TV.

My fury was vast and terrible. Almost fighting for breath, I stood, picked up a large china bowl from the mantelpiece, said 'Excuse me', and when their attention was on me, dropped it onto the fireplace, where it shattered.

My mother shrieked.

'That's what I think of you,' I said, 'and that's what I think of the Americans.' I walked out of the room, slamming the door behind me. My rebellious phase had begun.

My parents took note of the fact, but reacted by ignoring anything I said or did which seemed to indicate that I was now in revolt against society. This infuriated me. I felt that the least they could do was to argue with me, to get upset and begin asking me where they had gone wrong. But no, they just ignored me, and the effect was to make me more militant than ever.

This should at least have impressed Vincent and Pendleton, but for it didn't, and I continued to be the least significant member of the triumvirate. Still, we went on organising and began taking the thing more and more seriously.

'Of course,' said Vincent at lunch time the following Tuesday, 'if the police find out what we're planning, they'll try to stop us.'

Pendleton shrugged. 'We can take that for granted.'

'I tried to tell you that,' I said, but was ignored.

'Hey!' said Pendleton. 'I've just had an idea. The place to march to is the golf club. My dad says there's a party of Americans playing there that day. And if they're golfers, you can bet your bottom dollar they're right wing.'

'Great,' said Vincent. 'We can march through the town and end up there... No, hang on, what about marching

223

from outside the town, so the police don't get any excuse to interfere?'

We discussed the matter. The golf course was sited at the northern limit of the town, the final stretch of road from the north running dead straight for a mile or so. At one side of it – the side opposite the club – there was a broad grass verge. We agreed that this would be ideal for the march.

In order that the police should have no opportunity of banning the event, we decided to broadcast the news by word of mouth only. We would tell everyone we could think of who might be sympathetic, and all would be honour-bound to tell no one who might, as Vincent put it, 'sell us down the river.'

'What if the police move in after we've started?' asked Pendleton.

'We fight!' I said with vehemence.

'We all sit down cross-legged and link arms,' said Vincent. 'That way they can't move us.'

But I was determined they should take notice of me. 'I say we fight!'

'Look,' said Pendleton, with the air of an adult explaining something to a child who is being wilfully obtuse, 'we're against all forms of violence. That's what we're demonstrating about.'

'We're not against the Vietnamese fighting the Americans,' I said.

'They don't *want* to fight the Americans,' said Vincent.

'Well,' I said, 'we don't *want* to fight the police.'

'Shut up,' said Pendleton. 'We have bigger things to discuss.'

We spent the next few days in a frenzy of activity, and I thought of little except the march. Our attempts to restrict the news to those who might like to join us, and above all, to make sure it should not reach anyone who might be unsympathetic, were not a success. By the afternoon of the following day, every pupil in Stambridge Grammar School was aware of it, known fascists such as Bill Thring not excluded. The best we could do was to disclaim knowledge of any demonstration when the likes of Thring asked us. At least there was no evidence that the adult world had any inkling of what was going on, and in this Vincent and Pendleton took comfort.

'Forget about Thring and his cronies,' said Vincent. 'We'll be all right as long as teachers and parents don't find out. Ten to one Carruthers would have nosed it out somehow, but my mother says she's heard we won't see him again till next week. No, this is to be a march of workers and youth, the forces which together will one day overthrow the capitalist system.'

'Right,' said Pendleton.

'What workers?' I asked, but they took no notice.

To my annoyance, almost everyone seeking knowledge of the demonstration went to Vincent or Pendleton. And John Quincey, who turned out to be violently anti-American – 'What sickens me about the bloody Yanks is that they think *they* won the war!' – actually thought *he* was telling *me* about it.

But I went on doggedly with my role in organising the event, and made sure I was too useful to be pushed aside altogether. It was me, for example, who pointed out that we were going to need at least one banner, for the head of the column, and I undertook to provide it. What form it should take, and what materials I might use in its construction, were problems I chose not to consider at the time I made the offer.

The final conference of the organisers took place at lunch time the day before the march, and Pendleton told us that, by his calculations, there would be a minimum of three hundred people.

225

'And the maximum?' I asked.

He shrugged. 'Probably not more than a thousand. It's hard to say. Quincey's brother works in the carpet factory, and he's on our side, so we should get a bit of support from there. News has reached the printing works too.'

'And don't forget Buggleby,' said Vincent. 'We expect a big contingent from there. And by the way, Tom, how's the banner coming along?'

'Fine,' I lied. 'You'll see it tomorrow. It'll take two people to carry it, of course.' The truth was that I now regretted having undertaken to supply the thing, but was confident I could produce something with the aid of a white sheet and some paint, both of which were to hand at home.

The major details of the demonstration were now settled. People were to turn up at the north end of the long straight before one o'clock, at which time first Pendleton, then Vincent, would address them. (I was to be a steward.) At one thirty the march would begin. During it, we would sing The Internationale and The Red Flag, and would chant anti-American slogans. We estimated it would take an hour before the tail of the march was at the clubhouse, and the early arrivals there would occupy the time with more singing and chanting. At three o'clock, Eric Crabbe would make the main speech, which would end with the burning of an American flag which Crabbe was going to bring. This would enrage the Americans, who could be expected to sally forth from the clubhouse and attack us. We would offer no resistance.

~

I spent the evening watching television and refusing to think about the banner. The following morning would be time enough.

By the time I had finished breakfast, the task could be postponed no longer. It was now almost ten o'clock, and

Pendleton and I were to leave in his father's car, which he had found some pretext for borrowing, at quarter past twelve. I took a pot of red paint, one of green, and a brush, from my father's workshop, and sneaked them up to my room, where I pulled one of the sheets from the bed, and began work.

It soon became clear that the task would not be easy, and that the paint was determined to leave its mark on the carpet, walls and furniture, as well as on the banner. I went to the kitchen for some old newspapers, gave the room what protection I could, and carried on.

'YANKS OUT OF VIETNAM', I painted in great red letters, and under it, in green, I tried to show an aeroplane dropping bombs. This went less well. Never much of an artist, I was so doubtful about the thing I drew that I felt obliged to label if B52 on the fuselage. My idea had been to show it dropping bombs on an innocent Vietnamese peasant, who would be represented by a stick figure with arms raised to the heavens, and mouth wide open in a yell of despair. (I probably had Picasso's Guernica in mind.)

Unfortunately, the belly of my B52 came uncomfortably close to the bottom of the sheet, and I was obliged to paint a horizontal Vietnamese peasant with a single bomb linking the underside of the plane to the lower part of his trunk. When I stood back and looked at the result, I was horrified to see that it resembled a child's attempt to show what he saw daddy doing to mummy one morning when he went into their bedroom.

I slumped down on the bed in despair, and thought about beginning again on the other sheet. But this was impractical, as I was not even sure that the work I had done so far would dry in time for our departure. And as I looked at my effort, it struck me that it might plausibly be interpreted as indicating my belief that the Americans

227

were 'fucking' the Vietnamese. It was thus daring to the point, and I was instantly proud of it.

The only thing that now concerned me was that the horizontal figure was not obviously a human being. So my final touch was a representation of facial features, and a balloon from the mouth, saying 'AAAGH!!' Satisfied with my efforts I replaced the paint and brushes in the workshop, gathered up the newspapers, and waited for the banner to dry.

Only then did I permit myself to think of the possible consequences. I had, after all, destroyed a sheet. I was so out of sympathy with my parents that damaging their property was positively satisfying to me, but they would not be pleased, and I was anxious to avoid having to pay for a new sheet. So I went to the linen cupboard, where I found, amongst other things, four single white sheets. This was more than I had expected. I put one of them on my bed, thinking it unlikely that my crime would ever be discovered, provided only that I could get my work out of the house unnoticed.

This did not turn out to be a problem. By the time Pendleton appeared, the paint was dry and I was able to fold the banner and take it downstairs and out of the house without attracting suspicion.

'That the banner then?'

'Yes, but keep your voice down.'

'Let's have a look.'

'No chance. It's a sheet from my bed. My parents mustn't see it. You'll see it on the march.' We walked to the car.

'Hang on. How's it going to be held up?'

'Hmm?... Oh yes. Rakes.' This was no more than the inspiration of the moment. The point had not occurred to me. I turned back and took two rakes from the garden shed.

~

It was disappointing. There were only seven people at the head of the long straight when we arrived at twenty to one, and two of these were Joe Vincent and Eric Crabbe. John Quincey was carrying a small blackboard on which he had chalked 'YANKS OUT'.

'What are the rakes for?' asked Vincent, after Pendleton and I had greeted his cousin with due deference.

'Holding the banner,' said Pendleton. To my irritation. He was hogging enough of the limelight already, and the banner was my domain.

Eric Crabbe then told us that he was sorry, but he had been unable to get an American flag. Pendleton and I said it didn't matter, but I at least was furious. I had been looking forward to the burning of the flag more than anything, with the exception only of the unfurling of the banner.

That too, however, was a disappointment. For a start, it was not so much unfurled as unfolded, and then there was the problem of attaching it to the rakes without making the slogan illegible and the picture unrecognisable. The trouble was that I had used the maximum surface area, but we had no means of fixing the banner in place other than tying it at the corners. In the end, we had to settle for tying the two top corners, and letting the bottom ones hang loose.

It was ten to one by this time, and there were now eighteen of us (Pendleton said he expected a 'great rush' in the final ten minutes, but where this rush would come from was not clear, since we could see all the way into Stambridge, and only a handful of people were straggling up the long straight towards us.)

When the banner was finally raised, it read 'ANKS OUT OF VIETNA', but I thought this was not a problem. People could surely work out what it meant. But

229

my effort did not create a favourable impression. Everyone looked at it in silence.

'What's it meant to be?' said Pendleton at length.

I looked at him for a moment in silent scorn, then shook my head and turned away. Then some of the girls started giggling, and I thought I had better give an explanation. But Joe Vincent beat me to it.

'It's clear enough,' he said, to my relief. 'That's an American bomber, a B52. It's bombing that guy on the ground.'

It proved difficult to find anyone to carry the banner. The general opinion was that I was an obvious candidate for one of the rakes, but I had no intention of surrendering my status as steward, and in the end we managed to persuade two third-year boys to hold it. I decided to disclaim responsibility for the thing if possible.

By one o'clock, there were twenty-two people present, with another dozen or so on their way up the long straight. Apart from Eric Crabbe, all were grammar school pupils. It was disappointing. Since it was apparent that the head of the procession would not have to wait long at the club for the tail, we decided to give everyone chance to arrive before Pendleton and Joe Vincent spoke.

'Quite a few people will probably turn up just at the club,' said Pendleton.

'They'd better,' I said. 'Looks like your estimate of at least three hundred was a bit high.'

'The important thing,' said Eric Crabbe, 'is that we do at least hold a demonstration, to express solidarity with the oppressed people of Vietnam.'

'Hear hear,' said Joe Vincent.

At twelve minutes past one, in front of thirty-four pupils of Stambridge Grammar School and Eric Crabbe, Bruce Pendleton was hoisted onto the roof of his father's car to address the demonstration. (He had established that

Lenin had made his most famous speech from such a podium, so it was clearly the correct revolutionary thing to do.) The fat brute looked nervous, and the ragged applause that greeted him as he got ready to speak had no noticeable calming effect.

'Comrades,' he began. 'The reason we are here in such numbers today,' (he was reading the speech) 'is that we wish to express our disgust with American imperialism...' He went on for fifteen excruciating minutes, every carefully-rehearsed phrase failing to rouse us even to mild indignation against the Americans. It was awful, and Joe Vincent's effort was no better. He too began with 'Comrades', he too spoke for a quarter of an hour, he too succeeded in arousing only boredom laced with embarrassment. By the time he was helped down off the car, it felt as if hours had passed since the moment Pendleton had been helped up, and our numbers had now shrunk to thirty-one.

We began the march, the 'ANKS OUT OF VIETNA' banner at our head. Passing motorists looked curiously at us. We tried singing The Internationale, but our attempt petered out half way through the second verse, as few of the demonstrators were prepared to join in. 'Yanks out!... Yanks out!' shouted Joe Vincent, to retrieve the situation, and a moderately successful chant was taken up.

Pendleton sprang to the breach as it died out, with a cry of 'Ho... Ho... Ho Chi Minh!' which was taken up with equal enthusiasm. The weather being fine, and the relief after the two dreadful speeches being considerable, the march went well, and our spirits had recovered by the time we arrived in the car park in front of the clubhouse at ten past two.

I was all for hoisting Eric Crabbe onto one of the cars, but this suggestion was rejected, and he finally addressed us from a large stone. He spoke from notes, but his speech was, if possible, worse even than the two we had heard earlier. He went into subtle and intricate detail about Marxist philosophy, and he spoke for well over the allotted half hour. Perplexed faces appeared from time to time at the window of the clubhouse, and Major Harrington came out to ask what was going on. In the full dignity of the office proclaimed by my home-made 'STEWARD' badge, I strode over to him.

'Hello Tom' he said, in a voice too friendly for my liking. 'What's all this then? Some sort of demonstration?'

'That's right,' I said, failing abjectly to sound aggressive. 'We want the Americans out of Vietnam.'

'Do you? Well, you've a right to express your opinion.'

'There's a group of Americans here today, isn't there?'

'Yes, there is. Most of them are still out on the course, but there's a few already in the clubhouse. Is it that chap Crabbe who's speaking? The young communist?'

'Yes.'

'Hmm. Oh well, fair enough. Just don't get in the way of the cars coming in and going out, will you? A few people in the clubhouse wouldn't mind running you down, given half a chance.' With a cheerful nod, he turned and went back into the clubhouse.

Such was the tedium of Crabbe's speech that most of his audience had turned their attention to my chat with the Major. But they were not close enough to make out what was being said, and I saw in this an opportunity to raise my profile. Adopting my grimmest expression, I went over to discuss matters with Pendleton and Vincent.

'Some of the bastards in the clubhouse are all for coming out here and laying into us,' I said. 'I told him we're not moving until we're ready.'

'Good,' said the two of them in unison, and we all turned our attention reluctantly back to Eric Crabbe's awful speech.

While he was talking, a number of people arrived at the course or left it, but none, to my chagrin, showed the least intention of attacking us. Some made it clear, by the assiduity with which they ignored us, that they disapproved, some stopped to listen for a few minutes, some greeted those of us whom they knew. But that was all.

By the time Crabbe had finished speaking, only nineteen demonstrators remained, and there was no flag-burning finale for those faithful few. The demonstration fizzled out.

When it was over, Pendleton and I thanked Crabbe for his contribution, then left him and his cousin, and walked disconsolately back up the long straight to the car. The rolled-up banner was under my right arm.

'Apathy,' said Pendleton. 'How can we ever change the world, if people everywhere are as apathetic as this?'

~

Two days later though, we were given an unexpected opportunity to show what we were made of, when bourgeois society at last picked up the gauntlet we had been so doggedly throwing at its feet. For Carruthers was back, and he announced in his normal blunt manner that he had heard that a long-established tradition of the school had been broken in his absence. Saunders cringed.

'The tradition is that, in break times, girls walk round the school clockwise, and boys anti-clockwise. I am not going to bother arguing about whether or not this is a good thing. I tell you simply that this tradition will remain as long as I am headmaster. If anyone wishes to flout it from now on, that person will have me to reckon with.'

Pendleton came out of assembly fuming. This time, he asserted, Carruthers had gone too far, and he, Pendleton, was not going to stand for it. Nobody else said anything, but a number of us followed him out at morning break,

233

waiting to see what he would do. The suspense was most agreeable.

Carruthers, unusually for him, was standing at the door, gazing fixedly ahead. We walked past him, heads bowed, and Pendleton, the leader of a defeated army, turned left.

Epilogue: 1968

Walter Cardwell replaced the receiver and shook his head wearily.

'What was all that about?' said his wife.

'That was Jocelyn Carruthers. He says Thomas wasn't at the end of term service. And neither was Bruce, as if you couldn't have guessed.'

Mrs Cardwell looked anxious. 'Goodness, Walter, I hope they're all right.'

'Oh God yes, I shouldn't worry. You know those two. Probably just couldn't resist playing truant on their last day.' He resumed his place at the table, and poured himself a second cup of tea. 'I'd like to know what the little devils have been up to all the same.'

'Well,' said Mrs Cardwell, looking at her watch, he'll be back any time now if he wants us to think he was at the service. I can't think why he's turned out so different from Linda.'

'He'll be all right.'

'The house'll be quiet with both of them away.'

'Sane.'

Mrs Cardwell finished her tea, and stared at the leaves in the bottom of her cup. 'You don't think Thomas would take... drugs... at university? Lots of these young people do, you know.'

'Not him. He'll quieten down soon, you'll see.'

At that moment the door opened.

'Thomas!' they both cried.

Into the kitchen came a tall, dark-haired eighteen-year-old in the uniform of Stambridge Grammar School. The shocked reaction of the two adults was attributable to the state he was in. His blazer was torn, his left eye was blacked, and a trickle of blood had dried between his left nostril and his mouth.

'Something wrong?' he said. 'I'm your son, remember?'

'Don't you be so damn cheeky!' snapped Walter Cardwell.

'Thomas,' said Mrs Cardwell, 'how did you get into such a state?'

Thomas gave a weary and cynical sigh. 'You wouldn't believe me.'

'Try us,' said his father, looking him up and down with distaste.

'Today was the end of term service,' said the boy. 'Perhaps you knew. Well, I just happened to walk into a lamp-post on the way from the church to the bus stop. Please don't bother to pretend you believe me.'